THE SHIMMERING BLOND SISTER

ALSO BY DAVID HANDLER

FEATURING BERGER & MITRY

The Sour Cherry Surprise

The Sweet Golden Parachute

The Burnt Orange Sunrise

The Bright Silver Star

The Hot Pink Farmhouse

The Cold Blue Blood

FEATURING HUNT LIEBLING

Click to Play

FEATURING STEWART HOAG

The Man Who Died Laughing

The Man Who Lived by Night

The Man Who Would Be F. Scott Fitzgerald

The Woman Who Fell from Grace

The Boy Who Never Grew Up

The Man Who Cancelled Himself

The Girl Who Ran Off with Daddy

The Man Who Loved Women to Death

FEATURING DANNY LEVINE

Kiddo

Boss

THE SHIMMERING BLOND SISTER

DAVID HANDLER

MINOTAUR BOOKS
A THOMAS DUNNE BOOK
NEW YORK

This is a work of fiction. All of the characters, organizations, and events portrayed in this novel are either products of the author's imagination or are used fictitiously.

THOMAS DUNNE BOOKS.
An imprint of St. Martin's Press.

www.thomasdunnebooks.com
www.minotaurbooks.com

ISBN 978-0-312-57485-7

First Edition: October 2010

10 9 8 7 6 5 4 3 2 1

For Liesa and Miltie, who know why

THE SHIMMERING BLOND SISTER

Prologue

The Masked Avenger waited until he was absolutely positive she was asleep before he slipped soundlessly out of bed and tiptoed out of the bedroom—a man on a mission. Maybe his most critical mission to date.

Hell, there was no maybe about it.

His home lay in darkness. Outside, all was still and silent, even though it wasn't that late. Dorset was a bedrock New England town. Early to bed, early to rise, makes you healthy, wealthy, and . . . astonishingly boring. The Masked Avenger let himself out the back door and started across the lawn, his ears straining for a noise, any noise. He heard only the crickets.

He'd assumed other superhero identities over the years. Two of them. Secret identities that not a single living soul knew about. His first had been the Silent Thief, back when he was six years old. The Silent Thief operated in the quiet of Sunday mornings at dawn. He'd rise in the early light and creep down the upstairs hallway in his pajamas to the closed door of his parents' bedroom. Six mornings a week they awoke before he did. Sundays they slept in. He'd ease the door open carefully. Listen for their deep, steady breathing. Assured that they were asleep, he'd enter their room. An ocean of carpet lay between the Silent Thief and the chest of drawers next to his father's side of the bed. Mindful of the creaks in the floorboards, he'd slither his way across the room on his stomach, working his way deep into enemy territory, his heart pounding, mouth dry. It would take the Silent Thief five, sometimes ten, minutes to make it all the way around the bed. Then came the truly dangerous stage of his mission. The part that was absolutely not for the faint of heart. With a deep breath, the Silent Thief would spring to his feet and—standing there in full view of them now—steal the loose change that was scattered atop the dresser with his father's keys and wallet. Quarters and dimes, the occasional nickel. He didn't dare open the wallet and go for any bills. His father might notice those missing. Coins he never did. The Silent Thief would soundlessly snatch at least a dollar's worth with his small, moist fingers, then drop back down to the floor and slither gleefully back to his room—mission accomplished.

He kept his loot in an old tobacco tin hidden in the back of his closet. After two years of Sundays, he'd amassed a secret fortune of $107.25.

Until that morning when the Silent Thief was finally exposed—by his mother, much to his humiliation. She lay there that fateful Sunday morning, her breathing deep and steady as usual. Except one eye was wide open, watching him as he slithered along the floor. "What are you doing, sweetheart?" she whispered.

"I-I was looking for Jocko," he gasped hoarsely. Their cocker spaniel.

"Jocko sleeps in the cellar, not in here," she said reproachfully. Because she *knew.* Though she never said so.

He darted out of their room and never, ever dared go in there again. He spent his loot judiciously in the coming months on cheeseburgers, onion rings, and chocolate milk shakes at the fragrant diner near home, where he was forbidden to go because mother insisted that the food they served was unhealthy for a growing person.

But the Silent Thief was gone—never to return again. Superhero identities? Those were for little kids.

Until that warm summer night when he reappeared as the Midnight Watcher, a crusader vastly more cunning than the Silent Thief had ever dared to be. He was, after all, a sophisticated man of fifteen now. The Midnight Watcher didn't merely tiptoe out of his bedroom, he slipped out of the whole house. Waited until his parents had gone to bed. Then leapt out of his own bed and donned his special costume: black jeans, black windbreaker, black Converse Chuck Taylor high tops. He looked very cool in it. His bedroom window opened out onto the roof of the back porch. Out the window he'd go, then down the trellis to the patio, and off into the dark of night.

It seemed like a quiet neighborhood. Not much going on. But the Midnight Watcher knew better. He knew that a mere one street over from his own resided the beauteous, the incomparable, the one and only Donna Durslag. He knew that Donna's first-floor bedroom faced her parents' driveway, its window partially shielded by a large rhododendron. He knew that if he stood there in the Durslags' driveway, nestled in that rhododendron, he could watch Donna through her open window, completely undetected.

She was a dark-eyed dream girl with gleaming black hair and giant boobs. A senior at the same high school he went to. Not that she had any idea who he was. Donna was popular. Donna was a cheerleader. Donna dated the quarterback of the football team. Almost always, she'd be talking on her bedside phone when the Midnight Watcher arrived at his post. That was what she did. She talked to her girlfriends on the phone. Her room was very girlie-girl. Her bed was covered with stuffed animals, her walls with posters of insipid bubblegum music stars. Often, she'd be playing their awful music on her stereo. Which meant he couldn't hear a lot of what she was saying. But he could *watch* her, inflamed by his passion, as she lay there on her bed in a sleeveless top and shorts, talking and talking. She liked to lie on her tummy with her knees bent and her bare feet up in the air, swinging back and forth, back and forth. The Midnight Watcher was positively hypnotized by the sight of Donna's naked, succulent, pink toes.

He saw the rest of her naked only one time. Entirely, deliciously naked. It was a memorable night. It was also the night that marked the Midnight Watcher's final adventure. A summer heat wave was on. It had been a sweltering 98 degrees that day. The thermometer still hovered near 90 even late at night—and him all costumed from head to toe in black. Donna didn't have air-conditioning in her room. Just a ceiling fan. It must have been very warm in there. And her parents must have gone to bed early. Because when she came padding into the bedroom that night, fresh from her shower, Donna was stark naked. No T-shirt. No nightie. The Midnight Watcher couldn't believe his eyes. Donna Durslag was the first girl he'd ever seen naked. He was overwhelmed by the rich abundance of her curves. By the way her full, mouthwatering breasts jiggled as she walked. She came directly over to the window and flung open the curtains. Rested her arms right there on the windowsill. He stood there, inches away from her in the darkness. He didn't dare swallow or blink or breathe. She was so close he could see the dewy droplets of water on her rosy nipples. And smell her fresh, soapy scent. *Donna*. Standing there like that, he began to get incredibly excited. His heart pounding. His fifteen-year-old hormones raging out of control. That pulsating anaconda in his jeans so huge, so *alive* that he feared his entire being would explode in a pulp all over Donna's window. And so he, well, he did what any healthy, red-blooded American boy would do. Took matters into his own hand.

Unfortunately, it was at that very moment that the Durslags' next-door neighbors happened to turn on their porch light—backlighting the Midnight Watcher as he stood there in the rhododendron, one fist gripping his engorged pole. Naturally, Donna saw him. *It*. And so she, well, she did what any healthy, red-blooded American girl would do. Screamed her head off.

Her parents came running. Lights went on everywhere. Dogs barked. The Midnight Watcher sprinted away. Or tried to, hobbled as he was by his inflamed condition. So panicked that he ran *away* from home, then around the block twice. When he finally got home, he shimmied up the trellis and dove into bed with all of his clothes on, sweating and trembling. *Praying* she hadn't looked up at his face. Which she hadn't. He was lucky. Very lucky. But after that, the Midnight Watcher was no more. In fact, he said good-bye to superhero identities forever after that. Renounced them as a childish thing that he'd outgrown. And, frankly, was fortunate to have survived.

Until two weekends ago, when the Masked Avenger was born.

Out of necessity, he felt. To get even. Pay back each and every one of those rich old ladies who'd been looking down on him. He'd tried to shrug off their casual slights. Ignore their whispers. He'd turned the other cheek, been the bigger man. Sure, he had. But a man can only swallow so much. And then he must act. Has to act. Or he's not a man.

His costume of choice? A nod to his youth. Black nylon windbreaker, black jeans, black Chuck Taylor high-tops and—here was the new twist—a black wool ski mask. The Masked Avenger was a giver of gifts. His favorite means of announcing himself was the front doorbell. He'd left a dead skunk on Amy Orr's welcome mat because of *that way* she had of turning up her nose at him. And that no-good Kathy Fulton, the undertaker's wife, got a special gift, too. A customized addition to the sign outside of the Fulton Funeral Home. Right underneath the sober words *Burials and Cremations*, the Masked Avenger had scrawled: *And don't forget our homemade BBQ!* But those were special cases. Mostly, the gift that the Masked Avenger delivered in the dark of night was himself.

He'd ring the doorbell. Or tap on the kitchen window if he saw a light on in there. When the rich bitch appeared, he'd drop his jeans and wave good evening to her. Then he'd sprint off into the darkness, snickering with unbridled delight. To date, the Masked Avenger had treated seven of the old busybodies to an up-close, personal view of his equipment. To date, not one of them had the slightest idea who he was. Just some guy in a ski mask.

They were calling him the Dorset Flasher.

And he was absolutely *the* biggest story in town. Everyone talking about what a vile, awful monster he was. How his obscene behavior just *wasn't* Dorset. He'd definitely gotten the attention of that uppity black resident trooper, who was quoted on Channel 8 news as saying, "We're dealing with a seriously disturbed individual here." *Seriously disturbed*? The Masked Avenger paid her back but good. Took a nice late-night stroll up to her cottage and left her a custom-manufactured door prize.

The old ladies in town were so worked up that even Bob Paffin, Dorset's do-nothing first selectman, stuck his big red nose into it. That fool actually appeared on all four local Connecticut news channels to vow that Dorset would be a "safe zone" this upcoming weekend. "If the Flasher dares to strike again he will be very, very sorry," Paffin boasted.

The Masked Avenger couldn't resist such a clumsy dare. Not after it was reported in the local press that Bob and Delia Paffin would be hosting the monthly meeting of the Committee for Good Government tonight at their home on Frederick Lane. This being Dorset, the liquor would be flowing. This being August, many of the Good Government fossils and their wives would be gathered together out on the Paffins' screened-in back porch.

It was too good an opportunity for the Masked Avenger to pass up.

As he slipped silently out the back door into the darkness, he felt emboldened, excited, *alive*. In truth, the Masked Avenger had never had so much fun in his whole life. He darted across the back lawn and over the neighbor's low fence. The ski mask felt heavy and hot against his face in the warm, humid night air. But he could take no chances. He crouched there behind a lilac bush, his eyes scanning Dorset Street. A state police cruiser was parked right there in front of the firehouse. Another drove slowly past. A safe zone indeed.

He crossed the neighboring backyard and tiptoed his way onto Maple Lane, a short dead-end off of Dorset Street that ran into the Lieutenant River after less than three hundred feet. Rut Peck's house stood there in total darkness. The old postmaster had moved out. A dog started barking from the house behind his. Nan Sidell's big yellow Labrador retriever. The Masked Avenger waited patiently for the dog to shut up, then started his way soundlessly across Rut's weedy, overgrown front yard toward the bank of the Lieutenant River. All he had to do was follow the riverbank, and in less than a mile he'd be standing in Bob Paffin's backyard.

He was passing behind Rut's abandoned bunny hutch when he sensed that he was not alone. Someone was on his tail. The Masked Avenger came to an instant halt, breathing as quietly as possible. Hearing nothing now. Possibly his ears had been playing tricks on him. He started up again, creeping through the wild brush. But again, he swore he heard footsteps. Someone was definitely following him. Meanwhile, on Dorset Street, another state police cruiser went easing slowly by.

He started up again, moving fast across Rut's side yard. He was nearing the riverbank when he heard a scuffle in the darkness behind him. Maybe thirty feet back. Somebody, a man, let out a groan. And then the Masked Avenger heard a wet, sickening thud. It was, he imagined, the sound that a ten-pound sledgehammer might make as it smashed into a ripe muskmelon. Then he heard footsteps. All sorts of footsteps. Somebody crashing through the brush.

Somebody tripping and falling hard. Nan's dog started barking its head off again.

The Masked Avenger crouched there, wondering what in the hell was going on. He decided not to find out. Made it to the riverbank and took off, splish-splashing his way north, his chest heaving, the sweat pouring from him. He ran and he ran—until he'd made it all of the way to Beckwith Lane. When he got there, he yanked off the ski mask and shoved it under his windbreaker. Cooled off, caught his breath. Then he sauntered his way up the lane, just another villager out for an evening stroll. When he reached Dorset Street he circled around behind the library and crossed the soccer fields that were adjacent to the high school. Then he made his way back onto Dorset Street way over by Big Branch Road. As he strolled along, he could see the volunteer ambulance van and several cruisers clustered at the intersection with Maple Lane. Neighbors were standing there, gawking and talking. He blended in among them, listening to snatches of conversation.

"Dead as a doornail . . ."

"His whole head smashed in . . ."

"Lord, who would do such a . . . ?

"Oh, I think we know . . ."

The Masked Avenger said nothing. Whatever had occurred, he assured himself, had nothing to do with him. He drifted away from the onlookers and slipped back inside his darkened home, allowing himself a sigh of relief. All was quiet. Everything was fine.

Except it wasn't fine. Nothing was fine.

And nothing was ever going to be the same again.

One Day Earlier

Chapter 1

"Remember to breathe! Fill your lungs with breath! *Breathe*!"

Okay, okay—Mitch breathed. And shook. And sweated. The damned perspiration was streaming down his face. Or make that *up* his face, since the pose he was currently holding was a punishing form of torture known as downward facing dog. And the yoga studio at the Dorset Fitness Center was a steamy 92 degrees, same as outside on this Friday afternoon in August. No air-conditioning allowed. Not for a heat-generating Vinyasa class.

"Now step forward with your right foot into Warrior One," Kimberly commanded the class, which comprised Mitch and three pear-shaped middle-aged ladies who never got tired or broke a sweat. Next to them, Mitch felt like an overstimulated water buffalo. "Stay *strong* through your left leg!"

Mitch complied, wavering there on his mat in Warrior One pose—right knee bent, left leg strong—okay, semistrong—his hips square, core grounded, arms upraised to the sky. The truth? A gentle *poof* would have blown him right over. This was only his third try at yoga. He'd always had an aversion to things that make you go "Omm. . . ." But there was nothing New Agey about Kimberly's class. It was a brutal ninety-minute workout—a cross between Simon Says and a Navy Seals fitness certification test. Plus Mitch Berger was not a human pretzel and never had been.

But Hal, the trainer there whom Mitch lifted with three times a week, had urged him to try yoga to improve his flexibility and core strength. Why not, figured Mitch, a recovering *shlub* who'd taken off nearly forty pounds of man blubber after Dorset's resident state trooper had accepted his proposal of marriage and then dumped him in the very same week. Now that he and Des were back together again, he wanted to keep those pounds off. He ran two miles every day through the Peck's Point Nature Preserve. Lifted. Disdained all junk food. Most junk food. Actually, he'd thought he was in great shape when he signed up for his first class with Kimberly. He'd also thought yoga would be something gentle and soothing. Way wrong on both counts.

Right now this sadistic Zen drill instructor was sending them into their eighth nonstop round of sun salutations. Mitch flowed gamely along, every muscle in his body shaking. He felt certain that he was going to die there and then. By the time Kimberly mercifully allowed them to relax into *Savasana*—or Corpse Pose—it was not an exaggeration. Mitch didn't just melt into the floor. He *was* the floor.

Kimberly owned the Dorset Fitness Center, which occupied a spacious windowed corner of The Works, the old red brick piano works on the banks of the Connecticut River that had been converted into a food hall and shopping arcade. She was in her early thirties and quite desirable, if your taste happened to run to blue-eyed blondes who were lovely, leggy, lithe, limber . . . were there any other L-words to describe Kimberly? Lissome. She was definitely lissome. And she cared about people. Taught yoga twice a week to the inmates at York Correctional, the women's prison in Niantic. She also happened to be a Farrell.

Yes, one of *those* Farrells.

Kimberly did have a man in her life. She was engaged to some rich guy up in Cambridge who came to see her every weekend. Or so said Hal the trainer. Hal was a twenty-something jock who'd been recruited out of Dorset High by Boston College to play wide receiver. Hal wasn't big—no more than five feet eleven—but he told Mitch he'd possessed world-class shifty moves until he blew out his right knee freshman year. He'd dropped out of BC after that. Returned home to Dorset and, near as Mitch could tell, morphed into the village's preeminent stud muffin. Hal Chapman seemed to have his nightly pick of the college girls, secretaries and divorcées who found their way to the Connecticut shoreline every summer. This despite his truly appalling skullet haircut—a shaved head with a full-tilt mullet in back—and his rather broad snow shovel of a jaw. Hal also wasn't exactly the sharpest knife in the drawer. But he had broad shoulders, slim hips, a complete six-pack of abs and an easy, upbeat personality. The ladies loved him.

As the class lay there in *Savasana* Kimberly urged each of them to gaze inside with their third eye and focus on their *intention*. Mostly, Mitch's *intention* had been to survive until dinner. Although he was learning to use these introspective moments to connect more deeply with his new job. Mitch had been lead film critic for New York's most prestigious newspaper. When the paper got taken over by a huge media conglomerate, they'd made him over into their resident cutesy cable news quote-machine whore. Or tried. But he'd walked away from all of that—handed in his license to shill and rejoined his old editor, Lacy Nickerson, who'd just launched a prestigious e-zine devoted to thoughtful criticism of the arts. His *intention* now was to write about whatever was on his mind. Hold nothing back. Just run with it. Working for Lacy meant less money, but who wasn't working for less money these days? Besides, he had a contract to complete another film reference volume, *Ants In Her Plants*, which he hoped would do for screwball comedies what his first three bestselling guides had done for sci-fi, crime and the western. And now he was free to enjoy life in his antique post-and-beam caretaker's cottage out on Big Sister Island. He puttered in his garden. Played the blues on his beloved sky blue Fender Stratocaster. And spent as much time as he could with the lady in his life. All talk of marriage was off the table. They were just letting it happen. Mitch, the Jewish movie critic from New York City. Des, the West Point graduate who was six feet one, black and knew eighteen different ways to kill him with her bare hands.

After *Savasana* they sat cross-legged on their mats and said *"Namaste."* Then Mitch drank down an entire liter of mineral water and staggered to the showers, his arms so tired he could barely raise them over his head to shampoo his hair. But he did feel unbelievably mellow as he toweled off and put on his complimentary red *Saw IV* T-shirt, baggy shorts and rubber flip flops.

Hal was out on the floor working out a sexy young redhead in spandex. "Later, bro," he exclaimed, bumping knucks as Mitch oozed on by. Hal had a tendency to lay on the "bro" thing a bit thick, but it didn't really bother Mitch. Nothing bothered Mitch after yoga class.

The vast food hall, with its fragrant stalls and coffee bar and Parisian style seating area, was totally mobbed. It was a Friday afternoon, and during the summer the population of this quaint, historic New England village at the mouth of the Connecticut River doubled. It also developed a showier, more Hamptons vibe. Dozens of fashionably dressed young women with tanned legs and salon-streaked hair sat drinking iced mocha-whatevers and talking loudly on their cell phones. Mitch found himself looking forward to Labor Day, when Dorset's population would return to its normal seven thousand cranky Yankees.

Mitch bought some fresh buffalo mozzarella from Christine to go with the tomatoes and basil that were growing in his garden. Then he ambled over to the fish market in search of something to throw on the grill that night. As he stood there trying to choose between the striped bass and the sushi-grade tuna, Mitch found himself shooting glances at the woman next to him. She was an attractive, frosted blonde in her late forties or early fifties, fashionably put together in an aqua-colored silk top, tailored white slacks and a pair of Manolo Blahnik gold sandals that had to run at least six hundred dollars. The Hermès handbag she was clutching would easily go for at least twice that.

Mitch smiled to himself, thinking: *Yet another one.* Whenever he saw a shapely, good-looking blonde of a certain age, he always thought of Beth Lapidus, the sexy divorcée who'd lived in the apartment across the hall from him in Stuyvesant Town when he was thirteen. She and her son Kenny—a blinky, twerpy little ten-year-old whose nickname on the playground was Spiny. Beth Lapidus held an exalted place in the pantheon of Mitch's romantic life. She was his first true love. The unwitting object of his sexual awakening. God, how he'd adored her. Whenever he'd heard Beth's hallway door slam shut, he'd race to his bedroom window to watch her stride across the Oval, her hips swaying, blond hair shimmering in the sunlight. Mitch was heartbroken—truly devastated—when she got married to a rich Park Avenue eye doctor and moved to Scarsdale. He never saw her again.

Maybe it was the yogic glow on his face. Or maybe it was his stint as a big-time TV celebrity. But this particular frosted blonde was smiling at Mitch.

"Why, Mitchell Berger, it *is* you, isn't it?" Her voice was soft and slightly trembly. "I used to live across the hall from you in Stuyvesant Town. Beth Breslauer? I was Beth Lapidus then. My boy, Kenny, was always so fond of you."

Mitch swallowed, dumbstruck. Because this wasn't really happening. He was still on his mat in *Savasana*. Had to be . . . *Omm* . . .

"I'd heard that you had a place in Dorset," she went on. "I've been hoping we'd run into each other. I figured it was just a matter of time."

"You mean . . . are you saying you've moved here?"

Beth tilted her head at him fetchingly, much like Natalie Wood used to do. "Why, yes. I've lived here since the end of May."

"This is incredible. Why didn't you call me?"

"You're a big star now. I didn't want to bother you."

"As if. I was just going to get a fruit smoothie. Could I buy you one?"

He could. He did. They sat, Mitch trying his darnedest not to stare at her across the table. Beth wore her hair shorter now, cropped at her chin. But otherwise she'd changed remarkably little in the twenty years since Mitch had last seen her. Same curvy figure. Same plump, inviting lips. Same melting gaze from those big, dark eyes. Beth's face was remarkably smooth and unlined. No bags, no sags. He wondered if she'd had some high-end cosmetic surgery done. She looked as if she could afford it. She was wearing a lot of gold. Not ostentatiously, but it was there. Several rings on her soft, delicate fingers. A necklace, a bracelet, the Rolex on her wrist.

"My husband, Irwin, died last year," she informed him, sipping her smoothie. "We had eighteen good years together. And I liked Scarsdale well enough. But there's nothing worse than rattling around in a big house in suburbia all by yourself. So I sold the place. Just decided to do it and did it." Beth's manner, he realized, hadn't changed either. She somehow managed to convey helpless fragility and steely self-reliance at the same exact time. "I've bought myself a small apartment in the city, on East 62nd, and I have the condo here so I can be closer to Kenny. He's up in the Boston area. This way we get to see each other on weekends. He'll be coming in tonight after work. Mitch, I can't wait to tell him I've bumped into you."

"What does Kenny do for a living?"

Beth stuck out her lower lip fretfully. "I was afraid you were going to ask me that."

"Why, is it a deep, dark secret?"

"No, I just don't understand a word of it. He's a computer wiz. And apparently knows more about something called 'molecular modeling' than anyone in the country. He was on the faculty at

MIT. Now he designs research computer systems for pharmaceutical companies."

"Sounds pretty impressive."

"He's still the same Kenny," she responded, swelling with motherly pride.

"Beth, I'd love to get together with both of you. Where are you living?"

"In the Captain Chadwick House."

Mitch's eyes widened. The Captain Chadwick House was *the* choicest condo colony in town. The only one situated in the Dorset Street Historic District. Des's housemate, Bella Tillis, had been trying to grab up one of its precious units for ages. But they changed hands very discreetly and rarely, if ever, came on the open market. "It's impossible to get in there. How did you manage it?"

"It was no trouble at all," Beth answered with a shrug. "Your folks must be so proud of you, Mitch. How are they?"

"Oh, fine. They live down in Vero Beach now." Retired New York City public school teachers, both of them.

"And how do they feel about you and your fiancée?" she asked, arching an eyebrow at him.

"You've heard about us, have you?"

"Who hasn't? You and our resident trooper are the talk of the town."

"She's not. My fiancée, I mean. We're not engaged. We were. But we're not anymore. Although we're getting along great."

"And they're okay with the . . . differences?"

"You mean the part about how she carries a fully loaded SIG-Sauer and I don't?"

"You know what I mean."

"They just want me to be happy."

"That's all that any parent wants, Mitch. Kenny's engaged, you know. To a girl here in town named Kimberly Farrell."

"*Kimberly*? No way!" Although this sort of thing was not unusual in small-town Dorset, Mitch had discovered. It was a world of wheels within wheels. "She's my yoga teacher."

"Very sweet girl," Beth said with a noticeable lack of conviction. "Mind you, there's baggage. She was married once before—*very* briefly. A local fellow named J. Z. Cliffe. I don't suppose you know him, too, do you?"

"No, I'm afraid not."

"I can't help asking myself why it didn't work out. She and Kenny have discussed it, but Kenny won't share the details with me. He doesn't usually keep secrets. I suppose it's none of my business. It's just that I'm concerned. Kenny . . . he isn't that experienced when it comes to women. And he's done *really* well financially." Beth's mouth tightened. "There's also the matter of her father's notoriety. Dex and Maddee live across the hall from me. That's how the two kids met. Kimberly has been living with her folks for the past few months. Maddee needs the emotional support, I gather. Kenny ran into her one morning as she was heading off in her yoga gear. They struck up a conversation. Next thing I knew he was coming down every weekend to see her, not me. Please don't get me wrong, Mitch. He and Kimberly positively glow in each other's presence. I'm excited for him. For both of us, really. I'm loving my new life. I'm taking sculpture classes at the art academy. And I dash into the city whenever I feel like it. My girlfriends and I go to the theater together, shop til we drop, talk our heads off. I'm having a lot of fun."

And yet Mitch saw sadness in Beth's eyes. He saw loss. He knew all about these things. He'd lost his own beloved wife, Maisie, to ovarian cancer after only two years of marriage. Had spent months telling people how great he was doing when he was actually a lonely wreck. Although he figured Beth had to be dating someone by now. A woman who looked like Beth didn't stay alone for long. "Where are Kenny and Kimberly planning to live?"

"Up in Cambridge. She wants to keep the fitness center running. Her trainer, Hal, will manage it during the week. She'll come down on weekends to teach a few classes and keep an eye on her folks. The wedding's next month. Maddee has her heart set on a big fat Dorset wedding at the Yacht Club. Two hundred guests, an orchestra, the works. She's hoping it will get her back in the good graces of their former friends." Beth wrinkled her nose slightly. "I must confess, I have problems with her. And Dex I just plain can't stand."

"Well, you're not alone there."

Indeed, Dex Farrell was a pariah not just in Dorset, but all across America. As the head of Farrell and Co., the venerated credit-rating agency started by his grandfather, Dex Farrell was one of the Wall Street power brokers who'd been at the epicenter of the subprime home-mortgage meltdown. Dex Farrell had misrepresented the rating on hundreds of billions of dollars worth of mortgage-backed securities. His name was synonymous with Wall Street recklessness, dishonesty and greed. The only reason he hadn't been indicted for fraud was that federal prosecutors had concluded he was off his gourd. When pressed by a committee of the U.S. Congress to justify the high ratings he'd given to so many risky securities, he'd famously testified: "If it walks like a duck and quacks like a duck, then it's a duck." And then proceeded to start quacking. And wouldn't stop quacking even as he was being led from the chamber. His personal physician attributed Farrell's unusual behavior to an adverse reaction to a prescription medication for stress. Whatever it was, the disgraced Dex Farrell and his shamed wife, Maddee, had unloaded their shorefront estate in Dorset—where a lot of their blue-blooded, old-money friends had lost a lot of that blue-blooded old money—and fled to Hobe Sound, Florida. Recently, they'd slipped quietly back into town.

"There's no worthwhile cause that Maddee won't donate her time to," Beth said. "She delivers hot lunches to the housebound for Meals on Wheels. Stockpiles canned goods for the Food Pantry. Collects old clothes for the Nearly New shop at St. Anne's. She's quite the juggernaut. And so desperate to get back onto Dorset's A-list that it's kind of sad. Or it would be if she weren't always reminding me how many servants she had when she was growing up."

"And Dex?"

"He keeps to himself. Doesn't talk to a soul, near as I can tell. God, maybe. If he believes in God. Do you think swindlers like Dex Farrell believe in God? Or do they just worship money? I've always wondered about that."

"How do they feel about Kimberly and Kenny?"

"You mean because he's a J-E-W? They're okay with it. Kenny's the one who's not okay. He's *dreading* this fancy Yacht Club wedding of Maddee's. It's just not Kenny's style. Or Kimberly's. They're honeymooning at an ashram in the Himalayas, for pity's sake. Kimberly doesn't want to disappoint her mother. But if you ask me, it's *their* wedding and they ought to do what they want."

"Which is . . . ?"

"Get married on a beach somewhere at sunset with a few close friends."

"Well, if they change their minds, I have one." Mitch finished off the last of his smoothie.

"One what, Mitch?"

"A beach. And we get a sunset pretty much every day."

They headed back to the fish counter now to purchase their dinners. A glistening slab of striped bass for Mitch. Two slender fillets of sole for Beth. Dinner for one. Then he walked her out to the parking lot. Mitch got around town in a bulbous, kidney-colored 1956 Studebaker pickup. Beth was driving a frisky, red Mini Cooper convertible.

'I know, I know—it's too young for me," she acknowledged as Mitch stood there admiring it. "But I love it. And Kenny likes to drive it when he's here. Mitch, why don't you and your lady friend join us for dinner tomorrow night?"

"I wish we could, but she's not exactly free on the weekends these days. Not after dark anyhow."

Her face dropped. "Our village flasher, of course. How stupid of me. Well, what about an early drink? Say, five o'clock?"

"Sounds perfect. I can't wait to see Kenny again. It'll be just like old times."

"No, it won't. It'll be better." Beth gave him a good-bye hug, planting a warm, soft kiss on his left cheek.

Much to his horror, Mitch instantly flushed beet red. Couldn't help it. This was *Beth Lapidus*.

She drew back from him, her eyes widening in surprise. "Why, Mitchell Berger, are you blushing?"

"Absolutely not. I just took a hot shower, that's all."

"Of course you did, dear. Of course."

Chapter 2

THWACKETA-THWACKETA-THWACKETA...

It was the end of a hot mess of a day and Des was making a quick pit stop at her stuffy little cubbyhole in Dorset's Town Hall, a stately, white-columned edifice which smelled year round of mothballs, musty carpeting and Bengay. She had a mail slot there. Folks could leave her messages, tips, leads. Or slide notes under her door. Lately, she'd been swinging by a couple of times a day just in case someone had. Hoping for a break in this case. And *really* hoping to avoid a certain someone.

Thwacketa-thwacketa-thwatcketa . . .

The air-conditioner in her window was over twenty years old. All it did, besides make a racket, was wheeze gusts of warm, stale air. This was the downside of quaint—it generally meant cramped work spaces, outmoded wiring and mold. Hell, her heavy horn-rimmed glasses were fogging up. Des removed them, squinting at the newly printed fall school bus schedules that she'd found in her mail slot. Dorset's elementary, middle and high school were all grouped together in the Historic District. Mornings were always chaotic. A ton of busses and rushed parents pulling in and out at once. For the first week or so, Dorset's resident state trooper had to stand out there in the middle of Dorset Street directing traffic. It was a far cry from Des Mitry's heyday as a homicide lieutenant on the Major Crime Squad. One of only three in the entire state who were women. And the only one who was black. *And* the daughter of Deputy Superintendent Buck Mitry—the Deacon—who was the highest-ranking officer of color in the history of the Connecticut State Police. But, hey, she was totally fine with her new station in life. Just wasn't ready for fall yet. Today sure hadn't felt like fall. It had topped out at a sweltering ninety-four degrees. But Labor Day was less than ten days away. Teachers would be showing up for faculty orientation on Monday morning. The calendar didn't lie.

Thwacketa-thwacketa-thwacketa . . .

Des slid the schedules into her briefcase, allowing herself a weary sigh. It had been a brutal three weeks. Working seven days a week around the clock. She needed a blow. A nice long, lazy weekend. But she wasn't going to get one. Not until she nailed *him*.

The Dorset Flasher had exposed himself to seven elderly women in the Historic District over the previous two weekends. All of them wealthy, well-connected widows. He'd struck on Saturday and Sunday nights between 9:00 and 10:00 p.m. That first weekend, he'd rung their doorbells. When they answered there he was—in all of his glory. After word of his exploits got around, not one dowager in Dorset would answer her doorbell after dark. So the sick bastard had taken to waving his thing at them through their windows or sliding-glass doors. Des didn't have a very solid description of him. Frightened, indignant old ladies didn't make the greatest eyewitnesses. Plus he operated in the dark of night. All she knew was that he was of average height and weight. He appeared to be reasonably fit. He dressed in dark clothing and wore a black ski mask over his face. Des knew zero about his age or appearance. The old dears couldn't—or wouldn't—provide her with any helpful details regarding the particular part of his anatomy that he'd been so anxious to show them. Questioning them about it? Not Des's idea of a good time.

There had been two additional acts of malicious mischief in the Historic District on the very same nights that the Dorset Flasher had struck. A sign in front of the Fulton Funeral Home had been defaced. And a dead skunk had been left on Amy Orr's welcome mat. Des had no evidence that the same perp was responsible. Possibly there was no connection between the events at all. But her instincts told her it was the same nutso. Dorset was a very small town. It was also an affluent, picture-postcard town. A serial flasher exposing himself to rich old ladies was just the kind of story that Connecticut's local TV news stations ate up. They were all over the Dorset Flasher case. And all up in Des's grille. They weren't the only ones. A lot of Dorseteers were afraid to go out at night. She was under a lot of heat to nail the sick bastard. Translation: Dorset's *noodge* of a first selectman, Bob Paffin, was in her face even more than usual.

Thwacketa-thwacketa-thwacketa . . .

As she stood there in her sweltering little office, Des could feel the sweat trickling down her legs. She could not wait to floor it out to Mitch's place, strip off her uni and dive into the cool blue water of Long Island Sound. She was giving herself the evening off tonight. One evening to enjoy a cold beer and a nice meal. To feel Mitch's deft, sure hands on her. To relax and stretch and . . .

"Have you got any news for me, Des?"

Busted, damn it.

Dorset's snowy-haired, red-nosed first selectman stood planted right there in her doorway. "Folks are getting awful darned anxious," he reminded her. Bob Paffin was real helpful that way.

"I have nothing to tell you, Bob."

Which didn't satisfy him. "I need to be able to tell them that you're making good progress."

"Bob, we'll be out there with three extra cruisers tomorrow night. Believe me, the state police are taking this case very, very seriously."

Short of assigning a detective to it. But the state had limited resources and its detectives were swamped with far more serious cases. The Dorset Flasher hadn't raped or otherwise assaulted anyone.

Hadn't broken into a home. Hadn't stolen or destroyed anything of value. The sad reality was that he rated as nothing more than a high-profile nuisance. Which Des was totally fine with. She felt certain she'd nail him faster than any outside detective would. She'd cultivated strong contacts among Dorset's many stoned and disaffected young people. The Dorset Flasher, she felt certain, was one of them.

Bob Paffin stood there with a pained expression on his long, narrow face. "Des, you know I have every confidence in your ability. . . ."

Actually, what she knew was that Bob had gone over her head to Don Rundle, her troop commander, and complained about the piss-poor job she was doing. Dorset's first selectman had never considered Des "right" for the job and never would, despite the undisputed fact that she excelled at it. She tried very hard not to seethe with resentment whenever the meddlesome snake came near her. Sometimes she almost succeeded.

Mercifully, her cell phone rang. A 911 call. She listened to the dispatcher and then barked, "Bob, I've got to take this." Elbowing past him, she hurried out to her cruiser.

An intruder call had come in from the Captain Chadwick House, the eighteenth-century whaling captain's showplace that was one of the anchors of Dorset Street's tree-lined Historic District. It was a mammoth, brick mansion with wraparound enclosed porches and four acres of rose gardens and manicured lawns. Back in the 1920s, the Captain Chadwick House had been converted into a summer hotel. Then it was the Dorset Inn for a while. These days it housed the village's most exclusive luxury condominiums. Six very desirable units—plus an apartment over the garages for the live-in caretaker. The Farrells lived in one of the downstairs units. A New York widow named Breslauer lived across the hall from them. The other two downstairs units belonged to wealthy couples that had multiple residences around the world and spent only a few weeks out of the year in Dorset. The owner of one of the upstairs units had recently passed away. Her children were fighting over it. The other upstairs unit belonged to Bertha Peck, the indomitable eighty-eight-year-old widow who was the Heidi Klum of Dorset polite society. Bertha Peck decided who was in and who was out. No village blue blood dared to marry, divorce or sneeze without clearing it with Bertha. Bertha was rich. Bertha was powerful. Bertha *was* Dorset.

It was she who'd placed the intruder call. Bertha wasn't exactly a stranger to the 911 dispatchers. Just last Tuesday she'd dialed 911 to report that her toilet was stopped up. "Ma'am, you do realize that this number's for emergencies, don't you?" the dispatcher had pointed out. To which Bertha had loftily replied, "Young lady, my toilet isn't working. Allow me to assure you, that *is* an emergency."

The old girl was high maintenance. Downright dotty. But as first responder, Des had to play it by the book. As she parked her cruiser out front, her eyes scanned Dorset Street for any sign of a getaway driver idling nearby. She saw no one. Got out and rushed up the path to the front door.

The entry hall of the Captain Chadwick House was elegantly wallpapered and carpeted. A chair lift had been built into the grand staircase up to the second floor. Bertha's, from when she'd had hip-replacement surgery last year. She didn't need to use it anymore. Got around just fine now. Played a round of golf every afternoon at the country club with three other rich widows, who together comprised an octogenerian Heathers set.

When Des arrived at the top of the stairs she found the door to Bertha's apartment wide open. The lock did not appear to be tampered with but Des unsnapped her holster anyway. "Mrs. Peck?" she called out, rapping on the open door with her knuckles.

"Come in, Desiree!" Bertha sang out from somewhere inside of the apartment. "We're in here, dear!"

We?

Bertha Peck's grand-sized living room had a twenty-foot ceiling, a chandelier, wood-burning fireplace and a balcony that looked out over the rear lawn to the Lieutenant River. Her taste in décor leaned toward Victorian plush. Sofas and armchairs that looked like great big ornate pincushions. But the artworks that crowded her walls were quite modern and exotic. Bertha was a major supporter of the Dorset Art Academy and liked to display the originals she purchased at the annual student show—including one of Des's own horrifyingly brutal pen-and-ink drawings of a murder victim. This one a battered ten-year-old girl named Honoria Freeman. Giving artistic life to the murdered souls whom she encountered on the job was Des's passion and her salvation.

She found Bertha seated on the sofa in her den, calmly watching a rerun of *Seinfeld*. The episode where Jerry decides to buy his dad a new Cadillac. Bertha Peck was a dainty little thing who'd topped out at maybe five feet two back in her prime a half century ago. Now she was more like four feet eleven, and couldn't have weighed more than ninety pounds. Her linen summer dress was trimly cut, expensive and stylish. So was her cropped, layered hair, which she dyed an unlikely jet black. The round glasses she wore were also black, the saucer-shaped eyes behind them a piercing blue. Her lips were bright red, as were the nails on her tiny hands.

"Mrs. Peck, did you place a call about an intruder?"

"I most certainly did," Bertha responded airily. "He's *there* in the corner. I've taken care of him myself. But I still require your assistance, I'm afraid."

Des saw no one in the corner. Saw nothing. Frowning, she moved slowly in that direction until she reached the overstuffed chair that was parked there and saw . . . well, it was a small field mouse imprisoned inside of an overturned highball glass. The mouse was dead. Covered in blood.

First, Des reached for her cell phone to stop the other cruisers from rushing to the scene. Then she tipped her big Smokey hat back on her head and said, "Want to tell me what happened, Mrs. Peck?"

"I spotted him out of the corner of my eye," Bertha informed her proudly. "He was fast, but my own reflexes have always been well above average."

Des nudged the glass with her foot—and discovered, to her shock, that the poor creature was still moving. "He's alive."

"Of course he is. I'm no murderer."

"But . . . he's got blood all over him."

"That's not blood, dear. It's Clamato juice. I was having a Bloody Mary at the time."

"I see. And now you . . . ?"

"I want him removed from my residence, if you please."

"Of course, ma'am. Do you have a piece of cardboard I could use?"

Bertha went down the hall and returned with a shirt cardboard. Des slid it beneath the glass to secure the mouse in place, then carried it downstairs to the backyard and released it on the lawn. It ran away in a flash of red.

Maddee Farrell was out there fussing with the Captain Chadwick House's prized, fragrant Blush Noisette rosebushes, her pewter-colored hair drawn back in a tight helmet. Summertime could be very cruel to older women, Des reflected. Even those who were tall, slender and patrician. Maddee had no doubt been willowy and lovely when she was young. Now that she was approaching seventy, Maddee's sleeveless white blouse and pastel-yellow shorts revealed sticklike arms and legs that were mottled with liver spots. Her elbows were pointy, her throat shriveled. The poor woman looked like a famine victim. It didn't help that she had a street beggar's needy look on her deeply creased face. And wore too much lipstick that was such a ghastly shade of magenta.

"Why, good afternoon, Master Sergeant Mitry. Is everything okay with Bertha?"

"Everything's fine."

"Please tell me you've apprehended that awful pervert."

"I wish I could, ma'am."

"I'm afraid to go near a window after dark. We have a ground-floor unit. I—I could be his next victim, you know."

Des started back upstairs with the highball glass. Maddee stayed right on her tail, matching her step for step. When they reached Bertha's apartment, Maddee went barging into the lady's kitchen and started rummaging around.

Bertha stood in the entry hall, shaking her head. "I call her the trash Nazi, Desiree. Just watch, I guarantee you she won't return empty handed."

She didn't. Maddee emerged from Bertha's kitchen clutching an empty tonic water bottle as well as several used, gunky Ziploc freezer bags. "Bertha, you can get a nickel back on this bottle," she clucked. "And these Ziplocs can be washed and re-used."

"They're all yours, dear," Bertha said grandly. "Desiree, it might interest you to know that our Maddee has the largest privately held collection of used Ziploc bags in southern New England. What do you suppose she *does* with all of them?"

"And if you're discarding any other items of clothing, *please* let me have them for the Nearly New shop. I found several very nice sweaters of yours out in the garbage cans yesterday."

"Tell me, do your old Vassar classmates know that you've taken to Dumpster diving in your golden years?"

"We can get good money for them," Maddee plowed on, undeterred. "Or at the very least take them to the Goodwill bins behind Christiansen's Hardware. And honestly, Bertha, I do wish you'd called *us* about that mouse. Dex would have been only too happy to—"

"Make another sixty percent of my life's savings disappear?" Bertha demanded, turning savage. "Once was enough, thank you."

Maddee's eyes widened in shock, her magenta lips drawing back in a frozen grin that reminded Des way too much of death rictus. Blinking back tears, she scampered out of there.

"There," sniffed Bertha, "goes the cheapest damned woman I've ever met."

"Maybe she just cares about the environment."

"Like hell. Maddee Farrell's not eco-anything. She's simply a needy pest. Honestly, if I ever end up like her, I sincerely hope that someone will shoot me."

"Mrs. Peck, I'm always here if you need me. But disposing of a mouse is really something you should be calling Augie about." Meaning Augie Donatelli, the live-in caretaker.

Bertha made a face. "*That* beery do-nothing? I did phone his apartment. He didn't answer. Wasn't on the premises. Never is when I need him."

"Did you try his cell phone? He carries it with him at all times." Des happened to know this because the man was in the habit of speed dialing her four, five, six times a day to tell her how to do her job. Augie was a retired New York City police detective and full-time pain in the butt.

"He didn't answer his cell phone either. He's probably passed out drunk somewhere. I swear, when his contract comes up for renewal I'm going to make certain that the condo board cans him." Bertha batted her big, saucer eyes at Des. "But thank *you* for coming, dear. You're the one person who I know I can always count on."

Des returned downstairs and headed out back, to the row of garages. Augie's was the last one on the right. It was a double garage. His apartment upstairs was reached by a wooden staircase inside. Augie's shiny red Pontiac GTO muscle car from the sixties was parked inside, along with the John Deere riding mower and Gator utility vehicle that he used if and when he felt like working. Which he actually was as Des approached. The ex-cop was firing up the Gator, his left hand wrapped around a tall can of Ballantine Ale. The man had to be good for eighteen cans a day. He kept a supply in an old refrigerator next to his workbench.

"Mr. Donatelli . . . ?!" she called out to him over the roar of the Gator.

He shut off the engine, grinning at her wolfishly. Augie Donatelli had to be the most gleefully obnoxious sexist she'd ever met. The Notorious P.I.G. positively rolled around in the inappropriateness of his behavior. "I thought I told ya to call me Augie, sugar pie," he sprayed at her in his juicy Brooklyn bray.

"And *I* thought we had an understanding."

Augie took a swig of his ale. "We did?"

"You were going to be reachable by cell so I wouldn't keep getting nine-one-oned by Bertha Peck. Mice are your deal, not mine."

"Don't know nothing about that," he grumbled, rubbing a hand over his unshaven face. Augie was in his mid-fifties, with snaggly yellow teeth and brown eyes that were bleary and red-rimmed. His face was battered and bent-nosed. His droopy moustache, which harkened back to the Serpico Seventies, was flecked with gray. So was his black hair, which he wore unusually long. Almost to his shoulders. He wasn't particularly tall, but his shoulders were heavy and the arms that stuck out of his too-snug black T-shirt looked powerful. He had on a pair of ragged blue jean cut-offs, white tube socks and a pair of old-school Pumas. "But, hey, I'll get right on it," he promised, draining his Ballantine.

"You're too late. It's already done."

"So why are you busting my chops?" He fetched himself a fresh can from the refrigerator, moving with the cocky ease of a man who'd spent his entire career refusing to be intimidated by anyone.

"Bertha is talking about terminating your contract, that's why."

"I'm guessing you have a little something to do with that. Am I right, homegirl?"

"Wrong. That's not how I roll. And I am *not* your homegirl."

Their relationship had been antagonistic from day one. The very first words he'd said to her were, "Hey, mama, can I get some fries with that shake?" Her very first words in reply: "How would you like to spend the rest of the afternoon searching the driveway for your teeth?"

And it had gone straight downhill from there. Augie was always trying to goad her. Part of him was just kidding around. But not all of him. His eyes, when he turned serious, were cold, forbidding holes. Augie had a definite problem with the likes of Des wearing a uniform. She didn't know if it was because of her pigment, her gender or both. Didn't care, actually. The man was an ass.

He started up the Gator, Ballantine in hand, and eased it over to the Farrells' garage, which was open. Big, plastic tubs full of nickel deposit bottles were stowed in there next to their long, white Cadillac. On a Ping-Pong table there were a dozen or more black plastic trash bags stuffed with old clothing. Each bag had a label on it that read something like *Women's Sweaters: Petites*, *Men's Shirts: Mediums* or *Goodwill*. A cord of seasoned firewood was stacked against the back wall.

Augie began to fill the Gator's box-shaped cargo bed with armloads of wood. "That skinny old bitch Mrs. Farrell accosts me this morning and tells me they *must* have firewood on their porch *right away*." He paused to belch audibly. "I say to her, 'Lady, it's ninety effing degrees out.' But her husband positively swears the weather's going to turn sharply colder next week. And she says he chills easily. Must be that blue blood of his. Me, I'm a hot-blooded Mediterranean. I never get cold. Never screw people out of their life's savings either. If it weren't for that bastard, I'd be out fishing right now—maybe some nice, long-legged babe rubbing suntan lotion on my back. Instead, I have to put up with them and their crap. Get this—I was out sweeping the front walk this morning, maybe seven-thirty. I come back and I find that skinny old bitch *in my apartment*. You'll never guess what she was doing."

"Rummaging through your trash?"

"Exactamundo. She ain't all there, you ask me. And, boy, does she have her nose up in the air. Her and all of the other rich old broads in this town. You say hello to them and they act like you just took a leak on their shoes."

"Mr. Donatelli . . ."

"It's *Augie.*"

"What are you doing here?"

"Working. Why, what does it look like I'm doing?"

"I mean here in Dorset."

"Oh . . ." His face went slack. "My missus, Gina, always wanted to retire to a cozy little New England village. All those years in Mineola she kept saving brochures, magazine articles. It was her dream. But she never got the chance. The cancer got her."

"Is that why you retired from the NYPD?"

"*That* is none of your damned business."

She'd run a computer background check on him at the Troop F barracks. Detective Lieutenant Augie Donatelli had received four commendations for valor during his career. He'd been working out of the 24th Precinct on Manhattan's Upper West Side last year when he chose to retire after twenty-six years on the job.

"I'm here for the both of us," he grunted as he toted one more armload of wood to the Gator. His gait was not entirely steady. He was at least a six-pack into the Ballantine. "The job was dead to me. The city was dead to me. House was empty. So here I am, sugar pie. You got a problem with that?"

"No, Augie, I don't."

He got back in behind the wheel of the Gator, grinning at her. "Good, because I think I've got a break in our flasher case."

Des immediately felt herself tighten up inside. "I thought we had an understanding about that, too. You're not on the job anymore. And I don't discuss ongoing investigations with members of the public."

He shook his head at her in disgust. "Drop the act, will ya? I'll admit it—you're walking around with one of the top ten cabooses I've ever seen in my life. And I used to work *uptown,* if you follow what I'm saying. . . ."

"Actually, I'm trying really hard not to."

"But I was busting heads back when you were still in kindergarten. So be smart. I'm a resource. And I've got one doozie of a theory. If I were you, I'd listen to it."

"It's been a long, hot day. How about tomorrow?"

"You blowing me off?"

"I'm saying how about tomorrow." And hoping he'd forget that they'd ever had this conversation. Beery haze and all. "Have a good one, Augie." She tipped her Smokey hat at him and started down the driveway toward her cruiser.

Augie turn the Gator around and eased along next to her. "What time should I call you?"

"I'll call you."

"Know what? You have got some attitude on you, homegirl."

"I don't have an attitude. I treat everyone with respect. Why don't you give it a try sometime?"

"Wait, I got something else for you. I'm talking huge here. Has to do with our Beth Breslauer," he confided, glancing over his shoulder in the direction of her condo. "She and your boy Mitch are real tight, you know. They met for smoothies at The Works this afternoon."

"And you know this because . . . ?"

"I have the lady under surveillance."

Des came to a stop, hands on her hips. "You're following her?"

"She's quite some dish. I'd tap that in two seconds flat if it gave me a chance."

"Um, okay, I'm guessing *it* hasn't. Augie, are you aware that we have stalker laws in this state?"

"Who's stalking? The Works is a public place. So's the Mohegan Sun Casino in Uncasville."

"What about the Mohegan Sun?"

"I drove up there a couple of weeks back to see Billy Joel. The Piano Man did ten straight sold-out nights there. And, believe me, he put on a show. Pounded those ivories for two and half hours, sang his heart out . . ."

"You saw Mrs. Breslauer at the Billy Joel concert?"

"Outside in the parking lot. She was working it."

"What do you mean by 'working it?' "

"Trust me, that lady is not who she pretends to be," he explained, taking a long swig of his Ballantine. "This is one of the most fascinating characters I've come across in a long time. Ever hear of the Seven Sisters?"

"Sure, that's what they called the ladies' Ivy League back before the schools went coed. There was, let's see, Vassar, Bryn Mawr, Wellesley, Smith . . ."

"No, not *those* Seven Sisters. Geez, don't you hick troopers out here know anything?"

By now they'd reached the foot of the driveway. Des could see the Farrells seated on their screened-in porch. Dex Farrell was sitting in a rocker, reading a book. He was a severe-looking white-haired man with rimless eyeglasses. He didn't look up at them. But Maddee did—and promptly got busy making space on the porch for the firewood.

Across the street, John the barber was locking up his little shop for the night. He and a couple of his fellow volunteers from the firehouse next door were gabbing. All three of them waved at Des.

She waved back at them, then took a deep breath and said, "Can I give you a piece of advice, Augie? If you want to remain employed in this hick town, you'd better stop tailing your tenants and start fixing their leaky faucets. And you might want to cut back on the Ballantine, too."

"You *are* trying to get me fired," he snarled in response. "Nothing makes you people happier, does it?"

"By 'you people' you mean . . . ?"

"Don't play dumb with me, you bitch! You know what I mean. Can't stand having me around, can you? Afraid your little secret will get out."

"What little secret?"

"That you haven't got the slightest goddamned idea what you're doing!"

The men across the street could hear Augie quite plainly. Were missing none of this.

"Get hold of yourself, Augie," Des cautioned him quietly.

No chance of that. He climbed out of the Gator and charged toward her, staggering slightly. "They don't know the truth about you!" he roared, stabbing her in the shoulder with his finger. "But *I* do! *I* know you stepped over a dozen good men to get this job. And *I* know you stink at it!"

"You've had a few too many, Augie. Why don't you go up to your apartment and sober up?"

"Don't tell me what to do!"

She put a gentling hand on his shoulder. "Take it easy. I'm on your side."

"Like hell you are. Get your goddamned hand off of me. Get it off!" he hollered with a violent shrug of his shoulder. So violent that it rocked him back on his heels. Teetering, he lost his balance and came down hard on his butt in the driveway.

John and the others across the street were laughing at him now.

"You *shoved* me!" he spat at her, enraged.

"I did not." Des held her hand out to him. "Come on, let's get you up."

He bared his ugly, yellow teeth at her. "Get away from me."

"Take my hand, Augie."

He refused. Just sat there on the gravel like a petulant little boy.

"Fine, have it your way. But go home and sleep it off, will you?"

In response, Augie told her to do a very bad thing to herself. Then, in a menacing voice, he said, "Homegirl, you're going to be sorry you ever met me."

"Trust me, wow man . . ." Des showed him her wraparound smile. "I'm already there."

Chapter 3

In the city there was no such thing as autumn. There was summer. There was one cold, rainy weekend in October when all of the leaves fell off of the street trees. And then there was winter. But out on Big Sister, even though a torpid August haze hung low over Long Island Sound, autumn had already begun. Mitch saw its signs everywhere as he made his way down the beach to Bitsy Peck's house, bucket in hand. Orange leaves dotted the island's gnarly old sugar maple trees. A squadron of geese flew low overhead in a V-formation, heading due west. And a swarm of monarch butterflies were encamped in the cedars bordering Bitsy's place, resting up on their long migration south. Fall was coming for sure. It just wasn't in the air yet.

Bitsy had a mammoth, natural-shingled Victorian cottage with sleeping porches, turrets and amazing views in every direction. Her multilevel garden was truly spectacular. Hundreds of species of flowers, vegetables and herbs grew in her fertile terraced beds. It was Bitsy who'd taught Mitch the joys of gardening. She was out there right now, pruning away the yellowing vines on her heirloom tomato plants, the better to expose the ripening fruit to the sun's rays.

"It's the corn man," he called out to her, brandishing his bucket.

"Come ahead, young sir," Bitsy called back. "What's mine is yours."

She'd grown more than she could eat and had told him to take as much as he wanted. The best way to cook the fresh ears, he'd learned, was to plunge them into a bucket of cold water as soon he picked them. Then throw them on the grill to steam in their husks.

Bitsy was a round, snub-nosed little woman in her fifties who'd welcomed Mitch from the day he moved out to Big Sister. She was always happy to share her bounty and her wisdom. Also her insider's knowledge of Dorset. There wasn't anyone or anything that Bitsy Peck didn't know about. It was the Pecks who'd first settled Dorset way back in the 1600s. Bitsy was also someone who had been through a lot. She'd lost her husband right after Mitch came to town. And her daughter, Becca, was a recovering heroin addict. Even though the lady gave the impression of being a ditsy hausfrau, she was plenty tough and shrewd.

"I just ran into Beth Breslauer," he told her as he plucked a few choice ears from her corn patch. "Her name used to be Lapidus. She lived across the hall from me in Stuyvesant Town. Her son Kenny and I were pals growing up."

"Isn't that something? *Such* a small world." Bitsy paused from her labors, fanning herself with her floppy straw hat. "I could use a tall glass of iced tea. Care to join me?"

Mitch filled his bucket from her garden faucet and followed her to the shade of her wraparound porch. He took a seat in one of the rockers and gazed out at the Sound. There were no sailboats out. Not enough breeze. No gas-guzzling cigarette boats either—which had nothing to do with the breeze and everything to do with the economic times they were living in. The chesty boys could no longer afford their toys.

Bitsy came back outside with their iced teas and sat down next to him.

Mitch took a long, grateful drink before he said, "Beth's bought a place in the Captain Chadwick House. It's supposed to be impossible to get in there."

"It's very, very hard," she acknowledged. "I know of at least six ladies who'd love to buy a unit."

"And yet Beth swooped right in even though she's a widow from Scarsdale with no social connections here—that I'm aware of." He studied Bitsy, his eyes narrowing. "Nobody gets in there without a green light from Bertha Peck, am I right?"

"You most certainly are."

"And you're related to Bertha, aren't you?"

"We're second cousins by marriage. My husband's father was a cousin of her late husband Guy Peck, Jr."

"I don't get it. What kind of a connection could Beth possibly have with someone like Bertha Peck?"

Bitsy let out a merry chortle "Exactly what do you know about Bertha?"

"I know that she's the queen bee of Dorset polite society."

"That's Bertha Peck, all righty." Bitsy sipped her iced tea. "But what do you know about Bertha *Puzewski*?"

"Not a thing," Mitch said eagerly. "Do tell."

"Before Bertha married Guy she was a pretty little steelworker's daughter who'd danced her way to Broadway from Weirton, West Virginia. Bertha was a chorus girl when Guy met her. Check out her legs some time. They're still fabulous."

"I had no idea."

"That's because she reinvented herself as Yankee royalty. Trust me, the only finishing school she attended was the Billy Rose Aquacade at the 1939 World's Fair. *And* she got around in those days, too. Dated racketeers, gamblers, prizefighters. She was quite the little tootsie, our Bertha. There was a whole lot of whispering about her when she married Guy. I can still remember the old Dorset biddies saying that she'd once been the kept mistress of some mobster. Why, they practically made her out to be the Woman in Red." Bitsy paused, frowning. "I don't suppose that name will mean anything to someone your age."

"You're referring to Anna Sage, the madam who fingered John Dillinger for the FBI. She told them he'd be at the Biograph Theater in Chicago watching *Manhattan Melodrama*, an MGM gangster picture with Clark Gable, William Powell and Myrna Loy. It was the first on-screen pairing of Powell and Loy, who went on to make fourteen pictures together. Most notably their *Thin Man* series."

Bitsy stared at him with her mouth open. "Sorry, I forgot who I was talking to." She sipped her iced tea and resumed. "Bertha has outlasted all of those old ladies. There's hardly anyone left who knows her real story."

"Tell me, what have you heard about Beth Breslauer?"

"Not a whole lot, honestly. She doesn't socialize much. I understand that her late husband was an eye doctor in the city. I do know that Bertha prefers New York City doctors to the fellows out here. Maybe that's their connection. Maybe Beth's husband treated her."

"It turns out that Kenny is getting married to Kimberly Farrell, my yoga teacher."

"So I've heard. Kimmy went through school with my Becca. She's always been a real sweetheart."

"And yet Beth seemed a bit cool about her. Told me there was *baggage*. Kimberly's father, for starters. Her mother is hoping a great big wedding will get them back into the good graces of Dorset's elite."

"That's not too likely," Bitsy said with a shake of her head.

"Meaning people aren't ready to forgive him?"

"Meaning Dex and Maddee Farrell never belonged to Dorset's elite in the first place."

Mitch looked at her in surprise. "I thought they were upper crusters."

"You thought wrong, Mitch. Neither Dex nor Maddee is from

one of the founding families. To be quote-unquote Dorset you must be a Peck, a Vickers or a Havenhurst. The Farrells are merely wealthy New Yorkers with good social contacts."

"Whoa, time out. Bertha Peck is a chorus girl from Weirton, right?"

"Right."

"And no one in Dorset so much as farts without her permission, right?"

"Mitch, no one in Dorset farts, period," she pointed out, her eyes twinkling at him.

"So how come she's quote-unquote Dorset and they aren't?"

"Because she married Guy. Because she's Bertha. And because Dex behaved despicably." Bitsy gazed out at the water, her snub nose wrinkling. "My retirement portfolio is worth a fraction of what it once was thanks to that man. He will not be forgiven easily by me or anyone else."

Mitch rocked back and forth, sipping his tea. "Beth also has some concerns about Kimberly."

"I can't imagine why. Kimmy's a terrific catch for the right young man."

"I gather she wasn't the right catch for someone else."

"Oh, I get it. She's wondering about Kimmy's marriage to Connie Cliffe's boy."

Mitch knew the name Connie Cliffe. She was a high-end interior designer who had a mansion in the Historic District.

"Surely Beth can't be holding J. Z. against her," Bitsy went on. "A lot of us make that sort of mistake when we're young. Kimmy was barely out of Bennington when she met him. J. Z. was a good ten years older than she. Lordy, he must be forty by now. You've no doubt seen him working around the island. He's the house painter who does my place, Dolly's. . . ."

Mitch knew whom she meant now. The big, strapping guy with

the ponytail who'd been reglazing Bitsy's windows a few weeks back.

"That marriage lasted less than three months, Mitch. And, believe me, it wasn't Kimmy's fault. These things happen."

"What things happen?"

Bitsy considered her reply carefully. "Connie's a good friend. She and her husband, Fred, split up when J. Z. was a small boy. She raised him on her own, and that boy . . . how shall I put this? He was a real stinker, Mitch. The sort of rotten little rich kid who's always stealing things and getting into fistfights. By the time J. Z. was thirteen, he was into alcohol, marijuana, cocaine. Connie couldn't handle him. She sent him off to live with his father in New York City. Fred owned an art gallery in Soho, a couple of chic restaurants. He enrolled J. Z. in one of the best private schools. But he had no better luck with the boy than Connie did. J. Z. got himself kicked out of one school after another. Ended up out in New Mexico at a special school for problem kids. Where he did settle down. He even got accepted at Cornell. But he barely lasted a month there before he was back in New York City, working as a roadie for alternative rock bands, which I believe is a polite way of saying he dealt drugs. And used them. He and all of his rich, spoiled friends. They partied day and night, perfectly content to squander the best years of their lives. J. Z. always did well with the girls. He was handsome and wild and a bit dangerous. One night, he and a very pretty Park Avenue heiress totaled her BMW in East Hampton and almost killed someone. She was behind the wheel—and high on cocaine at the time. Went to jail for a year in spite of her daddy's pull. J. Z. ended up back out here living in Connie's guest cottage. By then he'd thoroughly fried his brains on drugs. What the kids call a homeschool Ph.D.—as in Permanent Head Damage."

"How did he and Kimberly hook up?"

"He was helping Courtney Borio paint the Farrells' house on Turkey Neck. Courtney was a burnout case himself from the Vietnam War. J. Z. went to work for him and, lo and behold, stuck with it. Kimmy was home from Bennington for the summer. The poor girl fell hard for J. Z. Convinced herself that with a little love and understanding, he'd do great things with his life. Dex and Maddee opposed the marriage, naturally. She went ahead with it anyway, naturally. Dex and Maddee bought them the condo in the Captain Chadwick House as a wedding present. That's how the Farrells came to own it. Gosh knows they couldn't get in there now if they tried." Bitsy let out a sigh of regret. "Kimmy and J. Z. didn't live there for long. She completely washed her hands of him. Took off for Oregon and didn't come back for years. Connie has never spoken one word to me about why Kimmy cleared out so fast—other than to say it was a private matter. Mind you, that didn't stop people from gossiping about what really happened."

"And what was the consensus?"

"That it was something of a sexual nature. Courtney Borio happened to be gay. He had a longtime thing going on with a fellow up in Chester. Anyhow, when Courtney first took J. Z. under his wing there was a lot of whispering that J. Z. might be . . . so inclined. When Kimmy upped and left him like she did, well, the whisperers thought they knew why. Not that anyone actually *knew*. But it made for a good, juicy story."

"What do *you* think happened, Bitsy?"

"I think J. Z. broke that poor girl's heart. Don't ask me how, because I have no idea. But I do know that J. Z.'s a breaker of hearts. He always has been. He can't help himself. That man can be . . . difficult. In fact, some people think that in order to get along with him you have to be able to speak psycho. Not true. But he's not all there. Still stoned on drugs half of the time, if you ask me."

"And yet you keep hiring him. Why?"

Bitsy's blue eyes locked on his and held them. "Because this is Dorset, Mitch. We may not be perfect. Far from it, in fact. But we always take care of our own. Never, ever forget that."

Chapter 4

A narrow dirt road snaked its way through the meadows and tidal marshes of the Peck's Point Nature Preserve, a peninsula that jutted out into Long Island Sound at the mouth of the Connecticut River. The dirt road ended at a barricade. Beyond it was the narrow, wooden causeway out to Big Sister Island. Des inserted her coded plastic security card to raise the barricade and then eased her cruiser *thumpety-thump-bumpety* out to the forty acres of Yankee paradise that Mitch was lucky enough to call home. There were five precious old Peck family homes out on Big Sister, not counting his caretaker's cottage. A decommissioned lighthouse that was the second tallest in New England. A private beach and dock. A tennis court. There was fresh, clean sea air. There was peace.

Quirt, Mitch's lean, mean outdoor hunter, came darting over to bump her leg with his hard little head as she climbed out of the car. Quirt was one of the two rescued strays she'd convinced Mitch to adopt. Des bent down and stroked him, feeling herself relax for the first time since she'd driven away from the Captain Chadwick House.

She kept a yellow string bikini at Mitch's that was positively indecent. She went inside the house, kicking off her shiny, black shoes. Peeled off her uni and ankle socks. Put the tiny thing on. She left her horn-rims on the bathroom shelf. Didn't need them. Didn't need to worry about her hair either, which she wore short and nubby. She grabbed a towel and started down the sandy path to the beach, feeling the sun-warmed sand between her toes.

Mitch was sitting on the float a hundred feet out, with his feet dangling in the water and a bottle of beer in his hand. The beer cooler sat beside him. He waved to her. Des waded in, then dove underwater and swam toward him, welcoming the water's delicious coolness all over her body. She surfaced and pulled herself, wet and shiny, up onto the float, stretching her fine self out next to him.

"Sorry, miss, but this is a private float. You'll have to pay a toll."

She leaned forward on her elbows and kissed him softly on the mouth. "Will that do?"

"We'll consider it a modest down payment."

Mitch pulled a Corona from the cooler and opened it for her. She took it from him, her eyes eating him up. She still could not get over how hard and cut he was. He'd been a flesh prince when she first fell for him—man boobs and all. Not anymore. He was a hunk.

She took a long, grateful drink of her beer, sighing contently. "I have been missing you all day, Armando." Which was her pet name for him now that doughboy no longer applied.

"Back at you, master sergeant. What took you so long anyhow?"

She told him about Augie, her voice rising with anger as she described the ugly little public scene he'd provoked.

Mitch studied her curiously. "You've dealt with drunks like Augie a million times. Why are you letting him get under your skin?"

"You mean aside from the fact he's a racist, sexist boor?"

"Seriously, why are you?"

She took another drink of her beer. "Because he was on the job. I don't like seeing what's happened to him. But enough about that fool. How was your day?"

"Great. I ran into an old flame. She lives right here in Dorset now. We're invited over for drinks tomorrow."

"I'm sorry, you just said what?"

He leaned over and kissed her, this time long and lingering. "Beth lived across the hall from me when I was a kid. She was a single mom. I looked out for her boy Kenny. Used to drag him to see old movies with me. He's a computer geek up in Cambridge now. Comes here every weekend because—get this—he's engaged to my yoga teacher, Kimberly. She's Beth's neighbor at the Captain Chadwick House."

"So this would be Beth Breslauer?"

"Her name was Lapidus when I was growing up," he said wistfully. "To me, she'll always be Beth Lapidus."

"Mitch, I would swear you're blushing right now."

"Am not."

"No, no, you totally are. Is something going on between you two that I should know about?"

"Why would you say that?"

"You just called her an old flame, remember?"

"Des, she was my very first big-time crush. I was thirteen and she was this incredibly sexy divorcee with knockers out to here."

Des glanced down at what was inside of her bikini top. Or, more precisely, wasn't. "Since when are you into knockers out to here?"

"All thirteen-year-old boys are into knockers out to here. Who was yours?"

"Who was my what?"

"First big-time crush."

Des stretched out on her back, gazing dreamily up at the milky blue sky. "George Michael. I had posters of that man plastered all over my room."

"Was this back when he was still with Wham or had he already embarked on his trailblazing solo career?"

"Hey, did I chump you about your first crush?"

"Yes, you did. And I'm very mad at you." He ran his hand up her smooth, bare flank, caressing her. "Very, very mad." Now he was licking the dried salt from her belly button. "Absolutely, positively furious." His tongue sliding lower and . . .

"Mitch, they can *see* us!"
"Who can?"
"The eye in the sky. Google Earth, NASA, whoever."
"Let 'em watch. Maybe they'll learn something."
She sat up, rearranging her teeny top. "I'll race you inside."
"What's in it for me if I win?"
"Oh, I think you know."
They were barely in the door before they were out of their suits. They jumped into the shower together and washed off the sand, hands all over each other. And then they were up in his sleeping loft taking it nice and slow and tender. It wasn't about performing. It was about *them*. And, God, was *them* something good.
As dusk approached they lay there in each other's arms, eyes glittering, unable to keep the silly grins off of their faces, not even trying. Mitch's indoor cat, Clemmie, lay curled up between them, purring. A sea breeze had picked up, cooling the airy little cottage.
"Can I interest you in some dinner, master sergeant?"
"You can interest me in just about anything right now."
Mitch put on a T-shirt and shorts and went outside to fire up the grill. She got into his No. 15 Earl the Pearl Knicks jersey and stretched out on a lawn chair, sipping a cold glass of Sancerre while he raided his garden for fingerling potatoes, tomatoes and basil. He put the potatoes on to boil, then flopped down in the lawn chair with a beer. They gazed out at the water, so comfortable with the island's quiet and each other that they felt no need to talk.
Except she did need to talk—about the case she was working. She had no partner to spitball with. Mitch knew this.
Which was why he blurted out, "How do you know for a fact that it's always the same guy?"
She frowned at him. He was never short of insights. Most of them whack. But, somehow, he did see things. "Um, okay, you're going where with this?"

"What if you're dealing with a *gang* of flashers? It's not as if the ladies have given you anything more than a vague description, right? Average height and weight. Wears a ski mask. For all you know, each lady could have been visited by a different weenie waver."

"You're not wrong about that. But why are you thinking it?"

"Because this whole thing's a goof."

"Mitch, it's no goof."

"Yeah, it is. It's just the kind of dorky stunt a bunch of bored teenaged boys would pull off. Like the Mod Squad, remember?"

"Who could forget them?" There had been five of those boys—high school garbage heads who'd taken to spray painting obscene graffiti all over Dorset. "And that was no goof, Mitch. They almost burned down Center School, as you may recall. But keep talking."

"You're not dealing with a sexual predator who's out there preying on attractive young women. He, or I should say they, have strictly chosen rich old ladies. Plus you've got that petty nuisance stuff in the mix. The dead skunk. The funeral home's sign. I'm telling you—it's a bunch of pimply kids. That also explains why it always happens on the weekend. Because their parents go out to dinner or the movies on the weekend. They aren't around to keep an eye on the little weasels. Tell me, have any of the ladies said the perp was . . . why are you smiling?"

"You said *perp*. You're just so cute when you do that. Sorry, go on."

"Have any of them described him as being, you know . . . ?"

"Locked in the upright position? Not a one. And, believe me, it has really, really been fun talking tumescence with the old girls."

"So he gives them a limp wave and then he runs. Which means he's *not* doing this for a sexual thrill." Mitch got up to check the grill. The fire was ready. He put the corn on to steam and sat back down next to her. "I'm telling you, girlfriend, this is no pervert. It's a gang of pranksters."

"Okay, I'll admit that it plays your way—in the abstract."

"What about in the real?"

"Not so much. We've got profiles of every kind of human depravity you can imagine—and then some—in our criminal data bank. Your flasher is typically someone who has no gang to run with. He's lonely, sexually frustrated and often confused about his sexual orientation. But it's funny that you brought up the Mod Squad. I talked to one of them today—Ronnie Welmers. He's a junior at Middlebury College in Vermont now. Had a summer job on campus that ended two weeks ago. He's been home visiting his dad since then."

"Hmm, interesting. Are you liking him for this?"

"Not really. Ronnie's cleaned up his act. Plans to go to business school."

"Wait, I thought you just said he's cleaned up his act."

"But he still likes to hang with his 'homeys,' as they so quaintly put it here in Funky Town, USA. I kept that boy's ass out of jail. Ronnie owes me big time. Told me he's been to a couple of keggers, caught up with old friends. Some of whom still go to the high school. All of them were talking about the Dorset Flasher. And he swears that not one of them has the slightest idea who he is. It's the best-kept secret around. They all think it's pretty hilarious."

"It does have its humorous side, you have to admit."

"Mitch, there's nothing funny about it. This guy is ruining my life. We patrolled the Historic District *in force* last weekend. And yet, somehow, he managed to hit four more old ladies without us getting so much as a glimpse of him. I'd swear he was getting around the village via the sewer system except—"

"Sure, sure. Just like Harry Lime in *The Third Man*. God, did Orson Welles slay in that film or—?"

"*Except* Dorset doesn't *have* a sewer system. Meanwhile, I've busted my hump working my way through every single loser boy in Dorset. Anyone who's been picked up for drugs, stealing, fighting in the past five years. Swamp Yankees *and* rich kids. And I've gotten absolutely nowhere. Whoever he is, he's smart and he's careful. He doesn't wear a wristwatch or rings on his fingers. Nothing that could identify him. He leaves no traces behind. Not a single shoe print. He defaced the funeral home's sign with a plain old Sharpie that you can buy anywhere. A friend of mine rushed that dead skunk through the lab up in Meriden for me. No fingerprints. He wore gloves when he handled it." Des took a sip of her wine. "I've got a theory, too. And I would never admit this to Bob Paffin in a million years. . . ."

"What is it, Des?"

"That we're dealing with a bright, pissed-off sixteen-year-old boy who has been marinating in self-pity all summer. And when school starts he'll crawl back into the woodwork and the incidents will stop."

"If that's the case then how are you going to catch him?"

"I'm not going to catch him, Mitch."

"You mean he's going to get away with it? That's not a good ending."

"We don't always get happy endings. This is real life."

"Doesn't matter. Trust me, girlfriend, you still need a rewrite."

Darkness was falling by now. He put the fish on to cook while she went inside and made a salad out of his ripe, juicy tomatoes, fragrant basil leaves and the buffalo mozzarella. She dressed it with olive oil and balsamic vinegar, then mashed up the fingerling potatoes with a drop more olive oil, plain yogurt and a whole lot of fresh dill. After that she set the table, lit the candles and opened another bottle of Sancerre. By then the grill chef was coming in the door with the smoky striped bass and steaming ears of corn.

"Actually, I did have one promising lead," she told him as they dove in, starved. "I haven't said anything because you happen to know the guy. I can talk about it now because I've crossed him off of my list. But you can't breathe a word of this, deal?"

"Deal," he promised. "Who are we . . . ?"

"Hal Chapman, your skullet-head trainer."

"Hal? No way!"

"Yes way. Hear my thing, okay? The principal at the high school poked around in some old files for me. Back when your boy Hal was fifteen, he got in trouble for behaving inappropriately toward a female classmate."

"Behaving inappropriately how?"

"He exposed himself to her out by the bleachers at lunch. The girl's parents declined to press charges so the law didn't get into it. School handled it internally. Counseling and so forth. And Hal was a model citizen after that. Even got a full ride to play football at Boston College."

Mitch nodded. "He blew out his knee freshman year and dropped out."

"He bitter about it?"

"Doesn't seem to be. He's always cheerful. A good trainer, real enthusiastic. He lives in his parents' old house on Griswold Avenue. They've retired to North Carolina. His dad worked for Electric Boat, I think. I don't know a whole lot more about Hal—aside from the fact that he does pretty well with the ladies."

"He does *real* well," she said, munching on an ear of corn. "I shadowed him this week. Tuesday night he got busy with this hot little hostess, Celine Sullivan, who works at the Rustic Inn. She spent the night at his place. Wednesday night he was with Shaun English, that tall, good-looking young thing in the Town Assessor's Office. He spent the night at her place. And last night your boy had himself a double-header. First he got sandy-rumped at Bluff Point with a young married lady named Lisa Neville. She's a client of his at the club. Her husband travels a lot on business. After Lisa went home to the kids,

Hal got busy down at Rocky Neck with Doreen Joslow, another of his clients. Also married. You've got to admire his stamina. Like I said, I've crossed him off of my list. He just doesn't fit the profile. He's not lonely. He's not angry. And he's for sure not sexually frustrated. That man's out there living the dream."

Mitch's phone rang. He took the call on the wall phone in his kitchen. Des glanced at her watch. It was 9:45. Late for someone in Dorset to be calling.

"Oh, hi, Bella," she heard him say into the phone. "Yeah, she's right here . . . No, no, it's okay. . . . Uh-huh . . . Okay, I'll tell her. . . . I don't know, ten minutes tops." He hung up and returned to the table with a troubled look on his face. "Bad news, girlfriend. He just struck again—at your place."

Her place was a snug two-bedroom Cape on a hilltop with a great view of Uncas Lake, which was two miles up the Boston Post Road from the Historic District. The front-porch light was on and the garage door was open, throwing all kinds of light out onto the short driveway. Also meowing. The eight feral strays she and Bella had rescued over the past two months were presently residing in cages in there while not-so-patiently awaiting good homes. Bella's jeep and Des's four-year-old Saab were parked out on the street. Des pulled her cruiser into the driveway with a screech and jumped out. Mitch was right on her tail in his pickup. He'd insisted upon joining her.

Bella, a short, feisty widow from Brooklyn in her late 70s, stood there in the garage doorway, hands on round hips, looking like an angry Jewish avocado in her dark green tank top and shorts. Also lopsided. She was wearing only one sneaker. The other foot was bare. Bella had been Des's neighbor back in Woodbridge when Des and Brandon were still married. It was Bella who'd saved her when Brandon took off. Bella who'd become her unlikely best friend and housemate—although she was always searching for a little place of her own.

"Believe me, the *last* thing in the world I wanted to do was ruin your romantic evening," she apologized as Des rushed toward her. "You've had *no* time for each other since this yutz started waving his pizzle all over town. I hope you weren't making wild love on the kitchen floor, all slathered in lavender oil."

"Bella, have you been watching *The Young and the Restless* again?"

"I happen to find daytime drama very stimulating."

"Yeah, I can tell that."

"It's cool, Aunt Bella," Mitch assured her. "We were just getting ready to wash the dishes."

"*Wash the dishes*?" Bella was incredulous. Also way disappointed. "Do I need to draw you two a map?"

"Talk to me, girl. What happened?"

Bella gestured to the front porch, where her missing sneaker lay discarded on the pavement. "The welcome mat is what happened," she answered, hobbling over there. "I was sitting at the dining table, e-mailing my grandson Errol. He's Ezra and Babette's boy. Very nice boy. A first-year dental student at UCLA. He's dating a girl from Thailand. I don't know how serious it is but—"

"You were at the dining table," Des prompted her. "And . . . ?"

"The doorbell rang."

"What time was this?"

"Nine thirty-seven, according to that little clock on my computer screen. I went to the door and I asked who it was. Believe me, there was no way I was opening it. Not with that nut on the loose. No one answered me. So I turned on the porch light and looked out through the peephole. I didn't see anyone. I waited a minute, then finally I opened the door, walked outside and . . ." She made a face. "That's when I stepped in it."

It was a turd. A very large, very fresh turd that had been deposited on Des's sisal welcome mat. She bent over for a closer look, her nostrils crinkling.

"I'm sorry if I compromised the evidence by squishing it."

"Bella, don't even go there. I'm just sorry your sneaker's ruined."

"Oh, no. It's not ruined. I'll bleach it. I'll boil it. Whatever it takes. That little pisher's not going to cost me a perfectly good pair of New Balances. And when you catch him I'll have a little present of my own for him. Let me tell you—if a rotten punk ever tried pulling this on Gates Avenue in the old days, we'd have made him eat that whole thing for lunch between two slices of marbled rye."

Des popped the trunk of her cruiser and donned a pair of disposable latex gloves, then grabbed a plastic evidence bag and a tongue depressor. A cruiser pulled up behind her Saab. It was Trooper Olsen, who'd been part of her four-person team that tried to nail the Dorset Flasher last weekend. And would be out there again tomorrow night. Oly was big, blond and competent. She filled him in and asked him to start canvassing the neighbors. Maybe one of them had seen something, or someone, between the hours of 9:30 and 9:45. He got right on it.

"Well, this was a first," Mitch said when she returned to the porch. "The Flasher has never struck on a Friday before."

"He's also never gone after sworn personnel."

"Maybe Bella was his intended target, not you."

"Trust me, she wasn't. Bella, I need for you to think hard. This isn't just us talking now. You're a witness in an ongoing criminal investigation. Exactly what did you see?"

"I told you—not a thing. When I opened the door nobody was there."

"Did you hear a car door slam? Someone driving away?"

Bella shook her head. "Nothing like that."

"How about footsteps? Maybe someone running?"

"I didn't see or hear anything," Bella stated flatly.

"Maybe he parked his car down the road," Mitch said.

"Maybe."

"Do you need my sneaker as evidence?" Bella asked. "Because I'd like to start soaking it if you don't mind."

"Go right ahead and soak."

Bella picked her shoe up by the laces and headed into the garage with it. Des crouched next to the mat and used the tongue depressor to scoop a sample of the turd into the plastic bag.

"This is a positive development, right?" Mitch said. "You've got actual physical evidence now. Your lab can figure out how big the dog was and that'll point you to its owner. All dogs in Dorset have to be licensed, right?"

"They do, Mitch. Except there are a couple of holes in your theory. For one, he could have plucked this off of anybody's front lawn. And for another, this isn't just any old dog poop."

"How do you know that?"

"Because when I was with Major Crimes we shared the same facility up in Meriden with the state's K-9 Training Center. I've seen what your average mature German shepherd leaves behind. This here was produced by a bigger animal."

"There are plenty of breeds bigger than German shepherds. You've got your Great Danes, Irish wolfhounds. And then there are the really big boys like Saint Bernards and English mastiffs. There can't be too many of those in—"

"Mitch, I'm fairly certain that this didn't come from *any* dog."

"Oh, okay, then that's a whole different plot." He bent over, squinting at it. "It's not a cow pie. And I know horse droppings when I see them." His face dropped. "God, please don't tell me it's a bear."

"No, nothing as tabloid fantastic as that. I'm sorry to say that unless I'm totally wrong—and I'm not—the origin of this fecal specimen is human."

For a second, Des thought her he-guy was going to lose his striped bass. But he gathered himself, gulping, and said, "Well . . . that's good, too."

"Really? How so?"

"We've got a fresh human fecal specimen here."

"Still waiting for the good part, Mitch."

"The state forensic lab can extract the guy's DNA from it, can't they?"

"Actually, that's a big no. The DNA in human fecal matter is too degraded for them to get a profile. Has something to do with the microbes in the gastrointestinal tract. If I want a sample of this bastard's DNA, I need his blood or saliva, nasal secretions, hair . . ." She carried the bagged specimen back to her car anyway. Because that's what you did. You collected evidence. Never knew when it might prove to be valuable. She slammed the trunk shut, mustering a tight smile. "You may as well head on home. I have to help Oly knock on doors."

"Are you going to join me later?"

"Don't think so. I'd better hang with Bella. She's more freaked than she's letting on." Des softened her gaze at him. "I'm afraid our big evening's over. I'm real sorry."

"Don't be—shit happens." He flashed a boyish grin at her. "That was a once-in-a-lifetime opportunity. I had to go there."

"I knew that."

"I knew you knew." Just as he knew that he couldn't kiss her good-night. She was in uniform. The neighbors were watching. Public Displays of Affection were a no-no. "We're good," he assured her as he climbed back into his truck. "Don't you worry about a thing."

"I'm not worried," she said quietly.

Because she wasn't. She was furious. The Dorset Flasher had made this personal now. And she wasn't just thinking of him as some abstract loser boy any longer. She had someone very specific in mind now. Someone who was openly hostile toward Dorset's blue-blooded dowagers. . . . "*You say hello to them and they act like you just took a leak on their shoes. . . .*" Someone she'd clashed with that very afternoon. A public altercation that had left him flat on his butt and humiliated. He'd warned her that she'd be sorry. And now there was a turd on her welcome mat. Coincidence? Des Mitry didn't believe in the tooth fairy, clean coal technology or coincidences. What she did believe was that she had her man. He was a bitter, angry widower. He had a drinking problem. And he lived by himself smack-dab in the middle of the Historic District.

Oh, yeah, she had her man, all right. Augie Donatelli was the Dorset Flasher. Des had zero doubt. None.

The only tricky part was going to be proving it.

Chapter 5

Beth had a radiant smile on her face when she answered the doorbell. And was impeccably turned out in a coral knit top and white linen slacks. "I'm so thrilled to finally meet you," she exclaimed warmly, taking Des by both hands. "Mitch was always like family. I hope you'll think of us that way, too."

"Thank you, that's very kind. And real sorry about the gunny-sack," Des said, meaning her uniform. "But I'm on the job tonight."

"No apology necessary. Believe me, we'll all sleep better when that sicko has been put away." Now Beth gave Mitch a hug and said, "And don't you look handsome." He had on an untucked white button-down shirt and khaki shorts. "That shirt really sets off your tan. Or should I say sunburn?" Her brow furrowed with concern. "My goodness, you look awfully red all of a sudden."

"From my daily run," Mitch explained. "It was really windy out at the point."

"Of course it was, dear. Of course."

Beth's apartment was huge, with high ceilings, tall windows and polished oak flooring. The décor was elegant but impersonal. No quirky little keepsakes. It had the feel of an executive rental, Mitch reflected. There was a screened-in porch off of the dining room. He heard voices out there.

It was a long, deep porch that looked out over an expanse of lawn to the Lieutenant River. Beth had furnished it with a white wicker loveseat and armchairs. A glass table was laden with chilled shrimp, deviled eggs and cheeses and crackers. There was hard liquor, wine, a washtub full of beer and soda on ice.

Kimberly and Kenny stood there together, hand in hand, glowing with so much love for each other that Mitch, who was known among his fellow New York film critics as the Town Crier, instantly felt himself welling up. Kimberly looked absolutely beautiful. Her long blond hair was brushed out. And the sleeveless print dress she had on showed off her lean, muscular arms and legs. She and Kenny were the same exact height—if you ignored that Kimberly wore flat sandals and Kenny thick-soled trail hikers. Still, Kenny was no longer a little twerp. He stood a wiry five feet ten in his Hawaiian shirt and cargo shorts. Was built like a marathoner. And was a good-looking guy in a neo-wonky sort of a way. His thatch of brown hair was stylishly unkempt. He had a four-day growth of beard. And the eyes behind his wire-framed glasses were bright and earnest.

He rushed toward Mitch, and pumped his hand excitedly. "God, Berger, it's *so* good to see you again!"

"Same here, Lapidus."

"And I'm ready for you this time, I swear. All set? Here goes: 'I've met some hard-boiled characters in my time but you—you're twenty minutes.' "

"Easy. That was Jan Sterling to Kirk Douglas in *Ace in the Hole*."

Kenny's face fell. "Damn, I still can't beat you."

"And you never will. Kimberly, I can't believe you didn't tell me this doofus was your boyfriend."

"Honestly, I had no idea you two had a history," she confessed. "And when I found out about it, Kenny swore me to secrecy. He and Beth wanted to surprise you."

"Which I'm happy to say we did," said Beth, bustling in from the kitchen with a platter of piping hot cheese puffs, then bustling right back out again.

"Kimberly, you know Des, don't you?"

"Of course. We always get seated together at the Chamber of Commerce dinners. We're the only single women who are under forty. We even get our very own table—just us."

"That's because the wives make up the seating chart," Des said, smiling at her. "Consider it a form of flattery. That's what I do."

"Really glad to meet you, Des," Kenny said effusively. "I'm guessing that if you spend time with this guy you must be into old movies."

"I'm developing a healthy appreciation—with the notable exception of the Three Stooges."

"That's a gender thing," Kenny stated with great conviction. "There isn't a woman on Earth who can tolerate the Stooges. Don't know why."

"I do," Des said. "Because they're really, really stupid."

He frowned at her. "And this is a problem because . . . ?"

"Oh, God, you two *did* grow up together."

Kenny and Kimberly were both sipping bottles of Sam Adams. Mitch fetched himself one and a Diet Coke for Des. Also a small plate of devilled eggs, promising himself he'd be careful. He could eat his body weight in devilled eggs. As he devoured one, he noticed Kimberly studying him with a critical eye. "Uh-oh, am I hunching my shoulders? No, it's my feet, isn't it? They aren't hip width apart."

"Actually, I was just observing how tall and straight you're standing."

"Really?"

"You're doing real well in class, Mitch. Besides, your mat is a judgment-free zone. Yoga is all about the acceptance of our lack of perfection."

"Mitch can totally vibe with that concept," Des said. "You should hear him play *Purple Haze* on his Stratocaster."

Kenny let out a laugh, that same high-pitched whoop he'd had when they were kids—one part rebel yell, two parts Woody Woodpecker. "You wouldn't say that to him if you weren't wearing *that*." Meaning her holstered SIG.

"Actually, she would," Mitch told him. "My sound is something of an acquired taste. Kimberly, are your folks into yoga, too?"

"Not at all. But they're both very active. Father still does the same Royal Canadian Air Force calisthenics every morning that he's been doing since I was a little girl. Mother plays tennis and tends the Captain Chadwick Blush Noisettes like a demon. Mother's very particular about 'her' roses. Won't let Augie within ten feet of the things. They were planted way back in the fifties, I'm told. Tourists always stop to take pictures of them. The two of them will be along soon. Mother has this thing about always showing up twenty minutes late. Something she learned at finishing school."

Beth returned now with a platter of sizzling stuffed mushrooms. Set it down on the table, poured herself a glass of white wine and joined them.

"Des, did you know that this guy here saved my life?" Kenny said. "Real deal. If it weren't for Mitch Berger I would be embedded face down in the Stuyvesant Town playground to this very day."

"Lapidus, I think you're overselling it a bit," Mitch said.

"If that's the case then he's been overselling it for twenty years," Beth said. "Because that's how long I've been hearing this story."

"See, there was this incredibly hulking playground bully named Bruce Cooperman," Kenny continued, ignoring them both. "He was a total goon. And huge. At age ten he was already shaving. Everyone was terrified of him. Everyone except for Berger. One day after school, I'm shooting hoops on the basketball court and Bruce starts giving me all sorts of grief. Takes my ball away from me, knocks me down, puts his big, fat foot on my neck and won't let me back up. Won't let me *breathe*. I'm facedown on the pavement, preparing to meet my maker, when I hear Berger say, 'You're being kind of rough on the little guy, aren't you? Wanna try that with me?'"

"I stole that line from *The Dirty Dozen,*" Mitch interjected. "Clint Walker said it to John Cassavetes."

"Bruce backed right off *and* gave me my ball back. And he never, ever bothered me again—because he knew that if he did, he'd have to take on Mitchell Berger, King of the Playground. Berger used to take me to see his favorite old movies, too. Heck, he pretty much taught me what cool was."

"This is disturbing on so many different levels," Des said, awestruck.

"Don't mind her, Lapidus. She's just bitter about being on duty tonight."

"Ah yes, this would be the infamous Dorset Flasher. He strikes every weekend, I understand."

"That's correct." Des raised an eyebrow at him. "And you come down here every weekend, right?"

"Why, yes. Yes, I do. Got in last night around 8:30. I drove my Prius down. It's the light green one parked out front. I take Amtrak when I can but the train leaves Boston at 5:35 and sometimes I just can't get away that early. The next train isn't until 9:45, which means I don't get here until midnight. So I jumped in the Prius. Made it here in just under two hours. Man, you would not believe the highway mileage that bad boy gets if I keep the speedometer just under . . ." Kenny gulped, his eyes widening. "Whoa, you don't think *I'm* the Flasher, do you?"

Des shook her head. "The man I'm looking for hasn't got a love life. And you most certainly do."

Kenny and Kimberly beamed at each other as the doorbell rang. Beth answered it and came back out onto the porch with Kimberly's parents, Dex and Maddee. Beth's smile seemed fixed a bit tighter now.

The notorious Dex Farrell wore a blue-and-white seersucker suit, red bow tie, crisp white shirt and polished cordovan loafers. His gaze was probing behind his rimless glasses. If Dex had been a Hollywood character actor, Mitch reflected, he would have specialized in playing judges and senators. He had a big head of neatly brushed white hair, a strong, decisive jaw. His manner was that of a man given to serious reasoning and sound judgment. All of which was a total deception. In reality he was none of those things. His wife Maddee was tallish and painfully thin. She wore a yellow summer dress, a pearl necklace and a truly alarming amount of bright magenta lipstick.

Kimberly went over to greet them with Des in tow. Animated conversation ensued. Mitch was about to join them when Kenny held him back.

"I know this comes out of nowhere, Berger, but I have a slightly humongous favor to ask of you. Would you be my best man?"

"Lapidus, I'd be honored. . . . Wait, do I have to wear a tux?"

"I'm afraid so. And if you want to pass I'll certainly understand."

"For you, it's no problem. Consider it done."

Kenny let out a huge sigh of relief. "Thank God. Seriously, I may not survive the experience if you're not right there by my side. Maddee's insisting on a full-frontal Yacht Club freak show. I love Kimmy to death but her folks are . . . scary. Dex isn't what you'd commonly think of as All There. And Maddee's just *real* tightly wrapped. Plus she's one of those insular country club types who's never worked a day in her life. Mom can't stand her, though she adores Kimmy. Hell, how can you not? And as long as the two of us are happy, mom's cool with it."

Dex Farrell built himself a gin and tonic and sat on the wicker sofa with it, his gaze fixed out on the rather gaudy rose garden. Mitch fortified himself with four more devilled eggs and headed on over there. "Mr. Farrell? I'm Mitch Berger."

He stared at Mitch for a second before he said, "Of course you are, sir." Dex spoke very softly. And slo-o-owly. Forcing Mitch to lean in closer to him. "Please . . . join me, Mr. Berger."

Mitch flopped down next to him. "Only if you make it Mitch, okay?"

"She's a fine figure of a woman—your fiancée."

"We're not engaged. We were, but we're not anymore."

"My mistake. Sorry if I raised a sore subject."

"You didn't."

Maddee Farrell swooped down on them now like a protective mother hawk. "And this must be Mr. Berger," she exclaimed brightly.

"He prefers to go by Mitch," Dex informed her.

"Mitch, I've had have numerous opportunities to meet your lovely fiancée but I've never—"

"They're not engaged. They were, but they're not anymore."

"It's just *such* a pleasure to meet you at long last." Maddee was an anxious woman with a strained, almost desperate expression on her face. Tightly wrapped indeed. "I understand you've recently lost a good deal of weight. I mention this because if you have any clothes that no longer fit, we're always looking for items for the Nearly New shop at St. Anne's. Just drop them by any time."

"I'll be sure to do that," said Mitch, who'd already deposited his former wardrobe on the sidewalk in front of his apartment on West 102 Street. Every item was gone in less than sixty seconds.

Maddee studied him with keen-eyed interest. Mitch was still waiting for the lady to blink. "I hope you have an open mind."

"I certainly try to."

"My Dex is neither a monster nor a thief. Merely guilty of behaving like a gentleman. And for that he has been demonized, ostracized and—"

"Dear, kindly go away, will you?" Dex said to her quietly.

Maddee's eyes widened with alarm, as if he'd just smacked her in the face. "Why, of course," she murmured, scurrying off to the hors d'oeuvres table.

"Please excuse my wife, Mitch. Myself, I ask for no sympathy. I merely wish to live the remainder of my life in peace. I often think of a favorite quote of mine by Mencken: 'American jurisprudence has been founded upon the axiom that it is the first duty of every citizen to police his neighbors, and especially those he envies or otherwise dislikes.' Often overlooked these days, Mencken. Quite a shame. He possessed a fine, clear mind." Dex fell silent for a moment before he added, "I enjoy your essays on the cinema very much. I admire people who write with passion. Or do anything with passion. That's something I've lacked my entire life. I never wanted to head up Farrell and Co., you see. It was expected of me. And so, like a dutiful son, I did what I was expected to do. Unfortunately, some of the fellows whom I trusted—classmates of mine, good friends—did not. They turned their backs on sound financial practices and made our credit rating system over into a trillion-dollar game of three-card monte. Lying thieves, the whole lot of them. They fed me a steady diet of disinformation. I should have figured out what they were up to. Rolled up my sleeves, knocked heads. But I never loved the business enough to care."

"Forgive me for asking, sir, but if you didn't know what was going on why didn't you admit that to Congress?"

Dex stared at him in disbelief. "Point the finger at someone else? Where's the honor in that?"

"But it's cost you your career, your good name."

"Perfectly appropriate under the circumstances. It was my name on the door. Although I refuse to beat myself up over it. I intend to thoroughly enjoy the time I have left on this Earth." Dex sipped his gin and tonic, gazing out at the roses again. "Why are we here, Mitch?"

"I'm here because Kenny and I were friends back when we were kids."

"No, I mean all of us. The human race. Have you a favorite thinker on the subject?"

"Yes, I do. My favorite philosopher has always been Mays."

"Mays?" Dex repeated. "Don't believe I'm familiar with Mays. First name is . . . ?"

"Willie. He captured the essence of our existence with eight simple words: '*I see the ball. I hit the ball.*' "

Dex stared at him blankly. "You're pulling my leg, aren't you?"

"Only a little. The truth is I have no idea why we're here. Do you?"

"Yes, I believe I do," Dex answered firmly. "Drop by some time and we'll discuss it over a glass of lemonade. No need to call. Just come by. I cherish stimulating conversation."

Beth's doorbell rang once again. She went inside to answer it, and reappeared this time with Hal Chapman in tow. Mitch's trainer wore a tight-fitting pink Izod shirt, tan shorts and flip-flops. His skullet was wet. He seemed to be fresh out of the shower. Also a bit ill at ease.

Mitch went over to say hey.

Hal bumped knucks with him, grinning. "How goes it, bro?"

"Good, thanks," he said as the master sergeant joined them. "Hal, do you know Des Mitry?"

"We've never met." Des studied Hal with those pale green eyes of hers. "But Mitch can't stop raving about your skills."

"It's my man here who does all of the hard work. I'm just there for him, that's all." Hal pulled a cold Sam Adams from the wash-tub and popped it open. "Kimberly said to stop by after I locked up for the night. Free shrimp, right?"

"And devilled eggs." Mitch helped himself to four more.

Kenny wandered over and said, "Good to see you again, Hal."

"And you, bro. "

"Lapidus, your mom tried to tell me what you do for a living. I didn't understand one word of it."

"I'm just a glorified geek, Berger. I used to work out of my rotten little apartment on Trowbridge Street. Now I have an office with thirty-two full-time employees, contracts up the wazoo. It's pretty neat."

"And you and Kimberly are going to live up there?"

"That's the plan. We'll keep house there during the week and spend weekends here so Kimmy can still teach a few classes and see her folks. I should think you'd be happy about this, Hal."

Hal stiffened, his nostrils flaring. "How would you know what would make me happy?"

"It's a promotion, right? You'll be in charge of the place Monday through Friday."

"Meaning *what*?" Hal demanded angrily, thrusting his jaw in and out. Mitch hadn't known this, but his trainer could turn from a gentle lamb into a red-faced rage monkey in the blink of an eye. "You think I'm some loser who's starving for crumbs?"

Kenny was aghast. "No, absolutely not. You're totally misunderstanding what I'm—"

"And why's *that*?" Hal was breathing heavily now. "Because I'm some stupid pinhead?"

Kimberly darted over to them, her brow furrowing with concern. "Kenny doesn't think that at all, Hal," she assured him, her voice low and soothing. "No one does."

Kenny nodded his head. "She's right. Chill out, man."

"*Don't* tell me to chill out!" roared Hal, shoving him roughly.

Kenny staggered back against the food table, rattling the dishware and glasses.

Mitch stepped between the two of them, suddenly feeling as if he'd been teleported back to the Stuyvesant Town playground. "Dial it down, Hal. Just take it easy."

Hal gave him a shove, too. "*Don't* try to tell me what to do!"

Mitch shoved him back. "I'm not *trying* to tell you. I'm *telling* you."

Des stood right there, in uniform, watching them—but opting not to intercede.

Hal took a deep breath in and out, shaking his head. "I don't know what I'm doing here. This was a bad idea. I'm sorry. I'm really sorry." Then he stormed out the screen door and out of there.

"Good lord . . ." Maddee Farrell gasped, watching him go.

"I shouldn't have invited him," Kimberly blurted out. "I'm sorry."

"It wasn't your fault, dear," Beth said.

"No, it totally was. Hal used to think he had a crush on me. Not that anything ever happened between us. I-I thought he was over it. I was wrong."

Kimberly wasn't alone. There was plenty of wrongola to go around, Mitch realized. He'd thought Hal was easygoing. And Des had called him a man who was living the dream. He wasn't. He was living the nightmare—in love with a coworker who had feelings for someone else. Clearly, the man was boiling with jealousy and resentment. So much that Mitch wondered if Kimberly was being totally candid with them. Had she and Hal been romantically involved at some point in the not-so-distant past? He wondered. Same as he wondered if Des could cross Hal Chapman off of her list of suspects after all.

He had no doubt that she was standing there thinking the very same thing.

Chapter 6

Real? Des was standing there thinking just how impossible men could be.

Because she'd been *so* tempted to step in when Hal went nutso on Kenny. It was her job to keep the peace. But she'd resisted the impulse, hard as that was. She had to. Men got into squabbles. They needed to blow off steam. They also needed to settle things in their own way. Which Mitch had done. If she hadn't let him do that—if she'd played mommy cop—then she'd have made Mitch look weak in front of his friend. He'd have resented it. Yet if things had gotten out of hand—like, say, if Hal had started swinging—then she'd have been guilty of standing there in her uni doing squat.

Sometimes, her job made a relationship with a man into a tightrope walk.

"You handled that like a seasoned pro, Armando," she said to him after Hal had fled.

"Thank you, master sergeant. Couldn't have done it without you. I knew you had my back."

"I've got your front, too, boyfriend. You're all mine."

There was a tap on the screen door now, but wasn't Hal. It was Augie Donatelli. "I'm here, Mrs. Breslauer!" he called out, standing there in a frayed New York Yankees T-shirt and plaid shorts.

"What does that awful man want?" Maddee sniffed.

"Believe me, I have no idea." Beth moved over to the screen door and said, "How may I help you, Mr. Donatelli?"

"It's *Augie*, hon. How many times I got to tell ya? Jeez, everybody's so damned formal around here." He leered at Beth through the screen door. He was definitely leering. "Came to take care of your leaky kitchen faucet."

"I'm entertaining guests right now," Beth pointed out.

"Yeah, I can see that." His eyes flicked around the enclosed porch. "How you doing there, Master Sergeant Mitry?"

"I'm fine, Augie," Des answered cooly.

"So now is obviously not a good time," Beth said to him.

"If you say so, hon, but I got a to-do list as long as my arm. Don't know when I'll be able to get back here."

Beth sighed wearily. "Fine, come on in."

He came on in, toolbox in hand, reeking of Aqua Velva and Ballantine.

"May I offer you something to drink?" Beth asked him politely.

"Nah, I'm good. Be out of your hair in a flash."

Beth watched him strut inside to the kitchen. "My shadow," she informed them miserably. "Wherever I go, he goes. If I'm at the post office, he's in line behind me, blabbering away nonstop. If I stop off at the drugstore, there he is again—asking me which brand of medicated foot powder he ought to buy. As if I'm interested in the condition of his feet. Why, I even ran into him one night at the Mohegan Sun Casino. I was meeting a friend there from New York. And there was Augie with that same smirk on his . . ." She shuddered. "Whenever he looks at me I feel dirty all over."

"You mustn't," Maddee said sharply. "*He's* the dirty one."

Dex, meanwhile, just sat and stared out at the Blush Noisettes. The man scarcely seemed *there*.

"Has Augie ever crossed over the line with you?" Des asked Beth.

"No, I can't say he's behaved inappropriately. It's just his manner, if you know what I mean."

"Oh, believe me, I know." Des steeled herself and headed into the kitchen. She found Augie on his knees under the sink, turning off the water. Which meant he was treating her to a really unwelcome expanse of hairy white plumber's crack. "We need to talk, Augie," she said, turning her eyes somewhere, anywhere else.

"If you say so, sugar lips. But maybe I ought to have a witness in case you try to assault me again, like you did yesterday."

"I never went near you, Augie."

"I guess we just have an honest disagreement about that." Mercifully, he climbed to his feet and went searching in his toolbox for a wrench. "Go ahead, say what you wanted to say."

"What are you doing here?"

"Fixing the faucet. What does it look like I'm doing?"

"Giving Mrs. Breslauer and her guests the once over."

Augie went to work on the faucet with his wrench. "And why would I want to do that?"

"You told me you have her under surveillance, remember?"

"Okay, true enough," he allowed.

"Why, Augie?"

"I have my reasons. Good ones. I was going to share them with you yesterday but you weren't interested—you and your fancy attitude."

"I don't have an attitude," she responded calmly. "But you sure do. You go out of your way to antagonize these people. I'm warning you, Augie, keep it up and they will bounce you right out of here."

"Don't threaten me, homegirl. And don't push your luck. I can still swear out a complaint against you."

"A complaint for what?"

"You pushed me to the ground yesterday."

"That's bull. You fell over all by yourself."

"Did not. But where I come from, only the lowest form of rat bastard swears out a complaint against a fellow officer. So we're good, you and me."

"I appreciate it, Augie. That's real decent of you. Since we're good, how about if we start over?"

"Start over how?"

"If you want to talk, one professional to another, I'm here to listen."

"No way," he snapped. "That window of opportunity is closed."

"What, you're punishing me now?"

He turned to face her, his arms crossed, one hand clutching the wrench. "Let's just say I don't care what other people think of me. Especially when those other people happen to be you."

"You have a grudge against me personally, Augie. Why is that?"

He stared at her with his cold, dark, cop's eyes. They were bottomless pools. He had stared down killers with those eyes. "Are you playing the race card with me now?"

"I'm not *playing* anything. Just wondering why you have such a big chip on your shoulder. You keep acting like you're the victim of some grave injustice. Want to tell me about it?"

He soaked that in for a moment before he said, "No. Are we done here?"

"Not quite. Did you stop by my house last night?"

"Why the hell would I want to do that?"

"You tell me."

Augie raised his chin at her. "You're talking about that little stink bomb somebody left you, aren't you?"

"It wasn't so little, Augie. And if you know anything . . ."

"If I *know* anything?"

"Now's the time to get out in front of it."

He shook his head at her in amazement. "You think *I* did it, don't you? You're actually accusing me of depositing my poop on your doorstep. Damn, homegirl, I don't know whether to laugh or cry."

"Why don't you try talking to me instead?"

He went back to work on the faucet. "Okay. If you want me to talk, I'll talk. Here's three little words for you: Go. To. Hell."

Chapter 7

As Mitch eased his Studey across the rickety wooden causeway toward home, he was grateful for his island sanctuary. He needed some time alone to reflect. That nice, simple little get-together at Beth's had gotten complicated in a hurry. It was so great to see Kenny again. He seemed like a terrific guy. Mitch was thrilled that his old friend and Kimberly were so madly in love. But then along came Hal, who it turned out had deep feelings for Kimberly *and* a world-class temper. Mitch was worried about a round two between Hal and Kenny. He was worried about Augie Donatelli's obvious and highly unwelcome interest in Beth. The ex-cop was so hot for Mitch's first love that he'd actually followed her to the Mohegan Sun, for crissakes. Mitch was also worried about the way Augie seemed to be getting under Des's skin. She'd had words with him in Beth's kitchen. And wouldn't tell Mitch a thing about what they had talked about. She'd been unusually tight-lipped. It baffled him. Kimberly's strange, remote father baffled him. So did her nervous, clingy mother. Hell, they all baffled him. His old life, the one he'd spent in darkened movie houses soaking up the world according to Louis B. Mayer, Sam Goldwyn and the brothers Warner had been so much easier to figure out. Everything was in black and white—even when it was filmed in Technicolor. Out here in Dorset, there were so many different shades of gray that it made his head spin like a gerbil wheel.

An old yellow MGA ragtop was parked at Bitsy's house. She had company tonight. Mitch could hear the loud, thumping rock music. Although, oddly enough, the music grew louder as he pulled up in front of his own place. Loud enough for him to recognize it as "Trouble No More" off of the Allman Brothers' landmark *Eat a Peach.*

The music was coming from his place.

As Mitch climbed out of his truck both Quirt and Clemmie came running up to him, yowling. Clemmie, who seldom went outside, seemed genuinely outraged. Wet clothes were draped over his lawn chairs, Mitch noticed. A pair of jeans, a T-shirt. Mitch didn't remember leaving them there. He hadn't. They weren't his.

He pushed open the cottage's front door, his heart racing, kick-ass music blasting—and discovered a naked stranger standing in the middle of his living room doing a low-down, hip-swinging boogie to the beat. In one hand he clutched a peanut butter and jelly sandwich, in the other a bottle of Corona.

Mitch flicked off the music first thing. Didn't matter. His bare-assed intruder didn't stop dancing. Just boogied on for another four, five, six seconds before it dawned upon him that the music had stopped. And swiveled around on one bare heel, gaping at Mitch in surprise.

"Can I *help* you?" Mitch demanded.

After a long, really long, moment of silence the intruder responded, "Other way around. Bitsy said you wanted my advice."

"I do?"

Apparently, there was not a reliable high-speed hook up between this guy's mouth and brain. After another incredibly long gap in time he said, "You're Mitch, aren't you? Or am I . . . Uh-oh, do I have the wrong house?"

"No, you came to the right place." Mitch studied him more closely. He was slope shouldered and sun-browned, well put together but going to flab, with high, hard cheekbones, uncombed blond hair and zonked-out blue eyes. About forty maybe. If Matthew McConaughey had a brother who'd inhaled way too many paint fumes, he would look just about like Mitch's naked stranger. "You're J. Z. Cliffe, aren't you?"

"That's what they keep telling me. Bitsy buzzed me out. Figured I'd just wait for you. Got hot so I took a swim. Got wet so I dried off. Then I got hungry." J. Z. remembered the sandwich in his hand and took a bite. "Then I got thirsty." He gulped down some beer. "Now we're all good. Glad to know you."

Mitch grabbed a T-shirt and a pair of boxer shorts from his wardrobe cupboard and tossed them to J. Z. "Why don't you put these on? Make yourself at home. What am I saying, you already have. Would you like to write my next column for me? How are you on the subject of icebox questions?"

J. Z.'s face got all scrunched up. "How am I on . . . hunh?"

"Never mind."

"Hey, sorry if I stepped on your turf, man. You can come over and help yourself to my stuff any time. What's mine is yours. I'm real casual about possessions." He stepped into the boxer shorts and pulled the T-shirt on over his head, then sauntered his way slowly around Mitch's exposed-chestnut post-and-beam living room, peering at the walls and ceiling. He moved with a rear-slung, rubber legged gait that reminded Mitch of R. Crumb's Mr. Natural. "Not that I'm trying to talk myself out of a gig or anything but your place looks pretty decent to me. I eyeballed the outside before you got here. You've got some minor blistering of your trim on the west side of the house. But you can go another year, easy. Unless what you're thinking is you want to redo the color in here because of aesthetic or spiritual reasons. Which I can totally get behind."

"Thanks for the info." Mitch fetched himself a beer from the refrigerator. "But Bitsy and I were talking about you in connection with another subject."

J. Z. frowned at him. "I paint houses, man. What else could I . . . ?"

"Kimberly Farrell."

"Kimmy?" He squinted at Mitch with one eye shut, which was either his way of trying to act inscrutable or he needed glasses. "What about her?"

"It's a personal matter."

"So this isn't a professional get-with?"

"No, it's not."

"In that case . . ." J. Z. retrieved a plastic baggie from Mitch's dining table and removed one of the dozen or so hand-rolled joints that were tucked inside. "Care to partake?"

"No, thanks, but you go right ahead," said Mitch, who had to admire the strict line that J. Z. drew between work and play.

There were matches on the old glass-topped rowboat that was Mitch's coffee table. J. Z. flopped down in the easy chair and fired up the joint, toking on it deeply. "Are you into her? Because I can totally dig that. Kimmy's shmoking hot. But you're too late, man. She's engaged to some computer geek up in Boston. Besides, don't you have a thing going with our resident state . . . ?" He froze, staring down at the lit joint in his hand. "Uh-oh . . ."

"Don't worry. I don't care about that. Actually, I'm the computer geek's best man. Kenny Lapidus is his name."

J. Z. observed a moment of silence as he sat there processing this. "Okay . . ."

"And you and Kimberly were married very briefly a few years ago."

"A million years ago," he recalled with a fond, faraway look on his face.

Mitch sat down on the love seat across from him. Clemmie moseyed over and jumped in Mitch's lap, eyeing this stranger guardedly. "I was wondering what happened between you two."

"Don't take this the wrong way, man, because I'm not a hostile or confrontational person. But why's it any of your damned business?"

"It's not," Mitch acknowledged easily. "And if you don't want to talk about it I can totally respect that. But I've looked out for Kenny since we were little kids, okay? I just want to make sure he's not getting into something he doesn't understand."

J. Z. treated Mitch to his one-eyed squint again. "No problem, man. Happy to help a brother." He took another pull on the joint, holding in the smoke for several seconds before he let it out. "Were you ever young and stupid?"

"I like to think I still am."

J. Z. flashed a lopsided grin at him. "Good answer. But were you ever young and stupid in a place like Dorset?"

"I grew up in New York City."

"Totally different universe. I spent a lot of good years in the City myself, but I ended up back here. And, trust me, it can really suck. A young guy's going to do his wild thing, you know? Trouble is, when you do it here in Dorset *everyone* finds out. You get trashed one night and wrap your car around somebody's sycamore tree? Bam—word's out that you're a messed-up druggie. You boink a girl and never call her again? Bam—you're a no-good louse. And here's the thing, here's the thing: No one *ever* forgets. Twenty years can go by and the old prune-faced biddies will still be talking about you. Know why? Because every babe you ever hook up with was, is and always will be somebody's sister or cousin. Or her uncle works for somebody who knows your mom. Or whatever. It sticks to you like glue for as long as you live. Even if it wasn't even your fault. I mean, sometimes it's *her* fault, right? Or nobody's fault. But, wait, because here's the real pisser. Are you listening . . . ?"

"Yes, I'm listening."

"The truth doesn't matter," J. Z. proclaimed. "Hell, people don't even *know* the truth half of the time. Doesn't stop them though. They make up their mind anyway. And talk about you just like you're a character in some soap opera. You have *any* idea what that's like?"

"Yes, I do, actually."

"Yeah, maybe you do. The old prune-faced biddies talk about you and the trooper lady, right? Well, me they've been talking about *forever.* Here, I'll give you a for instance. This guy Courtney Borio gave me a helping hand a long, long time ago when I was really down. Courtney was just a good guy, okay? He taught me a trade. Gave me a place in this world. What he did for me, I mean, this guy should be a local hero, right? Wrong. You want to know why? Because Courtney was gay. And so they all whispered about *the real reason* why he was being so nice to me. I don't roll that way, Mitch. Never have. I'm not judging. It's just not my thing, okay? But Courtney and me worked together for a long time—which, according to the old prune-faced biddies, meant that I *had* to be gay. Doesn't matter how many live-in girlfriends I've had over the years. To them I'm gay and always will be. Like I said, they never let the truth get in the way of a good story. And they're just plain *nasty*, man. I mean, just because a man's gay he can't have a friend who's not? How bigoted is that?" J. Z. glanced out of Mitch's bay window in the direction of Bitsy Peck's house. "I'm always happy to work for Bitsy. She's a cool lady, not like those old prune-faced biddies in the Historic District—my mom's so-called friends. They've never cut me any slack. Let me tell you, man, they're just lucky I don't hold a grudge."

"Why is that?"

"Because I'd make 'em pay for what they've put me through."

Mitch found himself leaning forward. "Make them pay *how*?"

J. Z. didn't answer him. His joint had gone out. He lit a match to it and got it going again, dragging on it deeply.

"J. Z., why did you move back here from New York? Why do you still live here? Feeling the way you do, I mean."

He shrugged his shoulders. "Where else would I go? This is my home. Besides, I'm working. Got a roof over my head. It's not much—just my mom's guesthouse. But it's mine. And I have a steady honey, Maggie. Real sweetie. The old prune-faced biddies talk nothing but trash about her, of course, because she slings drinks over at the Monkey Farm Café. She's not classy like them."

"Maggie works evenings?"

"Every weekend. Thursdays, too, if they get busy."

"What do you with yourself while she's working?"

He flashed a lopsided grin at Mitch. "We're doing it, man."

"These old biddies you were talking about . . ."

"Old *prune-faced* biddies."

"What do they have to say about you and Kimberly?"

"That the poor girl didn't know what she was getting into—about me being gay and all. And that when she found out the horrible truth, she dumped me."

"Which isn't what happened."

"Not even close, man"

"What did?"

J. Z. took a long swallow of his beer before he said, "I used to smoke a lot of dope in those days. Not like now. I was stoned *all* the time. I'm not trying to make excuses, okay? Just drawing you a picture. We'd been married a few weeks and it was going great. I was only, like, the second guy Kimmy had ever been with. She was just real enthusiastic and eager to please me. So one night she asks me if there's anything I'd like to do that we haven't done yet." J. Z. paused to ponder this, his brow furrowing. "Who knows what she really meant by that. I took it at face value and told her I'd always wanted to get into a threesome. She said 'Really, who with?' And so I mentioned this tasty friend of hers from high school. Cute little slice named Brittany. In fact, Brittany and me had kind of hooked up a couple of times before I met Kimmy. Anyway, that *wasn't* what Kimberly wanted to hear. And she completely freaked out. Started sobbing. Kimmy's incredibly sensitive. She *feels* everything. But, wait, because here comes the truly weird part: She said yes. Was all about wanting to make me happy. And so we ended up in a threesome with Brittany. Man, I thought I'd died and gone to heaven. Couldn't believe it was really happening. Not that it happened a lot. Just twice. But, my bad, I managed to mess it up."

"Mess it up how?"

"Me and Brittany kind of picked up where we'd left off before. I mean, since we were cool as a threesome I figured Kimmy wouldn't mind, you know?"

"And she did?"

"She *totally* did. Came home one day, found us in bed together and just completely lost it. I said to her, 'This isn't what it looks like.' And she said, 'Really? Because it looks like you're screwing my best friend.' Kimmy couldn't handle it, man. Told me I had no soul. That I was dead inside. Next thing I knew she'd moved back in with her folks and we were toast."

"What about Brittany?"

"She split town. Ended up married to some businessman down in Austin. Has a bunch of kids." He finished off the last of his beer. "That's the real story, man. From the source. Naturally, the old prune-faced biddies vastly prefer their own version, which is that Kimmy came home and found me in bed with a *guy*. It fits together better with all of the lies they've been telling about Courtney and me for so many years. To this day they will swear to you that Kimmy dumped me because I'm queer. Let me tell you something, man. I have to make an honest living in this place. So I work for them. I take their money. But some day those old prune-faced biddies will

get what's coming to them. The bad you do comes back to you."
J. Z. ran a hand over his weathered face. "Who said that?"

"You did," Mitch replied. "Just now."

"No, like isn't that a line from a chick song? Natalie Merchant, maybe? God, I hate her."

"How are things between you and Kimberly now? Do you speak?"

"Sure. Wouldn't jibe with her whole Zenny self-image to snub me. Bad karma. We're cool. Well, not cool, but civil." J. Z. gazed out of the bay window again, only this time his eyes widened with alarm. "Whoa, it's getting dark," he gasped. "I have to clear out *right now.*" He grabbed his baggie of dope and jumped to his feet. "Is it okay if I wear your clothes home? I'll drop 'em off next time I'm out this way."

"No problem," Mitch assured him. "But what's your hurry?"

"I don't like the dark."

"Why not?"

"Bad things happen," he whispered, gulping with genuine fright. Or at least it seemed genuine. The man was quaking with terror.

"What kind of bad things?"

J. Z. Cliffe didn't answer him. He'd already gone barreling out the front door, leaving it open wide behind him. Mitch got up and closed it, then reached for his cell phone to call Des.

Chapter 8

That night, Des left her cruiser in front of the firehouse and patrolled the Historic District on foot. Oly and two other troopers were prowling the District in their rides.

The night air was warm and sultry. If there was a moon up there she couldn't see it. She strolled her way along the rows of exquisitely preserved colonial mansions, her big leather belt and holster creaking, eyes and ears open. She could hear the sound of TV sets coming from open windows. Someone somewhere was playing an unsteady version of "Stardust" on a piano. She saw a few folks out walking their dogs. And a pair of giggly young girls running down the street for home in their bathing suits, dripping wet from somebody's swimming pool. But hardly any cars drove by. This was not unusual. The real action in Dorset on Saturday night wasn't in the Historic District. The bars and clubs were down near the marina.

It was nearly nine o'clock when she came to a halt out in front of the Captain Chadwick House. Only one room was lit up at the Farrells' place. Dex and Maddee were watching television or reading, she figured. In contrast, there were lights on all over Beth Breslauer's condo. As Des started across the lawn toward the backyard she could see Beth through her kitchen window. Mitch's first love was doing the dishes. Kenny and Kimberly were with her, the three of them chatting merrily, laughing. Already one little happy family. Upstairs, Bertha Peck's unit was dark. She'd gone out apparently. Her garage door was down. All of them were down except for

Augie's. The man's vintage, red GTO sat there, gleaming under his garage's overhead light. There were lights on in his apartment upstairs, too. Music was playing. An old Neil Diamond record. She settled in among the arborvitae bushes that edged the property and crouched there, waiting for him to make his move.

Twenty minutes had gone by when she felt her cell phone vibrate. She glanced at the screen and took the call, keeping her voice down.

"I've got a hot prospect for you, girlfriend. I am talking *sizzling*."

"Mitch, I thought you weren't going to do this again," she whispered.

"Do what?" he asked innocently.

"Go Nancy Drew on me."

"I'd rather be classified as one of the Hardy Boys, if you don't mind. Either Frank or Joe will do. I'm not picky. And you're right, I was. But this kind of fell into my boxer shorts."

"Into your *what*?"

"Des, I can barely hear you. Why are you whispering?"

"Mitch, what do you want?"

He was calling to tell her about J. Z. Cliffe, the burnout case who painted houses around town. How J. Z. had just left Big Sister stoned off of his gourd and just plain out there. Why J. Z.'s marriage to Kimberly had fallen apart. And why J. Z. remained filled with anger toward the Historic District's "old prune-faced biddies."

"J. Z.'s girlfriend, Maggie, slings drinks weekends at the Monkey Farm," Mitch added. "That means he's been footloose and fancy-free every single night our flasher has struck. His mom, Connie, has a big place right there on Dorset Street. He lives in her guesthouse. Refresh my memory—is Connie one of the ladies who's been victimized?"

"That would be a no."

"Naturally. No way he'd flash his own mother, would he? Well, maybe he would. But let's not go there. I've already had a full dose of weird tonight." Mitch fell silent. "You're not excited. Why aren't you excited?"

"The man's a prospect, no question," she admitted.

"He should be home in ten minutes. Are you going to shadow him?"

"Can't. I'm sitting on someone else."

"Augie, am I right?"

"Baby, just let me do my thing, will you?"

"I can sit on J. Z. for you. I'll jump in my truck and head right over there."

"Mitch, this isn't Tombstone. I'm not deputizing you. And we're not, repeat not, doing this. I'll take it from here. Just watch a movie, will you?"

"The Mets are playing."

"Even better. I'll swing by your place later, if that sounds appealing to you."

"Extremely appealing. It so happens I picked up some lavender oil at the health food store today."

"And what are you planning to do with that?"

"Well, first I'm going to massage you with it from head to toe. And then . . ." And then he proceeded to describe in great detail what else he planned to do—much of it involving his tongue and her most private crevices.

"Um, okay, I'm hanging up now." She flicked off her phone and waited for her pulse rate to slow back down to under a hundred. Then she called Oly, who promised he'd swing by the Cliffe place right away.

A car pulled into the gravel driveway of the Captain Chadwick House with a loud thump and started its way around back toward the garage. Bertha Peck's powder blue Mercedes 450 SL convertible. It was coming hard and fast and not particularly straight. The old girl was potted. Almost took out a row of Maddee Farrell's cherished Blush Noisettes before she screeched to a halt, using her remote control to raise her garage door. Bertha swung in way wide, very nearly scraping the side of her car as she pulled in. Then idled there for a moment with the rear half of the Mercedes still sticking out before she inched the rest of the way in and shut off her engine. She got out of the car, hit the switch to close the garage door and went tottering up the path to the mansion's rear entrance, humming to herself. A few moments later her living room lights came on upstairs. Then her bedroom lights. Then her bathroom light. After a minute, Des heard her toilet flush, and sincerely hoped it didn't choose tonight to clog up again.

By then her phone was vibrating again. Oly calling to report that there were lights on at Connie Cliffe's house but that J. Z.'s guesthouse out back was dark. His van was there. His old MG ragtop wasn't. Oly asked her if she wanted him to sit on the place. She suggested he resume patrolling but keep an eye on it.

Kenny and Kimberly came out onto Beth's screened-in porch now, Kimberly stretching herself out invitingly on the love seat. Kenny flicked off the lights so that the porch was in darkness. Des could no longer see the two of them. But she could hear their soft, intimate laughter. Crouched there in the arborvitae, she was starting to feel like a sleazoid peeper.

A few minutes after that, Beth came tiptoeing out of the same back door of the building that Bertha had just entered, closing it softly behind her. Beth wore a linen blazer and clutched her purse in one hand. She did not head for the garage. Instead, she started up the driveway toward the street, staying on the grass so that her footsteps wouldn't crunch on the gravel. When she reached the sidewalk she turned left and started down Dorset Street toward Big Branch Road, where the town's shopping district was. Where in the hell was she going? Des wondered—although not for long.

Because now there was activity at Augie's place.

First, he shut off the Neil Diamond concert. Then the lights inside his apartment. Then his garage went dark, too. She just caught sight of him in the darkness as he left the garage on foot, clad in dark pants and a dark long-sleeved shirt. He started his way across the expansive backyard, moving swiftly and quietly. Des took off after him, staying a careful distance back, one hand on her holster to keep the leather quiet. When Augie reached the low split-rail fence that marked the property line he paused, not moving, not making a sound. Des held her ground maybe fifty feet behind him, not moving, not making a sound. He seemed to be waiting for something. Or someone. Had he spotted one of the troopers cruising by? Was he on the lookout for Beth, his favorite stalkee? Because, hello, Beth had just gone the other way down Dorset Street toward Big Branch, effectively leaving him in her dust. It was so dark that Des couldn't tell *what* Augie was doing. She only knew that he didn't budge from his perch at that low fence for five minutes, ten minutes, fifteen . . .

Until suddenly he was on the move again. Climbing over the fence and moving with silent stealth across the parking lot that was behind the old grain and feed store next door. The building had been converted into law offices. Deserted on a Saturday night. It sat on the corner of Dorset Street and little Maple Lane. Directly across Maple Lane from it sat Rut Peck's farmhouse, which was currently vacant. Old Rut had moved into Essex Meadows and put the house up for sale.

Augie crossed the lane and plunged his way into Rut's wild, overgrown yard. Des stayed right behind him, moving as quietly as she could. It was becoming clearer to her now—how the Dorset Flasher had been able to elude her sweeps. The man was never out in the open. He worked his way across the village by way of people's backyards, driveways, little side roads. But she was on to him now.

And tonight she'd be right there to cuff him.

As Des pursued him across Rut's yard a dog began to bark from a nearby house. A big dog with a husky bark. There were only two other houses on Maple Lane. One belonged to Nan Sidell, a single mother with two young sons. Nan taught at the middle school. Did she have a dog? Des couldn't recall. But there were lights on at her place. The other house, which belonged to an old village handyman named Ray Smith, was dark. And Ray's truck was gone.

Des came to a halt in the blackness of Rut's yard, her ears straining. She couldn't hear Augie's footsteps now because of that barking dog. Couldn't make out his silhouette either. Damn, had she lost him? She yanked her Maglite from her belt and flicked it on, its beam pointed downward. Saw a shiver of movement in the thicket of bushes up ahead of her—*there*—and flicked it off, moving in that direction. Down toward the Lieutenant River. *Of course.* The river snaked its way through the entire Historic District. Its banks were the Flasher's own private highway. Mercifully, the barking dog fell silent now. Des could hear Augie moving his way through the brush again. Hear something else, too. A rustle in the brush *behind* her. Was someone else out there with them in the darkness? The dog? She turned around but saw no one, heard no one.

A car was making its way slowly along Dorset Street. It stopped when it reached Maple Lane, its high beams sweeping across Rut's yard as it turned in. It was a state police cruiser. It was Oly. He eased his way down to Nan Sidell's house and came to a stop. Des heard him get out. Right away, the dog started barking again.

Des took off, moving toward the riverbank out beyond Rut's house. Hoping, praying, she hadn't lost Augie's trail. Footsteps. She heard footsteps in the darkness again—someone crashing through the brush right behind her. No, *next* to her. Wait, no, all around her. She whirled, her flashlight's beam revealing nothing. Hell, what was . . . ? So fast now, too fast. Des heard a scuffle, a groan of pain, then a sickening thud. And now somebody was running again. She still couldn't see a living soul in the dense, overgrown thicket. But she definitely heard somebody and started running hard in that direction—until she tripped over something and fell hard to the ground, her flashlight rolling off into the weeds. Cursing, Des got back up and retrieved it, pointing it down at the object she'd tripped over.

Augie Donatelli lay there in the tall weeds at her feet with the back of his head bashed in.

He had a very surprised look on his face. He wasn't wearing a ski mask. Des saw no ski mask. He lay in a fetal position, as if he'd crumpled to his knees and then tipped over sideways. There was blood. A lot of it. And brain matter. A lot of it. A wooden baseball bat lay in the grass next to him.

Des sprinted through the brush after his attacker—only to find herself standing out in the middle of Maple Lane. She saw no one. Heard no one. Nothing. Just Oly's cruiser parked out in front of Nan Sidell's place. Oly was nowhere in sight. He must have gone inside the house. Nan's dog was still barking.

Cursing, Des yanked her phone off her belt and called it in.

Dorset Street was no longer quiet. Dozens of Historic District residents were out on the sidewalk, talking and gawking. Maple Lane had been closed off. The Major Crime Squad's techies were there from Meriden in their cube vans, along with a death investigator from the Medical Examiner's Office. So were news crews from Connecticut's four local TV stations, who were always up for a murder—especially when it took place in a ritzy village like Dorset. Rut Peck's overgrown yard was cordoned off, the crime scene lit up by the high beams of several cruisers. More cruisers were sweeping the neighborhood for anyone who was out on foot. Anyone who'd seen anything. Anything.

It was a 911 call from Nan Sidell that had brought Oly to the scene literally seconds before Augie's murder went down. Des knew Nan pretty well, having given a talk to the lady's seventh-grade class about drugs last semester. Nan was a fragile-looking little blue-eyed blonde whose husband had left her a while back for his rather dumpy secretary. Nan's two little boys were blue-eyed and tow-headed, same as her. Phillip, who was twelve, was lanky and tall for his age. Almost a head taller than his mother. Ten-year-old Peter was considerably shorter and pudgier.

"I've been keeping an eye on Rut's house ever since he moved out," Nan explained to Des, standing there barefoot in the middle of Maple Lane, her eyes huge with fright. Nan had her big yellow Lab close to her on a leash. Her two boys were right by her side. "Rut still has a lot of his furniture here. His silver, some antiques. I-I thought I heard someone messing around over there."

"Messing around as in . . . ?"

"Tromping around in the brush. Maybe trying to break in. I didn't know. And then Josie started barking her fool head off, so I figured I'd better call it in."

"You figured right, Nan. Did you see anyone fleeing the scene? Anyone at all?"

"I'm afraid not."

"How about you guys?" Des asked the boys.

Phillip shrugged his narrow shoulders. "We were in bed."

"Past our bedtime," Peter chimed in, nodding his head.

"Sure, I get you," Des said easily. "You'd turned in for the night, lights out. But Josie's got a mighty big bark. Maybe she woke you up. Did you hear anything? Or maybe go to the window and see somebody?"

The boys exchanged a long, hard look before Phillip said, "No." His voice was very firm. "Nothing."

"Nothing," echoed his younger brother, blue eyes gleaming.

The last to arrive from Meriden was a two-person team of homicide investigators from the Major Crime Squad, led by Lieutenant Rico "Soave" Tedone, who'd been Des's semibright weasel of a sergeant back in her glory days. Soave was still working on that goatee and shaved-head look. And still not quite making it happen. He was a bulked-up bodybuilder but way short and way, way insecure. Not that he had a thing to worry about. Soave was wired right into the Waterbury Mafia, the tightly knit clan of Italian-American brothers, cousins and in-laws who pretty much ran the Connecticut State Police. Soave's older brother, Angelo, and Angelo's brother-in-law, Carl Polito, were high up on the ladder—right there under Deputy Superintendent Buck Mitry.

Des made her way down to the foot of Maple Lane and said, "Evening, Rico. How's Tawny?"

"Big as an Escalade," he answered proudly. The man had finally married his girlfriend of nine years and she was currently expecting their first child. Real? Des found it hard to imagine Soave as someone's, anyone's, father. But it was going to happen. Life went on. "The baby's due any day now. I never know from one minute to the next when I'll be flooring it to the hospital."

"You're just lucky you got such quality backup, little man." His partner, Sergeant Yolanda Snipes, showed Des her huge smile. "Miss Thing, I have been missing you."

"Back at you, Yolie."

"What have you got for us, Des?" Soave wanted to know. "No, wait, don't tell me. It's Saturday night in quaint, cozy Dorset, where everyone is rich and WASP-y and perfect. So I'm going out on a limb here: It's whack."

"It's all that, Rico. And more."

"Break it down, will you?"

"*Break it down*?" Yolie let out a guffaw. "Sorry, is MC Hammer back in the house and no one told me?"

"My bad," he growled at her. The two of them bickered nonstop. It was how they communicated. "Please *run it* for us. Yo, is *that* cool enough for you?"

"Yo, I'm cool twenty-four/seven," Yolie fired back, her Latina's liquid brown eyes twinkling at Des. She was a brash, fearless, hard charger with braided hair out of Hartford's tough Frog Hollow section—half Cuban, half black and all pit bull. Yolie had put on twenty pounds of rock-hard muscle since she'd played the point for Coach Vivian Stringer at Rutgers. Her knit top was cropped at the shoulders, tattoos adorning both of her bulging biceps. Barefoot, she stood five feet nine. In her chunky heels she towered over Soave. Intimidated the hell out of him. Intimidated most of the men in the state police. She was tough, smart and she didn't do well around fools. "Talk to me, girl—how's your cute boy Mitch?"

"It's going great. We've never been happier."

"When are you two getting married?"

"It's going great. We've never been happier."

"I hear you. Won't go near there no more." Yolie heaved a sigh. "Me, I can't even get a man to ask me out for a cup of coffee. Don't matter whether he's black, white or mauve. . . ." She'd had a brief thing with Soave's cousin Richie back when Richie was on Narcotics, but he was married now. "Is there something wrong with my personal hygiene?"

"Not a thing, Yolie. You're terrific."

"Yo, can we talk about the dead guy now?" Soave demanded.

"First I'd better give you a little background, Rico. We have an ongoing situation that began two weekends ago. A certain party in a ski mask who's been—"

"This would be your weenie waver, right? Channel Eight was all over that. The news anchors could barely keep a straight face."

"Yeah, it's been a laugh riot—until now."

Soave raised his chin at her. "Keep talking."

"He's been leaving presents, too. I got a special delivery on my very own welcome mat last night—a nice, fresh turd of human origin."

Yolie blinked at her. "Ow, that's just disgusting."

"And our victim . . . ?"

"Mr. Donatelli moved here ten months ago. He was a widower. Also a retired New York City police detective."

Soave made a face. "Damn, that means his buds will be all over this."

"He lived and worked two doors down, at the Captain Chadwick House. It's a high-end condo complex. He was caretaker there, although the head of the board assured me he'd be getting bounced soon. The man was an obnoxious boor as well as a drinker. Never around when the tenants needed him. Plus he was borderline stalking one of them, a good-looking widow named Beth Breslauer." Des shoved her heavy horn-rimmed glasses up her nose. "Between us, I thought that *he* might be the Dorset Flasher. So I was tailing him on foot just now when it all—"

"Wait, wait," Yolie broke in. "You witnessed the murder?"

"Yes and no. I saw him leave his apartment. Pursued him as he made his way through the brush in the vicinity of the crime scene. I was definitely nearby when it happened. Heard a blow struck. Heard someone running away. Maybe one person. Maybe more than one. I can't be sure because I couldn't see a damned thing. A neighbor, Nan Sidell, heard someone prowling around and called it in. But she didn't see anybody either."

Soave thumbed his moustache, pondering this. "So, what, someone else besides you was following him?"

"That's certainly one possibility."

"Who would want to do that?"

"That all depends, Rico. If Augie was, in fact, the Dorset Flasher, then what we're looking at here could be an unsubtle form of payback."

He stared at her. "You mean like a vigilante killing?

"I do."

"Whoa, I don't like the sound of that at all. Is there another scenario?"

"That Augie was out here following the Dorset Flasher himself—once a cop, always a cop. Yesterday, he suggested to me that he might have an idea who our man was. I advised him to stay out of it. Could be he didn't follow my advice. Could be our Dorset Flasher graduated to the big time tonight."

"Killed Augie Donatelli to conceal his identity?"

"Exactly."

"Any chance it's none of the above?" Yolie wondered. "How about this neighbor? What's up with her?"

"Nan tips the scales at ninety-five pounds, tops, and has no motive."

"We know this for a fact?"

"Yolie, we don't know anything for a fact. And I have to lay something else on you folks that you're not going to like. Augie and I had a public altercation yesterday. He did a lot of yelling and ended up flat on his butt."

"You hit him?"

"I didn't so much as touch him, Rico. He was drunk, that's all."

"But there were witnesses?"

"Several."

"And now the man's dead and you were on the scene when it happened. Des, is there any way a district prosecutor could mount a reasonable argument that you're actually a suspect in this murder?"

"I'm afraid so. Let me make this next part easy for you, okay? No, I didn't do it. And, yes, I know I have to step far, far away from your investigation. After we're done here I'll give you all of my notes on the Dorset Flasher case. Every suspect I've looked at. We can sit down together over at Town Hall."

"Is that the place that smells like mothballs?" he asked.

"Always."

"Every time we set up there I swear I'm visiting my grandmother's house." He looked at Des uneasily. "We'll have to notify your barracks commander about this. You may be chained to a desk for the duration. Which sucks, but it is what it is. "

"I know this, Rico."

"Okay then." He rubbed his hands together briskly. "Let's have a look."

The death investigator was crouched over Augie, whose body was exactly as Des had found it. The bloodied baseball bat remained in the weeds nearby.

"This Louisville Slugger has seen a lot of honest playing time," Soave observed, bending over it for a closer look. "Handle's all nicked up. Ain't exactly current issue either—it's a freaking Mickey Mantle 125."

Yolie whipped out her Blackberry and went Googling. "You got that right, boss man," she said after a moment, peering at the bat for herself. "It was manufactured some time between 1964 and '72. The Mantle bats made prior to '64 had the trademark insignia under that oval label where it says Hillerich and Bradsby Co. This one here has the trademark in that circled 'R' after the words Louisville Slugger. It's a collectible. Worth north of two hundred in perfect condition. Beat up like this one maybe seventy-five."

"Augie was a native New Yorker," Des said. "And the right age to have been a Mantle fan. This could have been his bat. That totally works except . . ."

"Except what?" Soave asked her.

"I'd swear he wasn't carrying a baseball bat."

"So how did it get out here?"

"Good question, Rico."

Soave turned to the death investigator and said, "What can you tell us?"

"The victim suffered two blows," he answered cautiously. "One blow's to the left side of his head. The striking pattern's horizontal, suggesting that his attacker swung at him pretty much the way you would if you were hitting a baseball. That blow, I'm guessing, stunned him and sent him to his knees. The second blow, which was the fatal one, is an overhead chop. His attacker wielded the bat like an axe."

"Any idea about the attacker's size?"

"The blows are substantial. Not the Incredible Hulk, but no weakling either. As to height, that's difficult to gauge. If the victim was sneaking his way through the brush in the dark then we have to assume he was hunched over, not upright, which will significantly impact our calculations concerning the angle of the first blow. All I can tell you so far is that his attacker need not have been someone tall. Hopefully we'll know more after we get him on the table."

"So we're talking about a man of average height and weight," Soave concluded, shoving his lower lip in and out.

"Which happens to match the general description of the Dorset Flasher," Des said. "Unless . . . could his attacker have been a good-sized woman?"

"Don't see why not," the death investigator replied. "If she surprised him."

"Oh, I'd say Augie was good and surprised. Did you find a black ski mask on him?"

"No ski mask."

Soave moved away from the body now, Yolie and Des trailing along. "We'll search the neighborhood trash cans for that ski mask. And undertake a more thorough search of the grounds at daylight."

"I'd pay particular attention to the riverbank if I were you," Des advised.

"Will do," Yolie said.

"You folks ready to head over to Town Hall now?"

"First give us the short version," Soave responded. "If Augie Donatelli *wasn't* the Dorset Flasher then who are you liking for it?"

Des stood there, hands on her hips, mulling it over. "Persons of interest do come to mind. One is Hal Chapman. I'd crossed him off my list, but based on his behavior earlier this evening I'd have to put him back on."

"What kind of behavior?"

"He went semiballistic at a cocktail party over at the Captain Chadwick condos. I was there. You see, a childhood friend of Mitch's is getting—"

"I *knew* it!" erupted Soave, who'd never had any use for the unlikely civilian in Des's life. "I *knew* Berger would end up in the middle of this."

"His friend, Kenny Lapidus, is engaged to marry a local yoga instructor named Kimberly Farrell. Her father is Dex Farrell. *The* Dex Farrell."

"That thieving bastard cost me almost thirty grand," Soave grumbled. "I'd like to punch him out."

"You and everybody else. The Farrells live in the Captain Chadwick House. So does Kenny's mom, Beth."

"Is this the Beth Breslauer who the victim was hassling?" asked Yolie.

"The same. Hal's a trainer at Kimberly's fitness center. I knew he had a history—exposed himself to a girl back in high school. I also knew he was a major player with the ladies. But I didn't know until tonight that he's seriously into Kimberly. *And* has a major temper."

"Okay, who else do you like?" Soave pressed her.

"You'll also want to look at a local housepainter-slash-garbage head named J. Z. Cliffe," Des answered, not bothering to mention the source of this particular lead. "J. Z. has a grudge against the rich old ladies in town. His girlfriend works nights. And he used to be married to Kimberly."

"Sounds like this girl's smack-dab in the middle of it," Yolie said.

"I never trust yoga teachers," Soave blustered. "That whole mellow act of theirs is a complete crock."

"Time out. . . ." Yolie whipped out her notepad and pen. "Sometimes I just have to write this stuff down."

"And then there's Kenny," Des went on. "He's a big-time computer geek up in Cambridge. Comes down every weekend to see Kimberly. Before tonight he didn't strike me as a likely candidate to be our Flasher. But he's in play now. I saw him out on his mother's porch getting busy with Kimberly shortly before the attack. Once I took off after Augie, who knows where Kenny went."

"Kimberly would know," Yolie said.

"I saw something else just before the attack—Beth slipped out of the building and headed down Dorset Street alone on foot."

"Was she carrying a Louisville Slugger by any chance?"

"Just her purse, Rico. And she was headed in the opposite direction of the crime scene. Still, she was out and about when this went down. And she was feeling harassed by Augie. And here's one other thing you ought to know: Augie suggested to me that Beth Breslauer isn't who she appears to be."

"Meaning what exactly?"

"Damned if I know."

"Well, who does she appear to be?"

"A well-heeled doctor's widow from Scarsdale. When Mitch was a kid in Stuyvesant Town she was his neighbor. Her name was Lapidus then."

Soave thumbed his moustache as he considered all of this. "Des, let's be straight about one thing—do you or do you not believe that Augie Donatelli was the Dorset Flasher?"

She took a deep breath, letting it out slowly. "No, Rico, I don't."

"You've changed your mind about him?"

"Yes, I have."

"Why?"

"Because we're standing here looking at him, that's why."

Later, she climbed the narrow stairs up to Mitch's darkened sleeping loft and crawled into bed next to him, stretching her naked self out against him.

"Gee, mom, is it time for school already?" he murmured.

"Very funny."

"What time is it?"

"Just after three. Go back to sleep, baby."

"Not a chance." He kissed her, running his hands up and down her back. "Just give me ten more seconds to wake up and I'll go fetch the lavender oil."

"Not tonight. Go back to sleep, okay?"

"Something's happened. What is it?"

"Somebody beat Augie Donatelli's brains in. I found him in the bushes next to Rut Peck's house."

"My God, who . . . ?"

"Either he was attacked by the Flasher or by someone who thought *he* was the Flasher. That's the working theory, anyhow."

Mitch's sleeping loft wasn't wired for electricity. He struck a match to light the oil lantern. She promptly blew it out.

"Don't you want to talk about this?"

"I'm all talked out," she replied. "Until nine a.m., which is when I'll be getting my head chewed off by my barracks commander."

"Why will Rundle be pissed at you?"

"Because I was tailing Augie when it went down. Hell, I was practically on top of the crime scene. *And* I had that public scene with him on Friday."

"They don't think *you* killed him, do they?"

"There are some people around town who definitely will."

"Which people?"

"The ones who want me gone. Don't approve of me."

"Like First Selectman Bob Paffin, for instance?"

"Well, yes, now that you mention it." She snuggled against him, hugging him tight. "Or do you think I'm being a paranoid nut job?"

"When I was growing up my parents used to tell me that there were people out there who hated us on spec—simply for being Jews. I didn't think they were nut jobs. And I don't think you are. In fact, I know you're not."

"Rundle will probably chain me to a desk until the case is closed."

"All because you were out there doing your job tonight?"

"Basically. The good news is that Soave and Yolie are on it."

"Not to worry then. They'll figure out who killed Augie. Or I should say Yolie will. Mr. Potato Head will just puff and preen and say dorky things." Mitch had reciprocal warm, fuzzy feelings for Rico. He cradled her face in his hands, his own face very close to hers. "Nobody who knows you—really knows you—will believe you had anything to do with it. And anyone who does think that, well, you'll never win them over in a million years. So screw them."

She caressed his cheek with hers, kissing him softly. "I don't know what I'd do right now if I didn't have you."

"Now you know exactly how I feel every minute of every day."

"How did I get so lucky?"

"Luck had nothing to do with it, thinny. I chased after you."

"Did not. I'm the one who chased after you."

"I was just letting you think that. It was my play all of the way."

"Armando . . . ?"

"Hmmm-mmm . . . ?"

"Go get the lavender oil."

CHAPTER 9

"FOUR MORE, BRO! GIVE me *four*!"

Mitch and Hal had the Dorset Fitness Center to themselves at eight o'clock on a Sunday morning. Hal was putting him through a punishing set of reps on the pressing bench. Mitch's pecs and delts were popping, the sweat pouring off of him as Hal's favorite music mix, which leaned heavily toward Metallica, blared from the sound system.

"Now give me *two*! Come on, pump it, pump it. . . . *That's* what I'm talking about!" he exulted as Mitch aced his final rep. "Okay, give yourself a ten-minute blow on the bike. You earned it."

Gasping, Mitch climbed aboard a stationary bike and started pedaling.

Hal handed him a bottle of water, clearing his throat uneasily. "Listen, I'm real sorry about the way I lost it at Mrs. Breslauer's cocktail party. I feel sick about it, bro. That badass stuff is *so* not me. I phoned Kimmy last night to apologize but she was so pissed she wouldn't even talk about it. Which I totally understand. As soon as she walks in that door I'm going to quit. I really shouldn't be working here."

Mitch gulped down some water. "How come?"

"I'm not over her, that's how come."

"You two were involved?"

"No, never. Kimmy doesn't believe in getting physical with anybody who she works with. That's how she put it to me, anyhow. And I've been fine with it—until she met Kenny."

"And now you're not fine with it?"

Hal shook his head. "Bro, Kimmy's *the one*. I've never, ever felt this way about a girl. I get my share of tail. That goes with the job. But it's Kimmy who I really want. And I can't have her. So I think I'd better move on."

"Sorry to hear it, Hal. Where will you go?"

"There's a decent club over in Old Saybrook. I can get some hours there."

"That's not exactly the same as managing this place. As a career move, I mean."

"No, it's not," he allowed. "But it'll be a whole lot better for my sanity."

The front door of the fitness center opened and someone came in wearing chunky heels that clomped hard on the tile floor. *A pit bull with jugs* was how Des had once described Sergeant Yolie Snipes. Indeed, she was the fiercest-looking woman Mitch had ever known. Yolie's inked up arms bulged out of her sleeveless top as she stood there at the reception desk, her cop's eyes flicking around. Mitch called out to her, waving both arms in the air. She came on over.

"Hey there, sweet thing," she exclaimed, a big smile creasing her street-hardened face. Chiefly, it was that one-inch box cutter scar across her cheek. It left no doubt that Yolie had lived the life. "Good to see you again."

He climbed down off of the bike and gave her a hug. "Back at you. Pardon my sweat."

She let out a huge laugh. "You kidding me? This is the best action I've had all year." Her gleaming brown eyes looked him up and down. "Damn, boy, you are cut."

"And I have this guy right here to thank—Hal Chapman, say hello to Sergeant Yolanda Snipes of the Major Crime Squad."

Hal nodded to her, his manner noticeably guarded.

"How's my girl doing this morning?" Yolie asked Mitch.

"She's not happy."

"Not to worry. We'll close this one out in no time."

"Speaking of *we*, where's . . . ?"

"On his way to the hospital. Tawny just went into labor—unless it's a false alarm. She's not due for another week. Chances are he'll be back in a couple of hours. But if it's the real deal then I'm flying solo until a new boss takes over."

Translation: If she worked fast she had a chance to break the Augie Donatelli murder case on her own. Yolie Snipes wasn't just hard-edged. She was ultra-ambitious.

"Nice gym you've got going on here, Hal," she observed, glancing around. "I do my lifting in a stanky basement. Here you've got sunlight, a river view. I am loving this. Is Kimberly Farrell around?"

"Not yet. She'll be in soon for her nine o'clock class."

"Cool." Yolie straddled a pressing bench, her thighs straining against the thin cotton of her tan slacks. "Okay if you and me talk while I wait for her?"

Hal shrugged his broad shoulders. "What about?"

"Last night's beating death of Augie Donatelli. I understand you're a potential witness."

His eyes widened. "I am? How can that be?"

"You attended a cocktail party in a condo at the Captain Chadwick House earlier in the evening, didn't you?"

"Well, yeah. Mitch was there, too. So?"

"So I need to account for your comings and goings afterward. That's what they pay me for."

"Uh . . . do I need a lawyer?"

"You always have a right to counsel. But if it was me, I wouldn't bother. This is strictly routine stuff. Is there an office where we can talk?"

"Right here's fine. Okay if my bro sits in?"

Yolie shot a glance over at Mitch. "In what capacity?"

"As a witness," Hal answered.

She raised her chin an inch. "You need a witness?"

"Let's just say I'll feel more comfortable if someone else is around. You don't mind, do you?"

She shook her head. "No, I don't mind."

"Good deal." Hal hunkered down on the bench next to hers, forearms resting on his knees. "What do you want to know?"

Yolie pulled a small notepad and pen from the back pocket of her slacks. "Where you were last night."

"What time are we talking about?"

"Let's say nine o'clock."

"I was with someone," Hal said, coloring slightly.

"I'll need the lady's name and phone number, hon."

"Look, it's . . . complicated, okay?"

"Complicated as in she's married?"

"Well, yeah."

"Not a problem. I won't mess up your thing. I can contact her at her workplace. Look, let me make this easy for you. . . ." Yolie glanced down at her notepad. "Is her name Lisa Neville?"

"How do you know about me and Lisa?"

"Because you've been under surveillance for a while—in connection with the Dorset Flasher case."

Hal gaped at her in shock. "I have? What on earth for?"

Yolie's gaze hardened. "We don't really need to go there, do we?"

"Damn, that was a *million* years ago," he responded angrily. "*And* it was a bum rap. She was my girlfriend, okay? We were getting it on. Got caught out on the bleachers one day during lunch. She panicked because her parents thought she was this perfect little angel. So she put it all on me. The principal, Mr. Jaffe, knew what the real story was. Everyone did. He convinced her parents not to file charges against me. And they didn't. How did you even find out about it?"

"Dorset's resident trooper is a first-class detective, that's how."

Hal looked over at Mitch. "Did you know about this?"

"Des doesn't tell me everything she's doing." Which was the truth. Just not in this case.

"We're right back where we started, hon," Yolie said patiently. "The woman you were with last night?"

"Her name's Terri," Hal answered grudgingly. "She was a drop-in on Friday. Blonde, slammin' good bod. Not a local girl."

"Terri's last name?"

"I wish I could remember. I just hooked up with her that one time. I think it began with an E . . . Edsen, maybe?"

"Did she sign in?"

"I'll check." Hal went over to the front desk for the sign-in book and returned with it. "Sorry, she just signed in as Terri E."

Yolie had a look for herself. "She pay you with a credit card?"

"Cash. It's like eighteen bucks for a drop in."

"You have a phone number or address for her?"

"Nothing."

"Well, what did she tell you about herself?"

"That she'd been staying in Dorset with friends for the week."

"Do you remember their names?"

Hal shook his head. "All she said was that she was visiting an old college roommate and her dull husband."

"From . . . ?"

"Excuse me?"

"Visiting from . . . ?"

"New York. She was a New Yorker."

"There, you see? Now we're getting somewhere."

"She told me she was heading back home today. Real sweet girl. We vibed real good when I worked her out. She stopped by yesterday to thank me and, you know, one thing led to another."

"She hit on you, is that what you're saying?"

"It happens," Hal said with a shrug.

"Did she say if she had a job?"

"Yeah, some kind of cube-farm gig. A big outfit that recovers money for people who don't know they've lost it, or inherited it or something like that. I don't remember exactly. I was more interested in trying to get her top off than I was in her career." Hal cleared his throat. "Sorry, don't mean to be offensive."

"Not to worry, hon. I've heard worse. What time did you hook up?"

"Eight-thirty. She met me at the espresso bar out in the food hall, then I drove us to the beach in my ride."

"Where'd you park?"

"At White Sand Beach. We strolled down to this nice secluded little spot that I know about."

"Anyone see you?"

"Nope."

"What do you drive, Hal?"

"A Tahoe." He gave her the year and license number.

"You say Terri E met you at the espresso bar. How did she get there?"

"She drove, I guess. There were a lot of cars parked there. The food hall's open until midnight on Saturday night. When I brought her back it was still plenty busy."

"What time was this?"

"Eleven-thirty or so."

"Where did you drop her?"

"In front of the main entrance. She gave me a kiss, got out and then I took off."

"You didn't see her get into a vehicle?"

"Nope."

"Did she tell you where in New York she lives?"

"In the City, I think. But I'm not positive. Like I was saying, I was—"

"All about getting her top off. Yeah, I'm there."

The front door opened now and Kimberly came gliding in wearing her yoga clothes and a look of complete serenity.

"Over here, Kimmy!" Hal called out, visibly relieved by her arrival. "This here's Sergeant Snipes of the Major Crime Squad," he explained as Kimberly approached them. "She's investigating Augie Donatelli's death."

Kimberly smiled at Yolie warmly. "Good morning, Sergeant. If there's anything I can help you with please feel free to ask."

"Actually, I do need to ask you a few questions."

"Sergeant, could I borrow Kimmy for just one second first?" Hal interjected. "I mean, if you don't mind."

Kimberly said, "Hal, if this is about Beth's party don't worry about it."

"I didn't sleep a wink all night," he confessed miserably. "I totally embarrassed myself."

"And now you should let that feeling go." There was no trace of annoyance in Kimberly's voice. Only gentle kindness. Was Mitch witnessing the mystical power of yoga or the chemical effects of strong prescription antidepressants? He wondered—because her calm was pretty amazing. "It was just a silly moment, Hal. Silly moments are like those big puffy clouds in the sky. They blow away and then they're gone. I believe in you. I want you here. So just forgive yourself and move on, okay?"

He looked at her doubtfully. "Are you sure about this?"

"I couldn't be more sure."

"Well, okay. . . ."

A young couple came in to work out. Hal headed for the counter to sign them in.

"About those questions . . . ?" Yolie said to Kimberly.

"Ask away, Sergeant."

"This is my cue to take off," Mitch said.

"No, please don't," Kimberly said to him. "Kenny will be here in a sec. He was going to take my class but I'm sure he'd much rather hang with you. Shall we go in my office, Sergeant?"

"Or we can just talk right here," Yolie offered, shooting a quick glance Mitch's way. He knew why. She wanted him to be Des's eyes and ears. Wanted him to report back to her. Soave wouldn't play it this way, but Soave wasn't around. "If you don't mind, that is."

"Not at all, Sergeant. What is it you wish to know?"

"Where you were last night at, say, nine o'clock."

"With Kenny at his mother's place. I usually stay there with him when he's in town. He's not allowed to spend the night in my room until we're married. Unlike Beth, my mother's a little bit old-fashioned and a whole lot religious."

"Does she attend that lovely white Congregational Church?"

"No, St. Anne's on Old Shore Road. My folks are Episcopalian. Or, I should say, mother is. Father hasn't gone to church in twenty years. But she goes every Sunday, come rain or shine. She's there right now. I just helped her load up before I came here."

Yolie frowned at her. "Load up?"

"Her car. She collects bags of old clothing for the Nearly New shop. It's one of her causes. And, trust me, she is organized. Every item of clothing is bagged by category, by size, by gender. And she's been reusing the same black trash bags for so long that they're practically nothing but holes. But my mother never throws anything away. Is your mother like that, too, Sergeant?"

"My mother OD'ed on smack when I was baby."

"I'm so sorry."

"Don't be," Yolie snapped. "I ain't looking for your pity."

Kimberly flinched, taken aback. "At nine o'clock I was out on the porch."

"With Kenny?"

"No, he'd gone inside to answer some e-mail on his laptop. 'It'll just take a minute,' he says. It's usually more like two hours. He's a workaholic. I'm always trying to get him to chill out."

"Where was he answering this e-mail?"

"In his bedroom. Our bedroom."

"Mrs. Breslauer has a ground-floor unit?"

"Yes."

"There are windows in this bedroom, correct?"

Kimberly raised an eyebrow at her. "What are you suggesting?"

"Not a thing. Just trying to nail down whether you can be absolutely sure he was in that room at the time of Augie Donatelli's death. And you can't be."

"Kenny barely *knew* Augie. . . ." Kimberly's lower lip began to quiver. "Besides, he wouldn't have anything to do with violence. He's not like that."

"Trust me, girl. Right place, right time, we're *all* like that."

"Not Kenny!" Tears began to spill from Kimberly's blue eyes. So much for yogic serenity. What was it J. Z. had said about her? She *feels* everything. "How could you even think such a thing?"

"Just doing my job," Yolie responded coolly. "Where was Mrs. Breslauer at this time?"

"All tired out from playing hostess. She told us she felt like crawling into bed and watching something stupid on TV."

"You're saying she was in her room, too?"

"That's right."

Meaning that Kimberly didn't know that Beth had slipped out the back door of the Captain Chadwick House just before Augie's murder and taken off on foot. *Or* that she was lying to provide a cover for Beth. Not that Mitch considered Kimberly particularly devious or conspiratorial. But how did he know for certain what lay underneath that sunny calm of hers? Did she *feel* hatred and rage just like other people did? Was she capable of acting on such dark human emotions? The short answer: he didn't know.

Kenny came in the door now and headed straight for the front desk to make things right with Hal. His manner was totally cordial. Hal's was, too. Smiles all around before the two of them bumped knucks.

Then Kenny moseyed over their way. "Okay, Berger, this time I know I've got you," he said eagerly. "Ready? Here goes: 'You want me to hold the chicken?' "

" 'I want you to hold it between your knees,' " Mitch answered promptly. "That's Jack Nicholson to the coffee shop waitress in *Five Easy Pieces*. Give it up, Lapidus. You'll never beat me."

"This man is a freak!" he exclaimed, shaking his head in dumbfounded amazement. "Kimmy, would you mind if I grabbed a coffee with him instead of taking your class?"

She squeezed his hand. "Of course not."

Mitch said, "I've been pumping iron for the past hour. I should jump in the shower real quick."

"Don't bother. I work with computer weasels, remember? If they change their socks once a week it's a miracle."

"Mr. Lapidus, I'm Sergeant Yolanda Snipes of the Major Crime Squad," Yolie spoke up. "I'm investigating Augie Donatelli's murder. Don't wander too far, okay? You and me need to log some face time."

Kenny swallowed nervously. "We do? How come?"

"Routine stuff. No big deal."

"Okay, sure. We'll be right outside in the food hall."

As Mitch and Kenny started for the door, Yolie grabbed Mitch and said, "If you speak to our girl, tell her I'll be in touch. I intend to keep her in the loop *and* busy. I don't want her to go crazy."

"Yolie, that makes two of us."

Most of the food stalls were closed on Sunday morning. But the bakery and espresso bar were doing a brisk business. The village's early birds liked to gather there over coffee to peruse the newspapers and gab away.

Mitch and Kenny ordered lattes and found a table. Mitch was still thinking about Yolie's line of questioning. He couldn't imagine that Beth, Kenny or Kimberly had anything to do with Augie's death. And yet, Augie *had* been borderline stalking Beth. And Beth *had* slipped out at the time of his murder. Kenny, it appeared, could have easily done the same. And Kimberly could have been unaware—or was playing dumb.

Across the table, Kenny was studying him intently. He had a serious look on his face. "I'm glad you've done so well, Berger. I've followed your career. Never miss one of your reviews. And I-I saw your wife's obituary. I thought about sending you a card but I didn't think you'd remember me."

"Are you kidding? Of course I would."

"Listen, this is kind of weird, but if I ask you something, man to man, will you promise to tell me the truth?"

"I promise."

"What the hell's going on with my mom?"

Mitch took a sip of his coffee. "I'm not sure what you mean, Lapidus."

"I mean, do you know who she's seeing? Because she's got a man in her life, I'm positive. Not that she's said one word to me. Which isn't like Mom at all. We always tell each other everything. We're best friends. No secrets. Not ever." Kenny broke off, breathing in and out. "I'm figuring whoever this guy is, she's really ashamed. Like maybe he's married or something. Since Dorset's such a small town I thought maybe you'd heard some blowback or-or—"

"Slow down. What makes you so sure she's seeing someone?"

Kenny blinked at him. "I'm no dummy, okay? Last night she told us she was going to crawl into bed and watch TV. Maybe she fooled Kimmy—but not me. Who puts on perfume before she climbs into bed alone? Mom slipped out the back door, Berger. I heard her. I didn't hear her take her car out of the garage. So I'm figuring this guy must live within walking distance. Any idea who he might be?"

Actually a prime candidate did pop into Mitch's mind. A good-looking free spirit in his early forties whose girlfriend worked nights. J. Z. lived within walking distance of the Captain Chadwick House. And Beth would not want Kenny *or* Kimberly to know that she was getting it on with Kimberly's ex-husband. Because that was, well, sick. So sick that Mitch didn't even want to go there. Not out loud anyhow. "The guy doesn't have to live within walking distance, Lapidus," he said. "He could have been waiting down the street for her in his car."

"That's true," Kenny conceded.

"What time did Beth get home?"

"Four o'clock in the morning. I was wide-awake all night waiting for her."

"Did you talk to her about it?"

"No," he said abruptly. "She's a grown woman. Her love life really isn't any of my business. But I need to know. Seriously, Berger, you'd tell me if you knew anything, right?"

"Absolutely."

Kenny sat there gripping his coffee container tightly in both hands. "Mom's been through such a world of hurt ever since Irwin died. Irwin made her happy. Her life was a pleasure. Trust me, that wasn't the case after my father took off. When you knew us back in Stuyvesant Town, wow, every day was a struggle for Mom. All she ever did was work her ass off and take care of me. She never had any time for herself. Not that she ever complained."

"Do you ever hear from him?"

"From who?"

"Your father."

"I have no father," Kenny shot back. "I think he's out on the West Coast somewhere. He's an accountant or auditor of some kind. He remarried, started another family. But I don't know how many kids he has or-or what their names are. I don't want to know. I want nothing to do with that bastard. A guy who bails on his young wife and son the way he did. Leaving us to fend for ourselves. What kind of a man does that? When Kimmy and I start our family, believe me, those kids will know they have a father who loves them. No one should have to grow up like I did."

"And yet you did damned well, Lapidus."

"No thanks to him. It was Irwin who was there for me. Not that he ever got in my face or anything. He understood that he wasn't my father. But he gave me a push when I needed one. Taught me to believe in myself. Irwin wasn't a flashy sort of guy. A nebbish, really. But solid. And he worshiped the ground Mom walked on. Every morning at breakfast he'd tell her how beautiful she was. He was good to her. And he left her real fiscally fit." Kenny paused, running a hand through his thatch of hair. "Which, being honest, is my real concern. Mom's sitting on a mondo pile of dough. Not surprisingly, there are a million sleazeballs out there looking for a rich widow to prey on. She's a prime target. Trusting and kind. And still plenty attractive for a woman her age, don't you . . . ?" Kenny peered at him. "Wow, Berger, you just got *real* red all of a sudden."

"From my workout. I really should have taken that shower." Mitch sat back in his chair, sipping his latte. "I think you're underestimating Beth. She strikes me as plenty savvy. But I'll mention your concerns to Des. She can smell a shark from a mile off. Seriously, she's like Robert Shaw in *Jaws.* There's no need for you to worry about some schmuck moving in on Beth. It won't happen."

"That's awesome, Berger," he said gratefully. "Thanks."

"No prob. Except now *I* have to ask *you* something weird. Because there's something I still can't figure out."

"You want me to explain what I do for a living?"

"Oh, hell no. I'd never understand. This is about the Dorset Flasher."

"The late Augie Donatelli, you mean."

"Actually, they don't know for sure that Augie was the Flasher."

"Really? Stupid me, I just assumed. What *do* they know?"

"That the Flasher has been operating on the weekend. And that, by a strange twist of circumstance, you happen to visit Dorset every weekend."

"Wait, are you asking me if *I'm* the Dorset Flasher?"

"No, absolutely not. But I do keep wondering if there's some connection between your visits and his activities." Mitch's gaze locked onto Kenny's. "Is there?"

"Very good question," Kenny answered forthrightly. "I've been wondering about that myself. I solve analytical problems for a living, okay? That's actually what I do. And ever since this nut started waving his meat up and down the block I've been thinking: Why does this always happen while I'm here?"

"And where has your thinking taken you?"

"Berger, I don't have the slightest freaking idea."

Chapter 10

Des showed up at the Troop F barracks in Westbrook right on time, only Captain Rundle wasn't there. Which is not to say that her troop commander's small, plainly furnished office was unoccupied. Captain Richie Tedone of Internal Affairs was standing at the window watching the traffic whiz by on Interstate 95.

Soave's older cousin—and Yolie's one-time flame—was a key Waterbury Mafia player. A ball buster who'd been positioned in Internal Affairs so as to weed out anyone and everyone who dared to challenge their hold on power. The Brass City boys, according to the Deacon, always made sure they had a designated thug like Richie in IA. He was a chesty lug nut in his late thirties with tight, curly black hair and a twenty-inch neck. He wore a cheap, shiny black suit and an air of tremendous self-importance. The man was way smug. Also way into looking Des up and down as she stood there in the office doorway, his eyes unbuttoning her uniform, helping her off with her shoes and socks. She hadn't met a Brass City boy yet who didn't have a chocolate fantasy.

"Unfortunate bit of business last night, Master Sergeant Mitry," he said gruffly. "High profile, all over the TV news. Have a seat. We'll talk about it."

Des stayed in the doorway, on high alert. What in the hell was Richie Tedone doing here at nine o'clock on a Sunday morning? Why was IA even involved? "I thought I was here to see Captain Rundle."

"He'll be along. I just asked him to give us the room for a few minutes. Sit down."

She didn't budge. "If this is an IA inquiry then I'm entitled to representation."

Richie sat behind Rundle's desk, his stubby hands clasped before him. "It's not an inquiry. No notes. No tape recorder. I've got nothing up my sleeve," he assured her, waving his hands in the air like a second-rate magician. "I just want to have a conversation, okay?"

Des leaned against the door jamb, her arms crossed. "A conversation about . . . ?"

"You," he replied. "I've been keeping my eye on you, Master Sergeant. My cousin Rico claims you taught him everything he knows. He thinks you're wasted down here in scenic Dorset."

Des said nothing to that.

"Tell me, do you feel you're doing an effective job as resident trooper?"

"I do, captain. And the crime statistics back me up. They're among the lowest in the state, per capita."

"And yet you've had another murder on your watch." *Another* murder. "This time a highly decorated retired New York City police detective. Are you sure you're cut out for this particular post? Given your advanced level of training and expertise, I mean."

"Exactly where are you going with this, Captain? Because it's starting to sound a whole lot like an employment counseling session."

"Watch your lip." Richie glared at her. "There are going to be some major, major departmental changes taking place in the very near future. And, whether you know it or not, you're standing on a precipice. Your present predicament is—"

"Wait, *what* predicament are you—?"

"This is the part where I talk and you listen, okay? You had a physical altercation with the murder victim in front of several witnesses. That sort of ugly behavior will make it hard for you to remain in your current post. Damned near impossible, I'd say. Which is why you're standing out on that precipice." Again with the damned precipice. "The way I see it is you can go one of two ways. Either you move back up to Major Crimes or . . ."

"Or I'm out, is that what you're telling me? Because that's bull, Captain. I did *nothing* wrong. And the witness statements will back me up."

"Hell, I know that," Richie acknowledged easily, rocking back and forth in Rundle's chair. "Rico keeps lobbying to get you back. Swears you've paid your dues for that unfortunate misstep of yours a while back."

Meaning when she'd gone up against Superintendent Crowther. She'd been investigating a murder out on Big Sister Island. It had been her first visit to Big Sister. First encounter with a chubby widower from New York named Mitch Berger. The case led her smack-dab into the superintendent's own tangled role in a murder investigation thirty years earlier. They tussled. She won, as in solved the case. But lost, as in she was lucky she still had a job after the dust settled.

"There's always room for an effective team player on Major Crimes," Richie went on. "What would you think about coming back to the headmaster's house with the big people?"

"I'm happy right where I am, sir." Des glanced down the hallway. "Is Captain Rundle around?"

"I'm not done yet!" he snarled.

Des raised her chin slightly, studying him. "What is this, Captain? Why are you really here?"

He let out a short laugh. "You trying to tell me you don't know?"

"I'm not *trying* to tell you anything. I really don't know."

"Okay, fine. Play games if you want."

"I'm not playing."

Richie stared at her long and hard. "Who knows? Maybe you're not. He is an awfully hard nut."

"Who is?"

"The Deacon. Your da-da. Who'd you think we were talking about? Christ, for a smart girl you can be awful dumb. Anybody ever tell you that?"

Des drove her Saab up Route 9 alongside the Connecticut River in the direction of New Britain, the historic home of Stanley Tools. She was heading to Kensington, a working class suburb of the Hardware City. To the small, neat house where she grew up. She pulled into the driveway behind her father's cruiser and got out, glad that she'd changed out of her uni into shorts. It was ten degrees warmer away from the shore. And a whole lot stickier.

Buck Mitry had just gotten home from church. Des knew this because he was still dressed up for church. Her father believed in being dressed up for church. He believed in quiet, dignified charcoal gray suits. Owned at least half a dozen of them. He believed in white shirts, muted ties and shined shoes.

The screen doors were open, front and back. He didn't believe in air-conditioning. She could smell his coffee brewing in the kitchen. He drank at least ten piping hot cups a day, even in the swelter of August. Used to be a heavy smoker, too, but he'd quit as a twenty-fifth anniversary gift to her mom. In exchange, she'd left him for her high school sweetheart in Augusta, Georgia. He lived there by himself now. Unless you counted Cagney and Lacey, the two neutered strays Des had foisted on him.

He was standing there in the kitchen waiting for his coffee to be ready. He was a big man, six feet four, still straight and broad shouldered, though his brow was deeply furrowed now, his hair graying. He had the hugest hands Des had ever seen on any man. Had played first base in the Cleveland Indians organization for two years after high school before he met her mom and got serious. He took the state police exam back when they were looking for a few good black men. Rose steadily through the ranks to become the highest-ranking man of color in Connecticut history. He got there by being sober, honest and careful. He believed in obeying the rules. He believed that human emotions were a form of weakness that ought to be contained. That was why everyone on the job called him the Deacon. It was also why her mom had left him. "I have rediscovered laughter and joy," she'd told Des at her wedding.

"How are you, Daddy?" she asked, kissing him on the forehead.

"Getting along. Surprised to see you here, Desiree."

"Am I interrupting anything?"

"Not at all. I was just going to change into my work clothes and mow the lawn." He took off his jacket and hung it on a kitchen chair. Poured each of them a cup of coffee, sat at the kitchen table and waited for her to say something.

She sat across from him and waited for him to say something. The two of them were so much alike it was scary. It certainly scared her. Because she did not want to end up like him—closed off, distant, *alone*.

"I like your hair this way," he said to her finally. "Short."

She nodded in response. She'd lopped off her dreads over a year ago but he still hadn't gotten past his horror over them.

"How is your friend Mitch doing?" The Deacon actually liked Mitch, in spite of his pinkness. Thought he was a decent, kind-hearted man.

"Mitch is fine. Happy with his new job."

"And how about Mr. Brandon Stokes of the US Attorney's office?" he asked, curling his lip at her. Despite her ex's Yale Law degree and chiseled ebony good looks, the Deacon had never been a fan. Thought that Brandon smelled like a no-good player. Which, hello, it turned out he was.

"I wouldn't know, Daddy." She sipped her coffee. "It seems there's a lot I don't know."

"Such as . . . ?"

"I had a murder last night."

"I heard."

"Unfortunately, I had a public altercation with the victim on Friday."

"Heard that, too. Anything to it?"

"Nothing whatsoever. He was a drinker. He got out of hand. I dealt with him by the book and the witness statements will back me up. But that creep Richie Tedone just came sniffing around. Making all sorts of veiled threats about my future. It seems that I'm 'standing on a precipice.' Where do they even learn to talk like that?"

He lowered his eyes. "So it's come to that, has it?"

"Richie so much as told me that my 'predicament' has something to do with you. Care to fill me in?"

The Deacon was not one for rash responses. He considered his answer for a long moment before he said, "Desiree, there's no cause for you to be concerned about your future. It's not your job they want—it's mine."

"Daddy, what are you talking about?"

"Superintendent Crowther intends to retire at the end of next year. The Brass City boys want one of their own in my slot so that he'll be next in line to take over the whole operation. They've wanted my job for a long time. And now they're trying to use you to get at me. That's how they operate. I can guarantee you I'll be getting a phone call about this from your Captain Richie Tedone very soon."

"A phone call saying what?"

"That if I announce my retirement tomorrow they won't proceed with an IA investigation into your behavior. They'll even take a serious look at promoting you back to Major Crimes. Did he tell you there's always room at the headmaster's house for an effective team player?"

Des peered at him. "And if you *don't* announce your retirement?"

"They'll drag you through a full-frontal probe that will taint you for the remainder of your career—assuming you still have one by the time they're done."

"Daddy, those bastards have nothing on me, I swear."

"I believe you, Desiree."

"So tell them to go to hell."

"Ordinarily, I would. Unfortunately, I'm in a somewhat vulnerable position myself right now."

"You are? Why is that?"

He didn't answer her. Just sat there in suffocating silence.

"Daddy, what's going on?" she demanded.

"The vultures are circling, that's what," he answered at long last, staring down into his coffee mug. "Those Brass City boys swoop right in when they smell blood. Anyone who's even the slightest threat to them ends up getting—"

"Wait, I'm still missing something here. *Why* do they smell blood?"

"I'm taking a brief medical leave," he explained with a dismissive wave of his giant hand. "Incredibly minor matter. Some partial blockages in my pump that need rerouting. Just a simple plumbing job. But to them it's a—"

"Hold on just one second." Des's pulse had begun to race, and her palms were suddenly all sweaty. "Are you . . . you're having coronary bypass surgery?"

"At Yale-New Haven," he acknowledged, nodding. "On Wednesday."

"Which Wednesday?"

"This Wednesday."

Des gaped at him in shock. "You're having open-heart surgery this week and you don't tell me? The Waterbury Mafia knows about it and your only daughter doesn't? Jesus Christ, Daddy, how fucked up is that?"

"Watch your mouth, young lady."

"Were you *ever* planning to tell me? Or were you just hoping I didn't notice that you'd temporarily relocated your office to the ICU?"

"I didn't want you getting all hot and bothered," he explained with maddening calm. "You've got your own life. I'll be fine. Charlene's coming in from Scranton." His widowed older sister. "She'll stay with me when I get home. Honestly, it's nothing to worry about. Minor surgery, like I said."

"Damn it, Daddy, there's no such thing as minor open-heart surgery!"

He didn't respond. Just sat there drinking his coffee in self-contained silence. Des wanted to shoot him.

"Does Mom know?"

"No," he answered sharply. "And I'd rather she didn't, understood?"

"No, but okay."

"I won't be on the shelf for very long. The doctor said I'm looking at four to six weeks of rehab. Should be good as new after that. But in the meantime . . ."

"The vultures are circling."

"They are indeed. And, who knows, maybe they're right. Maybe this *is* my time to go. I can teach a class or two at the academy. Write training manuals. I've got a good pension coming. The house is paid for. Part of me thinks I ought to step down and enjoy life a little. Except for one minor detail."

"Which is . . . ?"

"Those bastards are *not* going to use you to drive me out. That will never, ever happen. I've put in thirty-two years on this job. I'll go when I'm good and ready—and not a minute sooner. I deserve that right. I've earned it." He got up and refilled their cups, his gaze softening slightly. "I'm just sorry you got caught in the crossfire."

"I'm the one who's sorry. I gave them an opening."

"No, you didn't. If it hadn't been this Augie Donatelli business they'd have made up something else. Is your ex-sergeant, little Rico, mixed up in this?"

"Hard to say. His wife's about to give birth to their first child."

"Just what the world needs—more Tedones."

"I do know that he's very loyal to them."

"They're loyal to each other. They understand loyalty. Hell, they prey on it. That's why they know I can't let you go down."

"They know squat. Listen, there's a really easy way to make this whole thing go away. They can have my damned job, okay? I'll quit."

"You will not," he growled. "You have your whole career ahead of you. Mine's behind me."

"No, it's not. You're fifty-six years old, Daddy. You've still got a lot of good years left. Which is exactly what they're afraid of—you being named superintendent. They're afraid you'll break up their little feifdom."

"Can't be done. Not by me anyhow." He puffed out his cheeks, sighing gloomily. "There's too many of them, Desiree. And they're too strong. And I'm tired. I've been getting tired a lot lately."

"You'll feel better once you get your heart fixed."

"That's what the doctor said. I don't know. . . ."

"Well, your doctor does. And so do I," she told him confidently, even though at that moment she could feel the whole world shifting underneath her feet. Her father had always been a tower of strength. Not once had she seen him give in to defeat. Not ever. This was a first. But it didn't sadden her. Quite the contrary. It made her mad. Really mad.

It was never a good idea to make Des Mitry mad.

The Deacon's cell phone rang.

He removed it from his belt and set it on the table, staring at its little screen. "Captain Richie Tedone—right on schedule."

It rang five times before the Deacon's voice mail took it. Then they sat there, staring down at their coffee mugs in silence.

"I want you to call him back after I leave," Des said finally. "Tell him you'll think it over. Let him think he's got you boxed in, okay? Don't show him your hand."

"My hand?" He let out a humorless laugh. "What hand?"

She got up and put her mug in the sink. "Just leave that part to me."

He looked at her suspiciously. "What are you up to, Desiree? What's going on?"

"They just made a huge mistake, that's what. They made this personal. And now they're going to be incredibly sorry."

"Why is that?"

"Because I'm going to make it personal, too."

Chapter 11

Some guy was waiting there at the security barricade. Looked as if he had been for a while. He was sprawled out on the grass in the shadow of his motorcycle, which was a wicked vintage Norton Commando. When Mitch pulled up there in his Studey, the guy stirred and climbed to his feet, slinging a knapsack over one shoulder.

"Nice bike," Mitch called to him through his open window. "Is that a '67?"

"Sixty-eight," he called back. "Inherited her from a friend. He started a family and decided it was time to part with his toys."

"Lucky you." Mitch used his coded plastic card to raise the barricade. "Are you waiting here for someone?"

"I'm waiting for *you*, dude," he replied. "You're Mitch, aren't you? Sure you are. I'd know you anywhere. Although the last time I saw you, up close and personal, you had a scraggly beard and a Jewfro yay-high."

Mitch studied this guy more closely. He was thirty or so. An unshaven rock and roller with a lot of wavy black hair, an earring and those soft brown eyes that women get jelly knees over. He was dressed in a sleeveless gray sweatshirt, torn jeans and black biker boots. He wasn't particularly tall but he was in shape—his biceps and pecs rippled. He was also intensely hyper, nodding his head up and down to a beat that he alone could hear.

"I've kept track of you over the years, natch."

"Natch?"

"And I'm a large fan of your work. It's Very."

"Very what?"

"Very, *Very*. It's my name, dude. Detective Lieutenant Romaine Very."

Mitch was still trying to figure out how they knew each other. He hadn't worn his babe-repelling chin spinach for at least ten years. "You're the Major Crime Squad guy who's taking over for Rico Tedone?"

"Not exactly, dude. I'm not local. I'm from the two-four." He fished his shield from the back pocket of his jeans. It was an NYPD shield. And the license plate on his Norton, Mitch now noticed, was a New York plate. "I was wondering if I could talk to you."

"What about?"

"Augie Donatelli. I'm kind of Dawgie's next of kin. The man had no family. Just me. He changed my diapers, metaphorically speaking. Broke me in when I was new on the job. He was a cop's cop. The best."

"I'm sorry for your loss, but what does this have to do with me?"

"I owe the man, okay? Have to make sure the state police out here do right by him. I've been trying all morning to find out what's up with the investigation. I hear you folks have an ongoing situation with a weenie waver, but beyond that I can't get squat."

"Again, why are you talking to *me*?"

"Because the detective who's running the show, a Sergeant Snipes, won't return any of my calls. And the unis won't let me within ten feet of Dawgie's apartment until she green lights me. I've got information, okay? I'm in a position to help. Word is you're tight with the resident trooper. Besides, you and me go back a few years."

"You said that before. I'm still not placing you."

"Really? I sat next to you all of the time in postmodern European lit."

"You went to Columbia?"

"Try to get the incredulity out of your voice, will you? It's insulting."

"Sorry, I didn't mean to . . ."

"I was a year behind you. Majored in Romance languages—which did me beaucoup good. Wore my hair down to my shoulders in those days."

"Hold on a sec. . . ." Mitch shook a finger at him. "You're the Jiggler."

"The what?"

"Your knee. It used to jiggle all through class and drive everyone nuts. Sounded like there was a woodpecker in the room."

"I had an energy situation, as in I had too much of it. Still do."

"And how did you end up becoming a cop?"

"It was a family thing."

"Your dad's on the job?"

"Not really," Very said, leaving it there.

"I'd like to help out, Lieutenant, but I really don't know anything."

"I'm down with that. I'm just asking you to listen. Can you do that?"

"Sure, I can do that. Come on out."

Very jump-started his Norton with a roar and eased his way across the wooden causeway behind Mitch. When they reached the cottage he killed his engine and climbed off, glancing around. "Stabbin' cabin, dude," he observed, his head bobbing up and down, up and down. "If you have to be out of the City, I mean. Me, I get ootsie if I'm not standing on good, solid pavement."

"I'm sorry, did you just say *ootsie*?"

"Why, you got a problem with *ootsie*?"

"No, no. It's a fine word. How long are you planning to be here?"

"For as long as it takes. I took some vacation time."

"Do you have a place to stay?"

"Figured I'd find a motel room somewhere."

"On the Connecticut shoreline in August—without a reservation? Good luck with that."

Inside of the cottage, Very made straight for Mitch's sky blue Fender Stratocaster, which was propped against his monster pair of Fender twin reverb amps, stacked one atop the other with a signal splitter on top. "Ow, mommy-mommy! Awesome setup, dude."

"I make some noise."

"I'll bet you do." Now Very went over toward the table where Mitch's computer sat amidst heaps of printouts, notepads and DVDs. "Mind if ask what you're writing about this week?"

"Icebox questions."

"Icebox . . . hunh?"

"It's an expression coined by Hitchcock. His way of shrugging off really obvious lapses in logic or credibility. He believed that as long as the audience was loving the movie they wouldn't care. Like, say, in *The 39 Steps* . . ."

"Never saw it."

"You never saw *The 39 Steps*? You must. That scene with the finger totally slays. Anyway, Robert Donat and Madeleine Carroll have to spend the night handcuffed together in a room in a remote country inn, okay? And she's convinced that he's an escaped killer on the run. It's really tense. Also pretty damned sexy for 1935. They're actually lying on top of the bed together, okay? And she's even removed her wet stockings. You're totally into the scene. So into it that, in Hitchcock's words, it isn't until you get up for a glass of milk in the middle of the night and are standing there at your icebox that you ask yourself: 'What did they do when one of them had to go to the bathroom?' Just like with his famous crop duster scene in *North by Northwest*."

"Okay, that one I did see. It was incredible."

"So incredible that it's not until later that you ask yourself why

James Mason went to the trouble of sending Cary Grant all the way to an Indiana cornfield when he could have bumped him off in any back alley in Chicago. And, by the way, who was flying that crop duster? Was it one of Mason's henchmen? Where did he score a crop duster that's outfitted with machine guns on such short notice? Did he steal it? Kill the real pilot?"

"None of which matters," Very conceded. "Because it's not real life. It's just a movie."

"Sorry, did you say *just* a movie?"

Very held up his hands in a gesture of surrender. "Whatever, dude."

"Can I get you something to drink, Lieutenant?"

"I could go for anything cold."

Mitch went in the kitchen and poured two glasses of chilled well water. Came back and handed Very one. "I have to tell you something you're not going to like," he said. "The resident trooper had serious issues with Augie. They even had an altercation on Friday. She said he'd been drinking."

"I'm sorry to hear that. But I'm not surprised. Dawgie didn't exactly roll with the times. He could be sexually inappropriate, politically incorrect, you name it." Very paced around the living room as he talked, bristling with intensity. "He started drinking a lot after his wife, Gina, passed. His fuse got shorter and, well, last year, he got into it with a black female officer over some totally minor detail on a case. Called her an inappropriate name in the squad room. You don't use that kind of language in the workplace. Or anywhere else. She slapped him. He slapped her back. Our captain tried to smooth it over. You know, let's keep this inside the room. She wouldn't hear of it. Was going to file all kinds of official charges. So the captain had to convince Dawgie to take early retirement." Very paused to gulp down some water. "All of which is to say he had a grudge against black female officers. Especially young, good-looking ones—which

I'm told the resident trooper is. Damned shame, really. Dawgie was in a position to provide her with some valuable intel. If he'd established a better rapport with her he might still be alive."

"What sort of valuable intel?"

Very yanked a fat manila file folder out of his knapsack and set it down on Mitch's coffee table. "You ever hear of the Seven Sisters?"

"Sure. There's Vassar, Bryn Mawr, Wellesley, Smith. . . ."

"Not *those* Seven Sisters. I'm talking about the crime family."

Mitch shook his head. "No, I can't say I have."

"Again, I'm not surprised. The Seven Sisters are one of the great untold stories in the annals of twentieth century crime." Very flopped down on Mitch's love seat, then jumped right back up again, pacing, pacing. "Dude, I am talking about a vast, highly sophisticated Jewish crime empire that dates back to New York's Lower East Side in the early 1900s. According to the birth records there were seven Kudlach girls—Eva, Sonia, Esther, Thelma, Fanny, Bea and Helen. All of them the daughters of Moses and Sarah Kudlach. Moses was a Russian immigrant who sold stuff off a pushcart on Orchard Street. Anything he could get his hands on. The old lady, Sarah, was descended from a long line of Roumanian street *gonifs*. Jewish gypsies, really. Her girls started learning the family trade as soon as they were old enough to walk. By the time they were six years old, each of them was fanned out across the city all day long, scamming people for money, picking their pockets, snatching their purses, watches, jewelry. Then they'd bring everything home for Mom and Pop to unload. A nice, tight, one-family crime ring. All of it small stuff. But they flourished. Especially after Sarah married each girl off. She chose their husbands carefully. Each one was a neighborhood guy with a legit trade—a tailor, watchmaker, pawnbroker, kosher butcher, auto mechanic, truck driver. Their businesses formed a network for moving stolen merchandise of greater and greater value. By the twenties the family had ownership stakes in high-end dress shops, jewelry stores, restaurants, parking garages. They'd also expanded into bookmaking and loan sharking. No bootlegging or drugs or prostitution. They concentrated on what they knew. They were careful. And smart. And, with one notable exception, they never came to the attention of the law. Just kept growing from one generation to the next, expanding their empire out of New York into Miami, Los Angeles, Las Vegas. You wouldn't believe the family tree, dude. Dawgie's got it here in his file somewhere."

"Lieutenant, are you telling me they still exist?"

"A lot of the third and fourth generation are totally legit—doctors and lawyers, college professors. Some operate businesses that were financed by criminal activity but are now totally clean. But, yeah, quite a few of them are still living the life. It's in their blood."

"And you're telling me all of this because . . . ?"

"You're tight with Beth Breslauer—or so it appears from the last roll Dawgie FedExed me. Here, I just got these yesterday. . . ." Very opened the file and handed Mitch a batch of eight-by-ten color photos.

Mitch flipped through them. They were surveillance shots of Beth and him drinking smoothies together at The Works on Friday afternoon. Buying fish. Chatting in the parking lot. Her kissing him good-bye. "I don't understand," he said slowly. "Augie was following me?"

"Following her. How well do you know the lady?"

"We used to be neighbors in Stuyvesant Town. I was friends with her son Kenny."

"That would be Kenny Lapidus," Very said, nodding, nodding. "He's shagging your yoga teacher, Kimberly Farrell, whose parents live in the same building as Beth Breslauer—which so happens to be where Dawgie lived, too."

"Welcome to small town life, Lieutenant. But why on earth was Augie following Beth?"

"Because Beth Breslauer's great-grandmother was Esther Kudlach, one of the original Seven Sisters. Esther's married name became Pincus. Beth's grandfather, Saul Pincus, was a major New York racketeer in the thirties. The only high-profile one of the bunch. Movie-star handsome. A real tabloid star—right up until the night he was gunned down eating a bowl of matzoh ball soup in Lindy's. Saul liked to live large. A thirteen-room apartment on Park Avenue for the wife and kids. And a penthouse on Central Park West for his mistress—a hot little bad girl who danced in the Billy Rose Aquacade. Her name was Bertha Puzewski. You know her as Bertha Peck."

So *that* explained it, Mitch reflected. Beth landed her condo in the Captain Chadwick House because Bertha Peck had been her grandfather's girlfriend. If any of this tale was actually true, that is. Big if.

"A freakin' gold mine," Very went on. "That's what Dawgie called the place. He had Dex Farrell, the world-class Wall Street swindler, in one unit. He had Saul Pincus' granddaughter living across the hall from Farrell. And Saul's old girlfriend parked upstairs, passing herself off as WASP royalty." Very sat back down in front of Augie's file, leafing through it. "Yeah, here it is—Saul and his wife, Minnie, had two boys, Sam and Nathan. Sam was Beth's father. He made his living as a bookie. Same as her first husband, Sy Lapidus."

"You mean Kenny's dad? No, you've got that wrong. Sy's an accountant, albeit a louse. He deserted them when Kenny and I were kids. Moved out west."

"He didn't desert them, dude. He was serving a nickel at the Fishkill Correctional Facility. Didn't move out to California until years later."

"That's not what Kenny told me."

"Then Kenny doesn't know the real story. Or he's not being

straight with you. It's all right here in the file," Very tapped it with his finger. "His dad's whole criminal history."

"Beth sold handbags at Bloomingdale's," Mitch said stubbornly. "She was a nice lady. Still is. She's not a criminal."

"I didn't say she was." Very looked at Mitch curiously. "You still with me? Because you look a little shook. I don't blame you. This is some crazy stuff."

"Very."

"Yeah, dude?"

"It's very crazy stuff."

The lieutenant resumed his pacing. Clemmie came padding down from the sleeping loft and watched this hyper stranger in her midst, highly suspicious. After giving the matter considerable thought, she voted with all four paws to go back upstairs to her nice, calm bed.

"The day Dawgie moved in he called and told me Bertha Peck smelled wrong," Very recalled. "The man just had a sixth sense when it came to phonies. She had him do a job for her, touching up some paint in her bedroom, and he spotted those old cheesecake shots of her on the dressing table. Professional studio stuff. When he asked her about them she clammed right up. So he got curious. Spent his days off at the Lincoln Center branch of the New York Public Library combing through old Playbills until he found her—Bertha Puzewski. One of his drinking buddies, an old-timer who used to work on the *Daily News,* remembered the tabloid items about her and Saul Pincus. A couple of months go by and, sure enough, Saul's granddaughter, Beth, bought a unit there. Right away, Dawgie got interested. Started filing reports of Beth's comings and goings. FedExing me rolls of film . . ."

"You just said 'rolls' of film again. It's a digital world. Who still . . . ?"

"Gina gave Dawgie an old school Nikon camera as a birthday

present not long before she died. No way he was switching to digital. He'd have been dishonoring her memory. Plus the man was a total trog. He wouldn't buy a laptop. Didn't do e-mail. He wrote everything out longhand. It's all right here in the file. Everything he sent me."

"Why you?"

"I happen to have a personal interest in the Seven Sisters."

Mitch narrowed his gaze at him. "Which is . . . ?"

Romaine Very didn't answer him. Just let the question slide on by.

"Well, what did he find out about Beth?"

"For starters, she has herself a boyfriend. His name's Vinnie Brogna. Ever meet him?"

"Can't say that I have, no."

"Vinnie calls himself a hairstylist. He owns Salon Vincenzo, which is that overpriced barber shop in the Comstock Hotel on Sixth Avenue. I happen to know that he runs a profitable bookmaking operation out of the salon. Also rotates a crew of high-end working girls in and out of the hotel for the pleasure of out-of-town businessmen. The dude's totally mobbed up. And I'm not talking any Seven Sisters here. He's in with the Albanese crime family. His wife, Lucia, is the niece of Big Sal, the family boss. Vinnie and Lucia have four kids, a nice big house in Great Neck. And, on the side, he has Beth Breslauer. He spends at least two evenings a week with her at her apartment in Manhattan. And he's out here on weekends whenever he can swing it. Vinnie likes the action at the Mohegan Sun Casino. The man's been known to drop twenty large in one night. Usually, he and Beth get a room together there."

Very handed Mitch more photos from the file. A photo of Beth climbing into a black Lexus on Dorset Street, halfway down the block from the Captain Chadwick House. A photo of her and a dapper middle-aged guy getting out of that Lexus at the palatial front entrance to the Mohegan Sun. Photos of them eating dinner together in a fancy restaurant, their heads close together, eyes gleaming. Waiting for an elevator. Embracing, kissing . . .

"My sources tell me that Beth and Vinnie have been a steady item for something like ten years."

Mitch's eyes widened. "*How* many?"

"Did I just stutter?"

"No, but that would mean—"

"She was seeing him while she was married to Irwin Breslauer, I know. And I'm sorry if that's a buzzkill but stay with me—there's more. I hear she's been pressuring Vinnie to marry her ever since Irwin died. Only, he won't leave Lucia. The man's a devout Catholic. Doesn't believe in divorce."

"But it's okay to screw around?"

"People are going to do what they're going to do," Very said with a shrug. "And, according to Dawgie, screwing's not the only thing those two have been up to. . . ." He fanned out another set of photos of Beth and Vinnie walking past a well-dressed couple in the casino parking lot. Beth apparently bumping into her. The lady's handbag falling to the pavement. Beth picking it up for her. Apologies all around. The two couples going their separate ways. "Pay particular attention to the other lady's right wrist, dude. Before the bump she's got a gold bracelet on. See it? After the bump, she doesn't."

"Lieutenant, are you suggesting that Beth *stole* the lady's bracelet?"

"Dawgie sure thought so."

Mitch studied the photos more closely. "Hell, these don't prove anything. Look, the lady's sleeve is hiked up before the bump. Here, afterward, it's not. For all we know she could still be wearing the bracelet and it's just covered up."

"Could be," Very conceded. "Except Dawgie believed otherwise.

He was convinced that Beth's still active in the age-old family business. And has been fencing her pickings through a cousin of hers who runs a pawnshop on Eleventh Avenue and West 41 Street."

"Lieutenant. I know this lady. She's no thief. Besides, she doesn't need the money. Kenny told me that Irwin left her very well off."

"You'd better get used to the idea that when it comes to his parents, your friend Kenny knows *bupkes*. Either that or he's gas facing you."

Mitch looked at Romaine Very reproachfully. "Do you have actual hard evidence that Beth has done anything wrong?"

"That's exactly what Dawgie was going after last night," Very responded. "Until somebody beat his brains in."

"Let me see if I've got this straight. . . . You're suggesting that his murder may have nothing to do with the Dorset Flasher and everything to do with Beth Breslauer trying to protect her secret criminal identity."

"Exactly."

Mitch shook his head at him. "I don't believe this."

"Believe it, dude."

"So some killer from this Seven Sisters crime family rubbed him out?"

"No, the Seven Sisters never get their hands dirty. Killing is strictly for thugs and goons. But her boy Vinnie knows thugs and goons through the Albanese family. He could have arranged for a contract hit easy. Somebody from out of town. Providence, maybe."

"Why do I suddenly feel as if I've wandered into a Scorsese film?"

"I need to get this information to the right people," Very said, his voice rising with urgency. "Help me get a foot in the door with this Sergeant Snipes, will you?"

"Not a chance. Once you bring up Beth's so-called connection to this so-called Seven Sisters of yours, she'll be dragged into an official state police murder investigation. She's my friend. I'm not going to throw her to the wolves based on Augie's say-so. Or yours. I want to talk to her first. Hear what she has to say." Mitch mulled it over for a moment. "But if you give me your word that the Seven Sisters won't come up then that's a different story."

Very frowned at him. "And how do I do that?"

"By telling Sergeant Snipes that Augie was tailing Vinnie, a well-known member of the Albanese crime family. Who, it so happens, has been dating Beth. And who, it so happens, doesn't take kindly to being tailed. You can flesh out the rest after I've had a chance to sit down with Beth—assuming there *is* more to flesh out. Which I highly doubt there will be."

Very paced Mitch's living room, back and forth, back and forth. "I can get with that," he agreed. "But I'd like to be with you when you talk to her."

"Why?"

"I have a personal interest, like I said."

"What kind of a personal interest?"

"There's a reason why it's called personal," Very shot back. "Look, either I come with you when you talk to Beth Breslauer *or* when I finally do get through to this Sergeant Snipes on my own—and, word up, I will—then she gets the entire package."

"Deal." Mitch reached for his cell phone. "I'll call Yolie."

Very froze. "Did you just say *Yolie*? Sergeant Snipes is *Yolie* Snipes?"

"Yeah, why?"

The lieutenant got a dreamy, faraway look on his face. "Woo . . ."

Mitch frowned at him. "*Woo* . . . ?"

"Just make the call, dude."

She got there in twenty minutes.

Mitch went out to greet her as she climbed out of her cruiser. "Thanks for coming, Yolie."

"No prob, hon. I was intrigued by your message. *So* mysterious." Yolie flashed a sly grin at him. "Plus I was hoping to accidentally run into Dorset's resident trooper."

"Des isn't here."

"She will be five minutes from now. Just spoke to her on the phone." Her gaze fell upon Mitch's visitor, who was lingering somewhat bashfully in the cottage doorway. "Who's the biker boy?"

"It's Very."

"Very what?"

"Very *Very*. That's his name. He's a police detective from New York City. Told me he's been trying to get you on the phone."

"Oh, right. I do have a gazillion messages from some lieutenant named, like, Romeo Very."

"Romaine."

"Mitch, I don't need a New York City hot dog sticking his nose in my case."

"I understand completely. But you may want to talk to him. He was tight with your murder victim. Seems to think he has information that can help."

Yolie heaved a sigh of annoyance before she waved Very on over.

He approached her slowly, the two of them sizing each other up like middleweights in a ring.

"You the detective who's been calling me?"

"That's me." Very showed her his shield. "And you're Yolie Snipes. No introduction necessary, believe me."

She drew back from him, her nostrils flaring. "We know each other?"

"We've never met, Sarge. But I'm a huge fan of Big East women's hoops. I saw you play at the Garden must be a half-dozen times. You wore number twenty-six. Averaged just under seven assists per game throughout your career. Played killer defense. And no one, but no one, settled her sweet self at the charity stripe like you did when you were shooting a free throw."

"Is that a fact?" Yolie growled. Although Mitch could tell she was warming to the guy. She'd settled into her left hip just enough so that she was no longer taller than Very. "Coach Vivian always told us it was to be balanced right."

"Oh, you were balanced plenty right," Very assured her. "Still are, from where I'm standing."

"Where you're standing, hon, is about a hundred and twenty miles outside of your jurisdiction. You got information for me?"

Very nodded. "Also some questions."

"What kind of questions?"

Very didn't answer her. His attention had been drawn to the Saab that was making its way across the causeway toward them.

"This must be your lucky day, Lieutenant," Mitch told him. "You're about to meet Dorset's resident trooper."

Des got out of her car wearing a polo shirt, shorts and an extremely troubled expression. Mitch really, really didn't like the way she looked. Something heavy was weighing on her. "Who's your friend?" she asked him quietly.

"Master Sergeant Desiree Mitry, say hello to Detective Lieutenant Romaine Very of the NYPD. He and Augie Donatelli were friends."

"*And* he thinks he can help," Yolie added dryly.

"Can he?"

"Dunno. All he's done so far is flap his gums about ball."

"Mitch told me that you and Dawgie didn't get along," Very said to Des. "That's messed up. And I'm sure it was entirely on Dawgie. He had his demons. I'll be real happy to tell you all about them sometime over a cup of coffee if you'd—"

"Is there a point here somewhere?" Des asked him.

"Yes, there is. The guy was like family to me, okay? He didn't have anyone else. And he didn't deserve what happened to him."

"Agreed," she allowed.

"You were saying you have questions," Yolie put in. "*What* questions?"

"Have your people conducted a search of Dawgie's apartment?"

She crossed her big arms in front of her chest, eyes narrowing. "Why are you asking?"

"Did they find a camera?"

"Yeah, an old-school Nikon. Top of the line model, all sorts of lenses."

"Was there any film inside of it?"

Yolie blinked at him. "I don't recall, offhand. But I'm sure they looked. We're very thorough out here, Lieutenant. We wear latex gloves. We floss our teeth daily." To Des she said, "Not that you asked, but I got what you need in the front seat of my ride. They're in the big white envelope." She meant crime scene photos. She knew Des. Knew Des would want to draw a portrait of Augie.

"You're the best," Des said, smiling at her gratefully.

"How about notepads?" Very asked Yolie. "Did they find any of those?"

"Don't recall any, no."

"Was his apartment locked?"

"Yes. So was his GTO."

"Did your—?"

"They searched the glove compartment and trunk. Found nothing of interest."

"Mind if I take a look around for myself now that you're done?"

"I don't mind—*if* you tell me what you're looking for."

"Nothing in particular. I'm just curious."

"You're curious, all right." Yolie's cell phone rang now. She glanced at the screen and took it. "Hey, Rico, how's Tawny doing? . . . No, no. You stay with her. She needs you right now. I can bring you up to speed tomorrow. . . . No prob, don't worry about it." She rang off, her face tightening with determination.

"Is Tawny okay?" Des asked her.

Yolie nodded. "False alarm. Hospital sent her home. She's seeing her doctor first thing in the morning. Rico will be back down here after that—unless the doctor says otherwise."

"So they're not assigning a different lieutenant to the case?" Very asked.

"Not yet," she replied. "Not that it's any of your concern."

"But it's huge for you." He'd picked right up on just how ambitious Yolie was. The man was no dummy. Not that Mitch had thought for one second that he was. "If you crack this by tomorrow afternoon it's a career maker. I can help you, Sarge. We can help each other."

Yolie rolled her eyes. "Lookie here, Romeo . . ."

"It's *Romaine*."

"You'll have to bring some game if you want stay on the court with me. You said you had information. . . ."

"Yeah, I'm getting there. First tell me about how Dawgie died, will you?"

"Two blows to the head. It went down in a neighbor's yard after dark. Someone came up on him from behind, near as we can tell. First blow sent him to his knees, second one finished him."

"Did the killer take his wallet?"

"Money and credit cards were still on him."

"Have you recovered the murder weapon?"

"At the scene. It was an old baseball bat."

"Wait, wait, don't tell me—a Louisville Slugger model 125 Mickey Mantle with a nicked-up handle. Dawgie'd had it since he was a kid. You found his prints and no one else's on it, am I right?"

Yolie frowned at him. "I just got word about the prints a half-hour ago. How did you . . . ?"

"Anyone who has enough game to ambush him would also be smart enough to wear gloves," Very explained. "Dawgie's wife, Gina, was terrified of guns. So he used to sleep with that bat underneath his bed in case someone tried to break in during the night. No doubt still did. He was your classic creature of habit. Since your techies are so thorough, they no doubt found the outline of it in the dust bunnies under there."

Yolie said nothing to that. Just stared at him.

"If he kept it under his bed," Mitch said, "then what was it doing out in Rut Peck's backyard? And how did the killer get hold of it?"

"Dawgie must have been carrying it."

"He wasn't," Des told him.

"How do you know that?"

"Because I was tailing him, that's how. He didn't have a bat on him."

"Time out, you just lost me. . . ." Very's right knee was jiggling, jiggling. He had to be the most hyper person Mitch had ever met. The man was a human hummingbird. "You were *tailing* Dawgie?"

Des nodded. "Your friend was doing a little freelancing, Lieutenant. Thought he might have a bead on the Dorset Flasher. I was sitting on the Captain Chadwick House last night. I saw him leave his apartment on foot and decided to shadow him. See where he led me."

"So you were in the vicinity of the murder scene?"

"I'm the one who found him. Tripped right over his body, in fact."

"And since you and he didn't get along, I'm guessing the bosses now have you chained you to a desk far, far away."

"Correct," Des said stiffly.

"Which sucks."

"Also correct."

"You folks are figuring one of two thing," he said to Yolie. "That this Dorset Flasher spotted Dawgie and took him out. Or that Dawgie was the Flasher and got taken out by someone looking to punish him. Am I right so far?"

"Well, yeah . . ." she acknowledged grudgingly.

Very shook his head. "No way. That's not what happened."

"How you know that?" she demanded. "You got special superpowers?"

"What else did your people turn up this morning?"

"Actually, I was just about to bring Master Sergeant Mitry up to date."

He flashed a grin at her. "Well, don't let me stop you."

"As if you could."

"You'd be surprised. I'm very resourceful."

"I'll just bet you are." Yolie opened her notepad, glancing through it. "Hasn't rained for a week. The ground near the body was bone dry. No shoe prints. But score one for your side, girl. The techies found fresh shoe prints down by the riverbank just like you said they would. Someone who appeared to be running away from the crime scene. Wearing sneakers, they think. They took impressions. They're working on them up at the lab right now. And the ME has the victim on the table as we speak."

"Has anyone turned up that ski mask?" Des asked her.

"Not yet," she replied, squinting down at her notes. "I hooked up with Rut Peck at Essex Meadows. He confirmed that his house is currently unoccupied. Ray Smith, his neighbor from across Maple Lane, was playing checkers with him at Essex Meadows when the murder went down."

"Checkers?" Very repeated. "I didn't know people still played checkers."

"At last, we found something you don't know," she shot back.

"Yolie, did you get anything more out of Nan Sidell?" Des asked.

"The neighbor with the barking dog? Oly recanvassed her this morning. She had nothing else for him. Why you asking?"

"I thought her boys might have been holding something back. Just a feeling. How about Dex and Maddee Farrell?"

"They heard the commotion afterward. Not the incident itself. Were in their den reading and listening to a Brahms Piano Quartet on National Public Radio. They're a pair of cuties, aren't they? Mrs. Farrell yapped at me nonstop. Mr. Farrell, the world's biggest scam artist, just sat there, staring at the wall. I was about ready to stick a pocket mirror under the man's nose. Make sure he was still breathing." Yolie leafed through her notepad some more. "We can cross their daughter's ex, J. Z. Cliffe, off of our list. He was throwing down tequila shooters at the Monkey Farm Café when it happened. His girlfriend Maggie Gallagher, who's a barmaid there, vouches for him. So do the bartender and couple of regulars. Hal Chapman's another story. He claims he was getting busy on White Sand Beach with a slammin' blonde named Terri. Married lady from New York who was in Dorset visiting friends. But he couldn't, or wouldn't, give me her last name—beyond the letter E as in maybe Edsen. Or the name of her friends. Or the make or model of her ride. All I've got is that she works for some big outfit that recovers assets for people." She raised an eyebrow at Des. "Maybe that's something you can sink your teeth into while you're chained to your desk."

Des nodded. "I'm on it."

"Which brings me to Kenny Lapidus . . ."

"Not a chance," Mitch said heatedly. "Kenny's no killer."

"We have to check him out, hon. That's what we do. Kimberly said he was in his bedroom e-mailing people at the time of the murder. That'd alibi out your average human, what with e-mails being time coded and all. But Kenny's a full-time practicing geek. There's no doubt in my mind that someone with his skills knows how to hack into a server and alter those time codes. Girl, I need you to nail down his travel schedule with Amtrak. Find out if any of the Dorset Flasher sightings occurred while he was in transit from Boston."

"Sometimes he drives down," Des pointed out. "Like this weekend, for instance."

"In that case we'll have to—"

"Wait, wait," Very interjected. "It sounds to me like you're Krazy Glued to this idea that the Flasher's your prime suspect. Unless, that is, Augie was the Flasher. In which case your prime suspect is, well, dead. But let's say your Flasher and your killer are one and the same person. This guy waves his thing on weekends, right, Sarge?"

"Right," Yolie affirmed.

"Today's Sunday. Will he be out there tonight?"

"My guess? He won't be flashing anyone for a good long while. But I'm stepping up our sweeps of the Historic District tonight just in case. There's always a chance this murder will embolden him. We're not talking about someone who has his head screwed on straight."

Very nodded. And nodded. "You have *any* other persons of interest?"

"Beth Breslauer," she replied. "The lady slipped out of her condo on foot shortly before the murder. But we still have nothing on her whereabouts."

"Um, okay, I may be in a position to help you there."

Yolie batted her eyes at him. "It's about time, hon. Step right up."

"Dawgie was keeping an eye on her."

"We already know about that," Des said. "Beth told me he was following her all over the damned place."

"It wasn't Beth who he was following," Very said with a glance Mitch's way. "It was the married man who she's been seeing on the quiet. He's a New Yorker. Dawgie got a bad hit off of him. Asked me to check him out. His name's Vinnie Brogna. Vinnie's hooked up with some baaad boys. A member of the Albanese crime family. And maybe he wasn't too happy about Dawgie's interest in him."

"Keep talking," Yolie said, keenly interested.

"The dude visits Beth every weekend he can get away. They hit the Mohegan Sun together. According to Dawgie's surveillance photos, it's not uncommon for Vinnie to pick her up down the block from her condo. Which just might place him right there on Dorset Street at the time of Dawgie's death, bat in hand. Or at least that's one possible scenario."

"What's another?" Yolie asked.

"That he hired an outside pro take him out."

"I don't suppose you have these surveillance photos, do you?"

"They're inside the house. Care to have a look?"

"Lead on, Romeo."

"It's *Romaine*."

"Yolie, we have to talk before I split," Des called to her. "Girl to girl."

"You got it," she said as she followed Very inside.

Mitch took Des's hand and squeezed it. "What's wrong with him?"

"Wrong with who?"

"Your dad."

Her pale green eyes widened. "How on earth . . . ?"

"You weren't answering your cell phone after you met with Rundle. I called Bella and she told me you'd just gone rushing off in your own car—to go see the Deacon, I figured. And now you show up here looking worried sick."

"He has to have coronary bypass surgery," she said grimly.

"When?"

"On Wednesday."

"And you're just finding out about it today?"

"He said he didn't want to worry me."

"And there's absolutely no reason to worry. My Uncle Miltie was back on the golf course in no time. It's actually fairly—"

"If you're about to say it's minor surgery, please don't or I'll have to slug you."

Mitch put his arms around her. She stood there stiff and unyielding. It was like hugging a six-foot length of cast iron. "Listen, he's going to be fine. And I'm here for you. We'll get through it together."

"Mitch, I'm really not up for this right now."

"Up for what?"

"*This*. The whole touchy feely thing. It's not me. So let's just not."

"If you say so, girlfriend."

"I do say so, okay? Because I can't. I-I really . . ." Then, with a shudder, she surrendered into his arms and sobbed and sobbed and sobbed.

Chapter 12

Captain Richie Tedone of Internal Affairs lived in a vinyl-sided raised ranch in a charm-free development of nearly identical vinyl-sided raised ranches in the Hartford bedroom community of Glastonbury—better known to Des as Shoot Me Right Nowville. Cousin Rico lived in the neighborhood. Half of the Brass City boys did, having abandoned the crumbling brick remains of Waterbury years ago for greener ChemLawn pastures. A red Chevy pickup sat in Richie's driveway next to a blue Dodge minivan. His slicktop was parked at the curb.

And Des was parked three houses down the street in her Saab, watching the place through the zoom lens of her Nikon D80. And waiting.

Richie was out in the driveway in a T-shirt and jeans, helping his little daughter learn to ride her tiny pink tricycle—pushing her along, yelling helpful encouragement to her as she pedaled around and around, laughing with delight. Richie's plump, dark-haired wife was weeding a flower bed, their newest arrival dozing in a stroller next to her. Just a typical Sunday afternoon in Richie World, where life was beautiful and nobody tried to put the screws to anybody.

Des waited. It was warm in the car. She had a chilled bottle of water for company. And her brain pain. It bothered her how easily Mitch had blown by her defenses. She hadn't said one single word about the Deacon. Yet Mitch *knew* from the second she got out of her car. How? *Because he's your soul mate, that's how.* It also bothered her that her father had purposely chosen to shut her out of his life. She was his only child. She cared about him. She loved him. How could he not tell her that he had a serious heart condition? *Because he's a stubborn butthead, that's how.*

There was some movement now Chez Tedone. The chesty lug nut was taking a call on his cell. Barking into it, one hand on his hip, ultra take charge. He flicked it off and went inside of the house. Came back out two minutes later with a gym bag. Heading out to hit the weights with a lifting buddy, it appeared. He kissed his wife good-bye, then hopped into the pickup, backed it out of the driveway and took off down the block.

Des waited until he was a safe distance away before she started up her Saab and went after him. She had good reason to. The man had smelled like a player to her. He'd sure leered at her like one in Captain Rundle's office—which was why she'd asked to speak to Yolie back at Mitch's house, girl to girl.

And here's what Yolie told her about Captain Richie Tedone of Internal Affairs who, contrary to popular wisdom, she had *not* been romantically involved with back when he was single: "We worked cases together, period. He was plenty hot for this, but I was not about to give him any."

"Why not, Yolie?"

"Wasn't interested in picking up an STD, that's why not. That man had seriously skeejie personal habits. No doubt still does, if that's your next question. Guys like Richie don't change their ways when they become family men. They just cheat on their wives."

"You think his wife knows any of this?"

"No way. Those Brass City boys go out of their way to marry girls who are sheltered, naive and—wait for it—dumb. Real, the man has *Mr. Sleazeball* tattooed across his forehead. You'd *have* to be dumb to marry that."

Mr. Sleazeball got onto Route 91, heading south in the direction of Middletown, which was where he'd turn off if he were heading to the headmaster's house in Meriden. He drove fast. Pushed it up to eighty. Des kept right with him, staying two cars back.

He wasn't heading to the headmaster's house. He stayed on 91 south past Middletown, all the way down to New Haven, the city that was one part Yale University for the privileged and two parts ghetto for the not-so privileged. Most of those black, some Hispanic. Richie steered his pickup onto Whalley Avenue, which took him around the historic, beautiful campus and into a business district that turned rundown fast. Liquor stores, check-cashing stores, fried chicken joints. Most everything was closed on Sunday. A few idlers hung out on the sidewalk doing nothing good.

When he got near Edgewood Park he made a left onto a street of ratty old three-story wood frame houses that had been broken up into apartments years ago. His destination was the Edgewood Vista, a 1960s-era two-story cinder block apartment complex that had been erected around a parking lot. The downstairs apartments had entrances right off of the parking lot. And bars on their windows. Richie pulled in and parked. Des parked across the street and watched him get out. He had his own key to one of the units. He let himself in, closing the door behind him. Des rolled down her window, reached for her camera and zoomed in on the door. It was apartment C. There was an air-conditioner in one of the windows. The curtains were drawn. She snapped a couple of pictures, then sat and waited. A couple of boys went by her in the street, dribbling a basketball and talking trash. A shirtless middle-aged man with ink all over his arms and chest was working on a Coupe de Ville in his driveway, sweat gleaming off of him. He paused now and then to sip from a can of beer and check her out.

Forty-five minutes later the door to apartment C opened. Des zoomed in and began snapping away as Captain Richie Tedone of Internal Affairs stood there in the doorway playing grab ass with a lanky, barefoot young black girl in a purple silk robe. The girl didn't want him to leave. Flung her body against his. They kissed and kissed. Couldn't keep their hands off of each other. His started roaming inside of her robe right there in the doorway—until she shoved him away, laughing. Des snapped two dozen nice, clear close-ups of all of this before Richie's girl finally shut the door on him. He swaggered back to his pickup, jumped in and roared his way out of there. Des ducked down so he couldn't see her as he drove by. Then she sat back up and kept her camera trained on the door to apartment C.

Richie's girl left twenty minutes later, teetering on sandals with four-inch stiletto heels—the better to show off her nice long legs and fancy purple toenails. . . . *Smile for the camera, honey. . . .* Her frilly pink minidress barely covered her butt. And that cascading canary yellow wig she had on looked about as real as spray-painted bubble wrap in the hazy summer sunlight. She was a skinny thing with broad shoulders and almost no hips. Des studied her through the zoom lens, frowning, as she unlocked the red BMW convertible parked outside of her unit and put the top down. Des snapped several close-ups of the license plate as the girl took off, leaving a trail of cheap perfume behind her.

Des promptly got out, locked the Saab and strolled across the street to the apartment complex's main entrance. Most of the tenants' names were scrawled on ragged pieces of masking tape over the mailboxes. On the mailbox for apartment C there was a powder blue note card with *Eboni* written on it in purple ink. The letter *i* was dotted with a little heart.

The building manager lived in apartment A behind a door that had a steel security grill. Des knocked. A mountainous black woman in polyester sweats opened it—unleashing all kinds of good smells from her kitchen. The TV was blaring in her living room. A half dozen little kids were sprawled there, transfixed by a cartoon.

"Afternoon, ma'am," Des said politely, flashing her badge. "I wanted to ask you a couple of questions if you don't mind."

"Who's in trouble now?" she demanded, instantly chilly.

"Nobody." Des showed her a big smile. "Know what? Your place smells just like my grandma's house. That's sausage and biscuits you're making, am I right?"

"Your people must be from the South, like mine," the woman allowed, thawing slightly.

Des nodded. "Georgia."

"Did you want to come in?"

"That's okay. This will only take a second. I like to keep an eye on the folks who've been of assistance to us. Make sure nobody's been coming around bothering them."

"Who we talking about, honey?"

"The resident in apartment C."

She looked at Des in surprise. "You mean Eboni with an i?"

"That's the person, yes."

"What kind of help you been getting from little Eboni?" Her tone of voice was downright mocking.

"It's part of an ongoing criminal investigation. I can't go into the details."

"And yet you show up here on a Sunday. Must be something pretty big."

"Let's just say Eboni did right by us. And I have concerns that certain individuals might try to retaliate or whatever."

"You don't have to waste no time worrying about that one." Again with the mocking tone. "Eboni's got a cop boyfriend."

"Is that right? New Haven city cop?"

"Don't know what kind. I ain't seen no uniform. But he's law, plain as day. You can tell by the way he struts around."

"And he visits her regularly?"

"Must be here three, four times a week. He takes real good care of little Eboni. Pays the rent on the apartment. Bought that BMW, too."

"Is Eboni working these days?"

"Some call it work," she sniffed. "Others call it something else. Not that I'm passing judgment. What the tenants do is their own business—as long as the rent gets paid."

"Has Eboni got any other regular men?"

"One or two. Not as many as before."

"You say he pays the rent. Does he write you a check?"

She let out a huge, rumbling laugh. "Where you think you are? People around here don't write no checks. They pay in cash. That's how come I got this security gate on my door. Management company put it in last year after I got ripped off twice. Installed a safe in my kitchen, too." She paused, puffing slightly for breath. "He puts the rent money right here in my hand the first of every month."

"How comes *he* pays you, not her?"

"If he give it to Eboni I'd never see it."

"Are we talking about drugs?"

"Wouldn't surprise me. Nothing about Eboni would surprise me."

"Did she sign a lease or is she here month to month?"

"Oh, there's a lease all right."

"Whose name is on it?"

"Eboni's. Mind you, that's strictly a what-you-call 'professional' name. The lease is in Eboni's real name."

"Which is . . . ?"

"Michael Toomey," she replied, stone-faced.

Des felt her pulse quicken. That explained why the girl's shoulders and hips had struck her as odd. Richie Tedone's skanky girlfriend wasn't a girl at all. She was a he—a drag queen. "Thank you for your time, ma'am," she said calmly, even though she was ready to *plotz,* as her friend Bella Tillis would say. "Next time I'm in the neighborhood I could use a few of those sausage and biscuits."

"Honey, you could use a few *dozen*. Don't you know that a man likes a woman who has some decent meat on her bones?"

Des got back in her Saab and headed straight for the Troop F barracks, where she parked herself at her unadorned steel desk and got busy on the computer. First she ran the license plate on that red BMW. The car was registered to Michael Reginald Toomey, Edgewood Vista Apartments, New Haven. Next she ran a criminal background check on Michael Reginald Toomey, age twenty, aka Eboni, aka Deelite. He/she had a long history of arrests for soliciting prostitution and possession of crack cocaine, dating back to when he/she had first been incarcerated at the New Haven Correctional Center at age fifteen. As Des scanned Toomey's criminal history, one particular case from two years back set off alarm bells in her head. She went trolling through all of the case files she could access. Then pieced together the rest of the story from the online archives of the *New Haven Register* and *Hartford Courant*. The case had received extensive coverage. Hell, even the New York City tabloids had covered it.

It went down in Sussex, a ritzy, shoreline commuter town in Fairfield County. Nothing but millionaires and their trophy mansions. On a tree-lined lane in one of those mansions it turned out that a high-end escort service—which is to say call-girl ring—had been quietly operating for months. The woman running it, who came to be known as the Suburban Madam, was a divorced mother of two, named Elaine Gruen. Elaine's husband had left her for another woman. Elaine got the mansion and child support in the settlement. But not enough income to maintain her Sussex lifestyle. So she'd dusted herself off and started her small business. She catered to a carefully screened clientele of wealthy gentlemen from not only the Connecticut suburbs, but New York, New Jersey and even Massachusetts. Her escorts collected five hundred dollars per hour, with discounted rates for overnight stays and weekend jaunts to resort hotels. The gentlemen contacted Elaine by cell phone or e-mail. She set up the engagements and kept half of the proceeds—which she split with her partner, Tiffany Nelson, a juvenile detention officer at the New Haven Correctional Center. It was Tiffany who recruited the Suburban Madam's choicest talent. Mostly, she chose the youngest, prettiest girls. But a handful were recruited for so-called special-needs clients—men who favored the company of heavy girls or tiny girls or, in some cases, girls who weren't girls at all.

It was a gold mine. Until, that is, the Sussex police stumbled onto it when they made a prostitution bust at a local motel. The girl, who'd recently been let go by Elaine for using drugs, was looking to cut herself a deal. Not to mention payback. The Sussex police called in the state's Organized Crime Investigative Task Force, which spent weeks combing through thousands of phone calls and e-mails. Elaine and Tiffany were eventually charged with violation of the CORA act and promoting prostitution in the second degree. Both women were sentenced to a minimum of three years at York Correctional in Niantic

Des sat there at her computer, frowning. *York Correctional.* Somebody in the middle of the Augie Donatelli mess had a York connection. Although for the life of her, she couldn't remember who.

There was more to the story. Elaine Gruen claimed that the task force's lead officer, Captain Peter Bartucca, had accepted sexual favors from one of her escorts. Elaine's lawyer went public with her accusation, screaming bloody murder. It got looked into by none other than Captain Richie Tedone of Internal Affairs. After conducting a thorough investigation, Richie found zero evidence that Captain Bartucca had engaged in any such behavior. "Mrs. Gruen's allegations," he told the *Hartford Courant*, "are a scurrilous, baseless, despicable attempt to sully the reputation of a fine public servant and family man."

The escort who Elaine Gruen said had provided Captain Bartucca with those sexual favors? None other than Michael Reginald Toomey, aka Eboni, aka Deelite.

Gotcha, Mr. Sleazeball.

Seated there at her desk, Des allowed herself the luxury of a satisfied smile. Then she took a deep breath, let it out and went to work trying to find Terri E as in maybe Edsen, who worked in a cubicle somewhere in New York and maybe—big maybe—had been getting busy with Hal Chapman while somebody else was beating Augie Donatelli's brains in.

Chapter 13

They took Mitch's truck.

Very rode shotgun, his head nodding up and down like a bobble-head doll as he took in the sights of the Historic District. "So how did a city kid like you end up in this colonial theme park?" he wanted to know.

"My wife passed away. I needed to make a change, meet new people. Besides, it's not a theme park—as your friend Augie would be only too happy to attest to."

"I hear you," Very said, his jaw muscles clenching. "How about you and the master sergeant? Any problems with the color thing?"

"That's for other people to think about. We don't."

"I've never gone there. I got pretty serious with a Korean woman when I was just out of the academy, but her family didn't want her dating a round eye. Plus she was into Renaissance fairs, which make me totally—"

"Ootsie?"

"I was going to say hurl."

"Sorry, my bad."

"She couldn't handle her parents' disapproval so she broke it off. But I still think about her sometimes. I'm just so damned tired of being by myself. Know what I'm saying?"

"Yes, I do."

"Don't get me wrong—I do okay when it comes to hookups. But the right woman? Someone who I can be *me* with? No fear? That's rare."

"Rare," agreed Mitch, who was wondering just exactly how he'd managed to wander into Lieutenant Very's personal eHarmony commercial.

"Talk to me about Yolie Snipes. What's up with her?"

Mitch smiled to himself. So much for wondering. "She's a rising star. Real smart. Comes with a lot of hard bark on her but she's honest and loyal. Des is real fond of Yolie. Me, too. But I'm kind of partial."

"Oh, yeah? Why's that?"

"She saved my life once."

"She got a steady man in her life?"

"No man at all."

"Get out! A gorgeous sister like that?"

"I don't think anyone has the nerve to ask her out. She can be a bit intimidating."

"I know. It's kind of a turn-on."

"So take a shot. Worst thing that can happen is she'll . . ."

"Just say no?"

"I was going to say beat the crap out of you."

Very's face lit up. "I can think of worse ways to spend an evening."

"Okay, Lieutenant, this is way too much information."

Maple Lane was cordoned off. A pair of cruisers were there to keep gawkers away. Also a mobile news van from one of the Connecticut TV stations.

Mitch pulled up in front of the Captain Chadwick House and parked. "Augie's apartment is around in back."

"We'll brace Beth Breslauer first," Very informed him.

"She may not be home."

"We'll find out."

"We could have called to let her know we were coming."

"Not how it's done, dude. You always drop in unannounced. Question a suspect before she has a chance to prepare her responses."

"So Beth's a suspect?"

"Everyone's a suspect."

Beth was home. And she could not have been more poised or polite when Mitch introduced her to Lieutenant Romaine Very of the NYPD. Not a trace of uneasiness. Not a frosted blond hair out of place. She was totally together. "This is such a nice surprise, Mitch," she exclaimed as she showed them in. "But I'm afraid Kenny's at the beach with Kimberly."

"Actually, we're here to see you."

"I have a few questions, Mrs. Breslauer," Very explained. "I'm not here in an official capacity. You're totally free to decline."

Beth tilted her head at him. "Questions regarding . . . ?"

"Augie Donatelli. He was like a father to me."

"I'm so sorry, Lieutenant."

"I understand he'd taken a personal interest in you. I'd like to talk to you about that, if you don't mind."

Beth glanced at the file folder that was tucked under Very's arm. "Certainly. May I offer you gentlemen a glass of iced tea? I was just having some out on the porch with my neighbor Bertha Peck. I'll ask her to excuse us."

"No need," Very said. "In fact, it'd be great if she stayed."

Beth's gaze narrowed slightly. "Whatever you say."

She fetched two tall glasses from the kitchen and led them out onto the porch. Bertha Peck sat on the white wicker love seat, wearing a trimly tailored linen summer dress and round, oversized glasses. She was a tiny, somewhat scary-looking old lady. Nearly ninety, but with glossy, coal black hair and big blue eyes that were slightly protuberant and more than slightly piercing. She sat very erect, hands folded in her lap. Her legs, as Bitsy Peck had advised Mitch, were still splendid indeed. Slender and finely shaped.

"Bertha, this is Kenny's friend, Mitch Berger," Beth said as she filled their glasses from the pitcher on the table.

"You're that movie critic who lives out on Big Sister." Bertha looked him over with keen-eyed disapproval. "The one who's been sleeping with our resident trooper."

"We're good friends."

"You're a lot more than that, young man," Bertha said sternly. "But I'd never make you two for a match. Not in a million years." Now she turned her gaze on Very. "And who is this handsome devil?"

"He's Lieutenant Very of the NYPD," Beth said. "A friend of Mr. Donatelli's."

"What does he want?"

"We're about to find out, Bertha."

Beth handed them their iced teas. They sat in the wicker chairs facing the love seat. Beth settled next to Bertha, who took a thirsty gulp of her own iced tea, smacking her lips. Mitch suspected hers was high octane. She liked her vodka, word had it.

Very jumped right in: "Mrs. Breslauer, has Sergeant Snipes questioned you yet about your whereabouts at the time of the murder?"

Beth blinked at him. "Why, no. Why would she?"

"Because she knows that you slipped out of here on foot shortly before it happened. You're unaccounted for, ma'am."

Beth shot a sharp glance at Mitch before she turned back to Very, stiffening slightly. "You said you're *not* here in an official capacity."

"Correct."

"So I'm under no obligation to answer you."

"Also correct. But if I were you, I'd be straight with me. It's the smart move."

"Why is that, Lieutenant Very?"

"Because whatever you say to her will become part of an official state police investigation. If you talk to me I may be able to keep it under wraps."

"You make it sound as if I *have* something to keep under wraps."

"Only because you do. You and I both know Dawgie wasn't stalking you. He was *tailing* you." Very opened the file folder and spread Augie's surveillance photos out on the coffee table before her. "You and your boy Vinnie."

Beth studied the photos, swallowing. "So . . . ?"

"So were you and Vinnie together last evening? Is that why you slipped out?"

Beth took a dainty sip of her iced tea. A blue vein pulsed slightly in her forehead. Otherwise, she gave every outward appearance of being calm. "Vincent picked me up down the block at nine o'clock. We caught Linda Ronstadt's second show at the Mohegan Sun. Ate a late supper at the Lobster Shack. Gambled a bit, then went up to our room. We left there at about four a.m. Vincent dropped me off here and kept on going so he could attend morning mass with his family in Great Neck."

Very flipped through some notes in the file. "According to Dawgie, Vinnie never spends the night here. He's never even *been* here."

"That was at my suggestion," Bertha interjected. "People in Dorset can be obsessively nosy when it comes to the love lives of their neighbors. Particularly when those neighbors are attractive single women. Maddee Farrell, for one, is a consummate busybody. I told Beth that if she wished to have any privacy, she would have to behave discreetly. So if you wish to blame anyone for her 'slipping out,' as you put it, then blame me."

"Why are we talking about 'blame' here, Bertha?" Beth's voice had an edge of defiance in it now. "I don't owe this man or anyone else an explanation for how I choose to live my life. Frankly, I resent the fact that we're even having this conversation."

Very said nothing to that. Just barreled in. "Does Kenny know about Vinnie? Or have you been hiding your affair from him, too?"

Beth stared at him coldly. "You're not a very nice person, are you?"

Very said nothing to that either. Just stared right back at her. The man was no lamb chop—not that Mitch had thought for one second that he was.

"It so happens that Kenny *doesn't* know about Vincent," she conceded, exhaling slowly. "I was married to Irwin when we first became involved. I wasn't particularly proud of myself. But I couldn't help it. I was in love with Vincent. I still am. We're incredibly happy together."

"Just to be clear about this—were you two an item back when Kenny's father was in prison?"

Beth lowered her eyes. "So you know about Sy."

"I know all about your grandfather, too." Very turned his gaze on Bertha. "I believe you were acquainted with Saul Pincus, weren't you, Mrs. Peck?"

Bertha took another thirsty gulp of her iced tea. "You believe right, young man. I was all of nineteen years old. Still had stars in my eyes. And, God, I was mad for Saul," she recalled, her small, wrinkled face glowing. "Our lovemaking was so intense I would nearly faint. It was never, ever like that with anyone else. Certainly not with my husband, Guy. But our love . . . Saul and I weren't meant to be. He died so young. It was very sudden."

"Yeah, he got suddenly shot in Lindy's."

"The poor dear was an innocent bystander to some awful gang squabble. He was just sitting there over a bowl of soup, minding his own business, when a stray bullet caught him right in the forehead." Bertha shook her head sadly. "The city was a dangerous place in those days."

Very let out a laugh. "Who do you think you're fooling, Mrs. Peck? Saul Pincus was rubbed out. The man was a big-time racketeer."

"*That* is a load of hooey," she said indignantly. "Saul was in the fur trade."

"I see. And what about the police case files and newspaper stories—are you telling me they're nothing but lies?"

"All lies. You shouldn't go by what the police or the papers say, young man. They never know the real truth about anything. Remember that in the future—assuming you have a future. You're awfully darned mouthy," she pointed out, her big blue eyes glittering at him. "Although you're obviously accustomed to getting away with it. You good lookers with your thick, wavy hair and bedroom eyes always do, don't you?"

Very shifted in his chair, looking slightly queasy. Evidently he wasn't used to getting hit on by a babe who was pushing ninety. The man was new to Dorset, after all. He turned his attention back to Beth now. "Mrs. Breslauer, have you ever heard of the Seven Sisters?"

Beth smiled at him indulgently. "Don't tell me you came here to talk about that old fairy tale."

"So it's a fairy tale?"

"More of an urban legend, like those stories you hear about werewolves living in the subway tunnels."

"In that case, why don't you tell me a little bit about your family?"

"Certainly. My mom and dad were fabric wholesalers in the garment district for more than thirty years. They're both gone now, I'm sorry to say. Mom's sister, Sadie, was a seamstress. And her husband, my Uncle Izzy, repaired transmissions at a garage in Long Island City. Dad's brother, my Uncle Nathan, drove a cab. . . ."

"Are you having a good time with this, Mrs. Breslauer?" Very glowered across the coffee table at her. "Your mother, Estelle, served two separate sentences for receiving stolen property. And your father, Sam, was a bookmaker. Not a big-time operator like his father, Saul, but he served time. So did your Uncle Nathan, your Uncle Izzy *and* your Aunt Sadie. I have their criminal histories right here. So stop disrespecting me, will you?"

Beth sat quite still for a moment, her plump lips pursed, manicured hands folded primly in her lap. Then she glanced at Mitch, smiling faintly, before she said, "They didn't want that life for me. I was the pretty princess. Special. And *so* smart. I graduated magna cum laude from Hunter College. Went to work at an ad agency on Madison Avenue. Married a reputable, hardworking young man. Sy was holding down a nine-to-five job in an office supplies store and going to accounting school at night. He got his accounting degree, too. We had plans. We had dreams. We had such a wonderful future all . . ." She broke off, her dark eyes puddling with tears. "Except it turned out I wasn't so smart. It wasn't until *months* after Kenny was born that I found out Sy was mixed up in my Uncle Izzy's bookmaking operation. I can't begin to tell you what a body blow that was. I was *so* ashamed. When Sy got arrested I hid the truth from Kenny. I didn't want him to know. I was terrified that he'd get drawn into that life himself. It has its allure, believe me. Particularly when you're young." Beth reached for her iced tea and took a sip. "I married Irwin to get Kenny away from it once and for all. Irwin never knew a thing about it. And Kenny still doesn't have a clue." She gazed down into her glass, breathing in and out. "But I must say, Lieutenant Very, that you're making my family out to be much more diabolical than they actually were. All of that fanciful nonsense about an organized underworld cabal called the Seven Sisters. It wasn't like that."

"So what *was* it like?"

"My people were Jewish immigrants who arrived at Ellis Island with nothing more than the clothes on their backs. They struggled and fought and did whatever they had to do to get by—even if that meant skirting the law now and then."

"Times were hard in those days," Bertha chimed in. "Believe

me, I know. My father was a dumb Polack who worked himself to death in the steel mills before he was forty. You're talking about poor people. Uneducated people who barely spoke the language. You're talking about the Great Depression and two world wars. Rough neighborhoods. Rough justice. Nobody looking out for you but your own kind. Everybody's family had to fight to survive."

"Mine ran small neighborhood businesses on the Lower East Side," Beth said. "Did they buy merchandise off of the black market? Yes. They did business with thieves of the lowest sort. Did they take bets and run numbers? Sure they did. If you owned any kind of a business—a candy store, a corner bar—that was expected of you. Did they get involved with loan sharks? You bet. There was no such thing as a fancy savings and loan for those people. Just an underground economy that operated by its own rules. Same as it still does to this day. You've been in one of those neighborhood bodegas in Harlem, haven't you, Lieutenant?"

"A million," Very grunted.

"Where do you think they get their cigarettes and razor blades—from reputable wholesalers? They buy them on the cheap from people who steal them for a living. Does that make them a part of a vast criminal conspiracy? No. They're just trying to get by—and hoping for a better life for their children. Just like I wanted for Kenny. After Sy got sent to prison I filed for a divorce. Went to work at Bloomingdale's because it paid better than the ad agency did. I met Irwin on a blind date. We used to joke about that—meeting an eye doctor on a blind date. Irwin was no George Clooney. But he was kind and decent and he came home every night. We were happy together."

"Meanwhile," Very put in, "you were *shtupping* Vinnie behind his back."

"You still have a lot to learn about life, young man," Bertha said reproachfully. "It's much, much more of a trade-off than you realize.

Just look at my situation. I was married to the dullest man on earth for forty-four years. Guy Peck was also a perfectly dreadful lover. He had zero appreciation of my needs. The Human Broomstick, I used to call him. And yet he gave me everything else I could ever want. So I was a good, dutiful wife to him—even though not a day went by when I didn't think about Saul. I still do. I still remember the cologne Saul wore. If I get the slightest whiff of anything even remotely like it I get weak in the knees. And that man has been dead for *seventy* years."

Beth studied Romaine Very curiously. "Why are you here, Lieutenant?"

"Augie Donatelli was my friend. I told you."

"So you did. But there's more to it than that. Why are you so interested in my family's history?"

"I have a long-standing personal interest in the Seven Sisters. That's why Dawgie kept me filled in about you."

"What *sort* of a long-standing personal interest?"

The lieutenant cleared his throat. "It has to do with my dad, okay? He shortened his last name when he struck out on his own. That's how it came to be Very."

"What was it originally?"

"Verichenko," he answered, gazing at her.

Beth's eyes widened. "Thelma Kudlach married a Verichenko. Manny, I believe. So that makes you . . ."

"Thelma's great-great-grandson. You and I are cousins, Mrs. Breslauer. I'm one of the family. And I know the real deal. I know that my grandmother started working the boardwalk in Atlantic City when she was five years old. And my grandfather picked pockets for a living—when he wasn't in jail. So don't try to tell me your family was just like everyone else's. And don't tell me the Seven Sisters is some urban legend. I *know* better, got it?"

Beth didn't say a word. No one did. There was only stunned silence.

Until Mitch said, "Beth, how did you and Bertha happen to hook up?"

Beth didn't respond. Just reached for her iced tea and took a sip, her hand trembling slightly.

"It was my idea," Bertha spoke up. "My attorney tracked her down for me. I wanted to meet her. Her grandfather was the great love of my life, after all. We got together for lunch in the city one day and became friends. Went shopping together. Took in the occasional matinee. I still enjoy a good musical—not that these girls today can dance. They're as graceful as Clydesdales. After Beth sold her place in Scarsdale she was looking to buy a condo out this way. I let her know when a unit became available here."

Very leafed through Augie's file once more. "Before he died, Mrs. Breslauer, your late husband lost a ton of money in the subprime housing meltdown. You were forced to sell that house in Scarsdale for significantly less than what it had been assessed at two years earlier."

"I wasn't *forced* to sell it." Beth was growing testy now. "I *chose* to. I got nearly two million dollars for the place, free and clear. And Irwin's investment portfolio still amounted to more than a half-million in good, solid stocks and bonds. *And* he'd taken out a substantial life insurance policy. My investment advisor has set me up so that I can live very comfortably without touching so much as one penny of the principal. Take it from me, Lieutenant. I *don't* need to pick anyone's pockets."

"Would it surprise you if I said Dawgie thought otherwise?"

"Nothing you can say about that man would surprise me."

"He tailed you and Vinnie to the Mohegan Sun. Were you aware of that?"

Beth made a face. "Of course. I spotted him right off."

"And how did you feel about it?"

"I was annoyed, naturally. But Augie liked to annoy me. Took delight in it, in fact."

"He thought you and Vinnie were working the place," Very explained. "Lifting handbags, jewelry and the like."

"Don't be absurd. We frequent the Mohegan Sun because Vincent enjoys the blackjack tables. Gambling happens to be legal there, you know. I get a spa treatment. We have a nice meal together. Go upstairs to our room and make love. He likes to keep the lights on. I like to be on top. Would you care for any more dirty details, Lieutenant Very?"

"No," he answered abruptly. "No, I wouldn't."

"Then kindly tell me why my personal life is any of your damned business."

"Because Dawgie was following you and now he's dead."

"You sound as if you believe there's a connection."

"Maybe there is. Vinnie does know people."

"You're thinking he put out a *contract* on Augie? Don't make me laugh. Vincent runs a hair salon. He's a family man."

"Yeah, the Albanese family. I've got your boy's criminal arrest record right here." Very stabbed the file folder with his finger. "Vinnie's been in the system since he boosted his first car when he was sixteen. He took a pop for breaking and entering one year later. Followed by armed assault. Followed by attempted extortion. Followed by . . . should I go on?"

"That's not necessary. . . ." Beth answered faintly.

"I'll have to talk to him as soon I get back to the city. Hear his version of where you two were last night."

"Go right ahead. At his salon, if you please. Not his home. He'll confirm everything I've said. Everything." Brave words. Except Beth didn't come off sounding brave. She sounded deflated. And her color wasn't very good all of a sudden. It was gray like putty. "May I pour you more iced tea, Lieutenant?"

"No, thanks. We're done here."

She managed a smile at Mitch. "I'll tell Kenny that you stopped by. He'll be sorry he missed you."

"Likewise. Could you give him a message for me?"

"Of course, dear. What is it?"

"Tell him I said: 'Chance is but a fool's name for fate.' "

"What the hell's that mean?" Very demanded as they started down the hallway toward the back door of the Captain Chadwick House. " 'Chance is but a fool's name for fate?' That some kind of a code?"

"It's a line from a Fred Astaire-Ginger Rogers movie called *The Gay Divorcee*. Not that Kenny will guess it in a million years. We've been playing the same movie game since we were kids," Mitch explained. "Kind of like you've been playing games with me."

"Dude, I don't know where you're going with that."

"Yeah, you do. You told me you became a cop for family reasons. Yet you were purposely vague. Now I know why."

"My dad took a job with the Port Authority of New York after he got out of Fordham. The man hated what he knew about the family. And he made sure I grew up hating it, too."

"You became a cop so you could right your family's wrongs, is that it?"

"Yeah, that's me—the gen-next righteous avenger." Very narrowed his eyes at Mitch. "Why, you got a problem with that?"

"You should have told me that you and Beth were related."

"You're right, I should have," he acknowledged. "Are we good now?"

"I don't know what we are, Lieutenant. But we're not good."

The back door of the building opened onto a brick path that led out to the garages. A precious dozen or so of those lush, flowering

Captain Chadwick Blush Noisette rosebushes lined both sides of the path. Maddee Farrell was pruning one of them back, a pair of garden gloves on her hands to protect against the thorns. Unlike Bitsy Peck, who tended her garden with a contented glow on her face, Maddee worked with feverish tenacity, every muscle taut, her jaw clenched. For her, that rosebush wasn't a pleasant diversion. It was a crusade. Dex was seated beside her on a folding canvas chair working on the Sunday *New York Times* crossword puzzle.

"Your roses look very nice, Mrs. Farrrell," Mitch observed.

"Why, thank you." Maddee flashed a tight smile at him. "It's not easy keeping them healthy, you know, what with the insects and diseases and ball-playing louts."

Mitch nodded politely, although he was unaware of any Captain Chadwick House resident who played any kind of ball, loutish or otherwise. "Mrs. Farrell, this is Lieutenant Very. He's a police officer from New York City."

Very nodded at her. "How are you, ma'am?"

"Rather alarmed, now that you ask," Maddee replied loftily. "We both are. Isn't that right, Dex?"

Dex didn't respond. Didn't look up from his puzzle. Didn't so much as acknowledge their presence.

"A man has been *beaten* to death in the middle of the Historic District, Lieutenant. This sort of behavior is simply not Dorset, I assure you. Why would anyone *do* such a horrible thing?"

"That's what the state police are trying to ascertain," Very replied.

"Thirty-six across, Mr. Berger," Dex said suddenly, tapping the puzzle with his pencil. "The clue is 'Actor Ray.' The answer would be . . . ?"

"That depends on whether you need four letters or six. If it's four then I'd go with Aldo Ray. You may remember him as Davie Hucko in the Tracy-Hepburn movie *Pat and Mike*. If it's six letters then they're probably referring to Ray Liotta, the star of *Goodfellas*."

"Two, three, four letters . . ." Dex murmured. "And Aldo fits. I already have the O. Thank you, Mr. Berger."

"My pleasure, sir."

"I hope you haven't forgotten my invitation. The world is full of lunatics and bores. Do stop by for some lemonade and a talk."

"I'll be happy to."

"Have you had any luck with that other matter?" Maddee asked Mitch.

"Other matter?"

"Gathering up your old clothes for the Nearly New shop. So many good, hardworking folks are doing without these days. Even if your things are a bit worn the Goodwill will gratefully accept them. Shoes, too, if any of yours are getting tight. It wouldn't surprise me a bit. The adult male's foot can grow as much as a full size larger, you know."

"I'll see what I can find," he promised her as he and the lieutenant continued down the brick path.

"Dude, is everyone in this town crazy?" Very wondered, shaking his head.

"Pretty much."

There were a half dozen garage bays not counting Augie's. His had yellow police tape over its locked double-wide door. Very yanked it away and punched a security code in the keypad. The automatic door promptly lifted open.

"How did you know his code?"

"Dawgie used Gina's birth date for everything."

Augie had a rider mower and a John Deere Gator in there. A tool bench. An old refrigerator. And, center stage, a gorgeous red, vintage Pontiac GTO.

"His pride and joy," Very said, gazing at it. "She's a '65. 389 V8, four on the floor, chrome rally wheels, dual exhausts. They called that color Montero red. He always wanted one when he was a kid. Bought it for himself last year off of some rich guy in the Hamptons."

"I never had the slightest idea, Lieutenant. I lived across the hall from Beth and Kenny for all of those years and I had no clue about her husband, her family, any of it. All I knew was that she was a nice lady."

Very stood there nodding, nodding. "She must have been a real honey in those days, too. Hell, she still is. Vinnie has good taste, I'll sure give him . . ." He frowned at Mitch. "Dude, you just got *way* red all of a sudden. You okay?"

"I'm fine. So kindly back off."

"Hey, whatever."

"You want to know something, Lieutenant? No one in this world is who or what they appear to be. That's the second most important thing I've learned since I moved to Dorset."

"What's *the* most important?"

"That WASPs have no idea what a real bagel is. Tell me the truth—was Augie right? *Is* Beth still in the family business? *Have* she and Vinnie been working the casino?"

Very ran a hand through his wavy black hair. "The truth? I honestly don't know. But I was definitely getting played just now by her and that old lady both. They're slick operators those two. Moved me wherever they wanted to."

"Meaning what? That they're hiding something more?"

"Oh, absolutely. I have no idea what. But I sure would like to know."

"How much of this do you have to share with Sergeant Snipes?"

"All of it, dude. Sorry, but this is a murder investigation."

"Understood."

Very pulled two pairs of white latex gloves from the back pocket of his jeans, tossing one pair to Mitch. "Never leave home without 'em," he said, grinning at him. Then he felt around underneath the GTO's rear bumper until he grabbed hold of a key case that was held in place under there with a magnet. He removed the key from the case and climbed the wooden stairway up to Augie's apartment. Yanked the police tape from the door and used the key to open it.

It was warm and stuffy inside Augie's one-room apartment, which smelled of Aqua Velva, stale beer and dirty laundry. The décor had the flavor of a hot-sheet motel room in Secaucus, New Jersey. All that was missing was the cheapo landscape painting on the wall over his unmade bed. For art, Augie had a pinup calendar from a tool catalog thumbtacked to his closet door. Miss August was a busty blonde wearing red suspenders, a tool belt and a smile. Augie had a Pullman kitchen with dirty dishes piled high in the sink. An olive green lounge chair that was set before a thirteen-inch TV. A footlocker that served as a coffee table. There was a battered old oak desk. A chest of drawers. On top of that there was a framed photograph of a pretty young woman with dark hair.

"That's Gina," Very said somberly. "He wanted to be buried next to her in Mineola. His plot's all paid for. I'll have him transported there after they release his body."

Mitch had a look underneath the bed. Augie's Louisville Slugger was gone, just as Very had said it would be. Mitch could definitely make out its outline in the thick layer of dust under there. "I don't get it—if this place was locked, then how did that bat end up out there last night? Des swore Augie didn't have it on him."

"Obviously, she was mistaken."

"What if she wasn't?"

"She *was.* Had to be. That's the only way it rolls. I'll search the desk, okay? You check out the footlocker."

There were newspapers and empty beer cans heaped on the footlocker. Mitch removed them and opened it. Inside, he found a stack of old *Playboy* magazines from the late sixties. Each issue had been tucked inside of a protective plastic sleeve.

"This guy was a serious collector," he said, sifting through them. "He has Barbara McNair's legendary nude pictorial from *If He Hollers, Let Him Go*. And here's the classic Ursula Andress spread from July, '66. Look at all of these—Julie Newmar, Pamela Tiffin, Stella Stevens. . . ."

"Anything in there besides old time peek-a-boobage?" Very asked as he riffled through the desk drawers.

"Baseball cards. Shoe boxes full of them. Looks as if he has the complete Yankees teams from '64 through '72. But there's not a thing in here that's the least bit current." Mitch closed the footlocker back up. "You having any luck?"

"Nada. No notepads. No nothing. Wait, here we go. . . ." He'd found his friend's Nikon in the bottom drawer. Checked its register before popping it open. "No film inside, damn it." Very got up and checked out Augie's bathroom. Poked around in the medicine chest. Then went prowling into the kitchen, flinging open cupboards and drawers and, lastly, the refrigerator. "Got something here, dude."

"What is it, lieutenant?"

"A cold six of Ballantine. I'm totally there. You want one, too?"

"Why not?"

Mitch joined him in the tiny kitchen and accepted a tall can of Ballantine Ale. Leaned against the sink, opened it and drank some down while Very peered inside the open refrigerator. It was empty except for the Ballantine, a carton of orange juice and assorted condiments. Clearly, the man didn't do much cooking. Very reached for the mustard jar, twisted its lid off and poked his gloved index finger inside. Then he screwed the lid back on and did the same thing to the pickle relish, the ketchup and the mayonnaise. It was a large jar of mayonnaise. And when Very plunged his finger in down deep—son of a bitch—he found a smaller jar submerged inside. He removed it from its goopy hiding place and rinsed it off in the sink. Inside of it there was a roll of 35mm Kodak film.

"Knew I'd find it eventually," he said with quiet satisfaction.

"I'm surprised that the crime scene investigators didn't."

"Had no reason to, dude. They weren't looking for it."

"What do you think is on it, Lieutenant?"

"Dawgie's last batch of surveillance photos, I'm hoping. That roll he FedExed me of you and Beth having smoothies together—when did he take those?"

"Friday afternoon."

"These must be from Friday night. Or maybe some time during the day on Saturday."

"Why didn't he get them developed? Why did he hide them?"

"No idea. But we've got to find out what's on this roll right away. Is there a place here in town that's open on Sunday?"

"No, but there's a quickie photo center over in Old Saybrook. It's in the shopping center across from the bowling alley."

"You telling me *that's* what people do out here to launch their payload? They *bowl?*"

"I can drive you over there."

"Not necessary. I'm on it. Just need you to run me back to your island for my bike."

"Are you sure?"

"Positive. I've got other business to attend to. Still have to find myself a place to stay tonight, for one thing."

"If you run into any trouble with that let me know. My neighbor, Bitsy Peck, has at least eight spare bedrooms and loves company. And why don't you come out for dinner later? If you don't get a better offer, I mean."

"Thanks, I'll do that." Very sipped his Ballantine, gazing around at his dead friend's dreary little apartment. "Not much to leave behind when you're gone, is it, dude?"

"No, Lieutenant," Mitch said softly. "It's not."

CHAPTER 14

"WHAT HAVE YOU GOT for me, girl? And, please God, make it good," blustered Yolie as she barreled across the lawn from her cruiser, fists clenched, jaw clenched, *clenched*. "Because I really need a break here, understand?"

Des was stretched out on one of Mitch's lawn chairs savoring the fresh sea breeze after spending so many hours at that damned desk—searching high and low on her computer screen, working the phone. Quirt lay underneath her, his tail swishing in the grass. The geese were flying overhead. The grill was lit. Augie's killer was still on the loose. The Dorset Flasher, who either was or was not the same person, was still on the loose. Her father was having his chest cut open in three days. It was just a typical Sunday evening in paradise. "I understand, Yolie," she said. "Chill out, girl. You're so wired you're giving off sparks."

"Damned media people keep messing with my head," she huffed in response. "*Demanding* I feed them something for the six o'clock news. What do you tell them when you have nothing to tell them?"

"That this is an ongoing criminal investigation. That you are pursuing numerous fruitful leads, are making excellent progress and have no new information that you can share with them at this time."

Yolie stuck out her chin. "Yeah, that's pretty much what I said."

"Then you should be fine."

"Rico *really* doesn't like me putting my face out there."

"Rico will *really* have to deal with it. Sit yourself down, will you?

You have to learn how to pace yourself. We'll talk it out over dinner."

Mitch had gone to fetch a bucket of sweet corn from Bitsy's garden. His own fresh-picked salad greens were taking a bath in the kitchen sink. Two organic free-range chickens were marinating in olive oil, lemon juice, rosemary and garlic.

He came trudging up the path now, a Corona in one hand, his bucket of corn in the other. "Hey, Yolie," he called to her. "Can I get you a beer?"

She shook her head. "No slow juice for me. I'm on duty tonight."

"In that case, how would you like a cranberry spritzer with a twist of lime and a sprig of my very own homegrown mint?"

"Do I *look* like some skinny East Side Gap bitch to you?"

"Down, girl," Des cautioned her.

Yolie puffed out her cheeks. "Sorry, Mitch. Didn't mean to bite you. I'm just a little stressed right now."

He grinned at her. "Really? I hadn't noticed."

"That cranberry . . . whatever sounds great."

"One spritzer, coming right up," he said as a buzzer went off inside the cottage. Someone was at the causeway gate. Mitch fetched his binoculars from inside of the door and had a look. "Ah, good, it's Lieutenant Very."

Yolie's eyes widened with alarm. "What's *he* doing here?"

"I invited him to dinner. Hope you don't mind." Mitch pressed the buzzer to raise the security barricade and then went inside to make her drink.

Des watched the New York cop ease his motorcycle across the wooden causeway, hearing its throaty roar.

"I-I had no idea he was coming. *None.*" Yolie sounded even more wound up now—if such a thing was even possible. "It would have been nice if you'd warned me, girl. Just a teeny-tiny heads-up, know what I'm saying? I've been wearing the same clothes since yesterday. Smell like I've been living in a damned Dumpster for the past . . ." She broke off, fanning her face with her fingers. "Am I acting whack?"

"Not at all. He's really cute. And Mitch thinks he's a nice guy."

"He does seem nice, doesn't he?"

Des got up and went inside. Mitch was in the kitchen putting the finishing touches on Yolie's drink. "Is this you pulling a Bella or what?"

"I don't know what you mean, Master Sergeant."

"You do, too, Mister Matchmaker."

"Ohh . . . I see where you're going with this. But you could not be more wrong. I had no idea Yolie was coming to dinner when I invited him."

She gave him a doubtful look. "Uh-huh. . . ."

"But now that you mention it I'm glad she's here."

"And why's that?"

"Because the guy's desperately lonely. And when I first mentioned Yolie's name to him he went '*Woo* . . . ' "

"*Woo* . . . ? What's that mean?"

"That he thinks she's hot."

"Mitch, he'd better not hurt her."

"What makes you think he'd do that?"

"He's a man, isn't he?"

"I *knew* it. Film noir weekend was a huge mistake. I should never have screened *Out of the Past* for you. Let's try to think positive, okay? Lieutenant Very isn't Robert Mitchum and Yolie's not Jane Greer. Just leave them be."

He started back outside with Yolie's spritzer and a cold Corona for the lieutenant. Des followed him. Very stood next to his bike yakking a mile a minute with Yolie, the two of them so hyper Des was sure they were about to lift right up off of the ground.

Mitch handed them their drinks. "Any luck finding somewhere to stay tonight, Lieutenant?"

"Afraid not. There isn't a motel room to be had anywhere."

"I just spoke to my neighbor Bitsy. You're welcome to bunk with her. She lives in that giant natural-shingled place over there. I can introduce you after dinner."

"Thanks, dude. Appreciate it."

"How did you make out with that other thing?"

Very took a long, thirsty gulp of his Corona. "I made out," he replied, leaving it there. Des had no idea what they were talking about.

Mitch checked the grill and decided the fire was good to go. Fetched the platter of marinated chicken from the kitchen and set the pieces on the grill to sizzle, arranging the ears of corn around them.

Very flopped down at the picnic table. "You get anywhere today, Sarge?"

"Not unless you call nowhere somewhere," Yolie grumbled, sitting down across from him.

"Your people still haven't turned up that ski mask?"

"No mask. It's gone. Or was never there to begin with."

"How about Dawgie's body? Did they find any hairs or clothing fibers on him?"

Yolie shook her head at him. "Nothing. And they can't tell us much more about his assailant than we already knew. He, or she, swung that bat right-handed. Height's anywhere between five six and six foot—depending on how low Augie was crouched as he crept through the brush in the dark."

Des took a seat with them. "How about the force of the blows?"

"Average strength for a man. Above average for a woman. Meaning we can cross Bertha Peck off our list. Except she's so tiny and ancient that she was never on it to begin with." Yolie took a sip of her spritzer. "Those shoe prints they found down by the riverbank? Tread pattern belongs to a pair of Converse Chuck Taylor All Stars. It's a unisex shoe. A man or woman could have been wearing them. Same old song—average-sized foot for a man, above average for a woman. They gave me their usual boatload of blah-blah-blah about the perp's estimated weight and corresponding height, for whatever good *that* does."

Des made a face. "Which isn't much."

"I don't even pay attention," agreed Very, nodding, nodding. "I've turned up big, fat perps with little, tiny feet. Pip-squeaks who wear a size twelve triple-E. That stuff's meaningless. Sure sounds good when they do it on *Law and Order* though." He peered across the table at Yolie. "So you're nowhere."

"As I believe I just told you." She turned her gaze on Des. "I'm still waiting to hear from *you*, Miss Thing. Got any news I can use?"

"I do. For starters, I tracked down Hal Chapman's alibi."

Yolie brightened. "This would be Terri E as in maybe Edsen?"

"It's *Ensor*," Des informed her. "Hal told you she worked for some New York outfit that recovers peoples' lost assets, right? I surfed the Web sites of a gazillion companies until I finally found one called Equitrust. It's headquartered in White Plains, not the City. I accessed their employee directory and found a Terri Ensor. Then I located a Gregory and Terri Ensor in West Nyack. Called them up and got Greg. Identified myself and asked him if his wife was home. Right away, he wanted to know why. I told him she may have witnessed a vehicular accident in Dorset last evening. He acknowledged that she was out here visiting a college friend, just got home this morning. He went and fetched her. When Terri got on the phone I told her I needed to talk to her about Hal Chapman. She said '*Who?*' I said 'You know, your trainer at the Dorset Fitness Center.' After a really long silence she went '*Ohhh. . . .*' Clearly, Greg was still standing right there and she was scared he'd find out. I told her I just needed to know if Hal was with her last night at nine o'clock. She wouldn't be called to testify in court. This was strictly off the record. But I needed to know."

Yolie stared at her expectantly. "And . . . ?"

"She backed him up, Yolie. Everything Hal told you."

"That's good work, girl. Thanks."

"Excuse me, did I say I was done?"

"You've got something more?"

"I checked with Amtrak on the comings and goings of Kenny Lapidus over these past three weekends. The first weekend that our Dorset Flasher waved hello, Kenny bought himself a ticket on the Northeast Regional that left Boston's South Station on Friday at 5:35 p.m. It arrived on time in Old Saybrook at 7:34. He caught a train back to Boston from New London at 10:20 p.m. on Sunday. Made it home just after midnight."

"Why did he leave from New London?"

"The late train doesn't stop in Old Saybrook on Saturday or Sunday."

"So he was here in town while the Flasher was doing his thing?"

"He was here," Des confirmed.

"No way," Mitch protested as he turned the chicken on the grill. "Kenny's *not* the Dorset Flasher."

"I'm not saying he is, baby."

"But Dawgie *was* all over his mother," Very pointed out. "Kenny had a definite motive for swinging that bat."

"How about the other two weekends?" Yolie asked her.

"Amtrak had no record of him purchasing tickets last weekend. He must have driven his Prius down. We already know he drove here this weekend. He told us so. What we don't know is whether he got here on Friday in time to leave that little present on my welcome mat."

Yolie considered this for a moment. "You think Captain Rundle would mind if you took a personal day tomorrow?"

"Captain Rundle would be thrilled not to see my long face hanging around his barracks. You want me to drive up to Boston and check out the security cams at the MassPike toll booths, am I right?"

"You are. Let's nail down exactly when Kenny came and went. I'll run his credit card receipts. Maybe he bought gas somewhere along the way."

"You people are wasting your time," Mitch argued insistently. "Kenny's a total wimp. Hell, *I* used to protect him from playground bullies. Do you honestly think a guy like him could murder a retired police detective?"

"It doesn't take balls to commit murder, dude," Very said. "Just desperation."

"We have to look at him, Mitch," Yolie added. "These Flasher incidents coincide with his visits. The victim was putting the screws to his mom, like the lieutenant says. And he has no one to vouch for his whereabouts at the time of the murder. Kimberly told us he was in his bedroom sending e-mails, but he could have slipped out the bedroom window."

"No way," Mitch shot back. "If he'd gone out the window Des would have seen him. She was staked out right there."

"True enough," Des conceded. "Except the window wasn't his only way out."

"What's that supposed to mean?"

"Kimberly was out on the porch, right? Kenny could have just tiptoed through the apartment without her knowledge and gone out by way of the front door of the building. Then I wouldn't have seen him."

"Maybe somebody else did," Very said.

"Maybe."

"Now that you mention it," Yolie said, "that scenario plays for Kimberly, too. She was alone on the porch. No one to vouch for her. And she's plenty strong."

"Why would *she* kill Dawgie?" Very asked.

"Because Kenny wasn't up for it. The man's a wimp, like Mitch said. What we don't know is why they'd go to such lengths to protect his mom. I mean, so what if Augie was hassling the lady? All she had to do was just Say No—unless he was a total creepaholic stalker, in which case Des would have gotten involved, right?"

"Actually . . . there's a bit more to it than that," Very put in slowly. "Another angle that I worked this afternoon with my man Mitch here."

Yolie glowered across the table at him. "*What* angle?"

"Augie was absolutely convinced that Beth Lapidus and her married boyfriend, Vinnie Brogna, were up to no good together."

"What *kind* of no good, Romeo?"

"It's *Romaine.* Are either of you ladies familiar with the Seven Sisters?"

"Wait one second . . ." Des said. "Augie asked me that on Friday. I thought he was talking about the colleges. He called me a hick."

"Yeah, that sounds like Dawgie."

"So what *is* the Seven Sisters?" Yolie demanded.

"A somewhat legendary Jewish crime family," he replied. "They got their start a hundred years ago on New York's Lower East Side. And still exist to this day. I happen to know a little about them because I'm a member of the family. So is Beth Breslauer. We're both descended from the same long line of thieves. The two of us are cousins."

Yolie looked at Des in amazement. "Okay, I didn't see that one coming, did you?"

"Not even."

"Wait, wait, there's more," Mitch said eagerly. "Beth's not the only one who's connected to the family. Back in the thirties, when she was a young chorus girl, Bertha Peck—nee Bertha Puzewski—was the mistress of Beth's grandfather, Saul, a big time racketeer."

"Okay, now this is just plain whack," Yolie said.

"Very," Des agreed.

The lieutenant looked at her. "Yeah, Master Sergeant?"

"Um, it's very weird."

"I'm down with that," he said, nodding, nodding. "Beth claims that she's kept her thing with Vinnie a secret from Kenny. He doesn't know about them. She never entertains the guy at her condo. Won't even let him pick her up there."

Des mulled this over. "So she's saying she slipped out the back door last night to go meet Vinnie?"

"Exactly. Told us he picked her up down the block and the two of them hit the Mohegan Sun. Saw Linda Ronstadt. Got themselves a room."

"The front desk can confirm whether or not her story's the real deal," Yolie said.

"Augie told you that Beth and Vinnie were up to no good together," Des said. "You still haven't told us what kind."

"He thought they were working the Mohegan Sun. You know, snatching handbags, wallets, jewelry. Beth insists not, naturally. And her criminal record is spotless, but . . ."

"Wait, why am I just finding out about this *now*?" Yolie demanded, glaring at Very.

"Because I'm telling you about it *now*. You want to hear my thing or throw down?"

"Did Augie have any evidence to back that up?" Des asked.

"He sent me some photos that, in his opinion, show Beth lifting a lady's bracelet. You can look at them and see what you think. Mitch has seen them."

"And I don't think they show Beth stealing a thing," Mitch said. "Augie saw what he wanted to see."

"The photos are inconclusive," Very acknowledged. "They for damned sure aren't anything a prosecutor could run with. And yet I'm *positive* that both Beth and Bertha were playing me this afternoon." He took a drink of his beer. "I found another roll of film hidden in his apartment, Sarge."

"Hidden *where*?"

"Inside a jar of mayo in the reefer."

Yolie glared at him once again. "We made a deal, remember? You promised you'd tell me if you found anything."

"Which is exactly what I'm doing."

"*How* many hours after the fact?"

"I had to get the roll developed, Sarge."

"Do you *have* to keep calling me that? Makes me sound like some grizzled old gee with a potbelly. Make it Yolie, will you?"

"Or Precious," Mitch said. "She really likes to be called Precious."

"I can shoot you, hon," Yolie reminded him.

"You wouldn't dare. You'd leave Des bereft."

"What's on this roll of film?" she wanted to know.

Very fetched the photos from his knapsack and laid them out on the picnic table, one by one, without comment. They were photos of Beth Breslauer. Beth on her screened-in porch in a shortie nightgown, sipping her morning coffee. Beth in a halter top and shorts, painting her toenails. Beth in a one-piece bathing suit soaking up some sun out on the lawn. Her figure was quite good for a woman her age. Toned and shapely. She was showing skin in most of the photos, and was generally barefoot. The longer Des looked at them the more they creeped her out. They'd been taken by a lonely voyeur who had a schoolboy crush.

"The fifty-year-old girl next door," Mitch observed, studying them closely. "A lot of these remind me of those old issues of *Playboy* in his footlocker—minus the R-rating, of course."

"I'm with you," Very said. "It's pinup stuff."

"And they aren't that recent, Lieutenant. See this one? The cartoon daisies behind her are in full bloom. That was in mid-July. This roll's been sitting around for weeks."

"Playing you how?" Yolie said suddenly.

Very looked at her blankly. "Sorry?"

"You said you had a feeling that both she and Bertha were playing you."

"Totally. They were holding something back. I'd stake my life on it."

"I'll have a go at her myself in the morning—minus Bertha. Squeeze her a little. See what pops out."

"And I can go at Vinnie in the City," Very said. "Dawgie's photos of him with Beth give me big-time leverage. I'll threaten to drag his wife in for questioning. No way he wants that to happen. Yeah, Vinnie I can squeeze plenty hard—if you want me to, that is. Your case, Yolie."

"Squeeze away," she urged him. "I really want to break this tomorrow."

"I know you do. We'll get there," he promised.

Mitch had fallen strangely quiet. Just stood there gazing out at a sailboat on the water.

"Are you okay?" Des asked him.

He looked at her, frowning. "Sure, why wouldn't I be?"

"Your dream girl isn't exactly who you thought she was."

"I'm fine, Des." He went back to the grill to turn the chicken. "Besides, this whole thing is much harder on the lieutenant. He's combing his own family's unsavory history. How does *that* feel?"

"Needs doing," Very said with a shrug. "I'm good."

Des nodded politely, thinking, *You are both so full of crap.*

"Me, I'm just plain confused," Yolie said. "If Augie's killing has something to do with Beth and Vinnie's activities, criminal or otherwise, then what about the rest of it? Was Augie the Dorset Flasher or wasn't he? What's the connection? *Is* there a connection?"

No one answered her. No one had an answer.

"I'm still waiting to hear the Berger version," Des said finally.

"My man's not a member of the reality-based community. His mind operates on an entirely different astral plane. He sees things that the rest of us don't."

"And this helps you how . . . ?" Very wondered.

Mitch, meanwhile, was standing there at the grill staring at the lieutenant, his eyes narrowing.

"Dude, why do you keep looking at me that way?"

"Because it's your family."

"Right, and I just said I'm . . . Hold on, are you thinking *I* killed Dawgie?"

"Why not? You showed up here out of nowhere waving a tin star . . ."

"Gold shield, actually."

"You knew the access code to Augie's garage. Knew where he kept the spare key to his apartment. Knew that he hid the murder weapon under his bed. Maybe he was about to expose one of the Seven Sisters' deep, dark secrets. Maybe—okay, here it is—maybe you didn't go straight after all. Yeah, that's it. You're actually one of them. A loyal family member. They planted you on the force, which Augie never knew about until now. And so you had to kill him to protect your cover. You've stuck around Dorset because you're trying to influence Yolie's investigation. Steer it toward Vinnie and away from yourself."

"That's . . . really awesome, dude," Very marveled. "Way cool. Except it's not real life. It's a movie with, like, Harvey Keitel."

"I was thinking more along the lines of Johnny Depp."

"No, Colin Farrell," Yolie said with tremendous certainty.

"Just out of curiosity, am I the Dorset Flasher, too?" Very asked. "Or is that an icebox question?"

"An icebox *what*?" Yolie wondered.

"Trust me, you don't want to know."

"You're not the Flasher," Mitch told him. "There's no connection between the two cases. He's just some horny, frustrated high school kid. Which is exactly what Des was thinking before Augie turned up dead."

"He's right about that," Des admitted.

"Mitch, you are one major-league twisted mother. I'm serious, dude. So what happens now? Do I pull a piece and try to shoot my way off of this island?"

Mitch frowned at him. "I haven't worked that part out yet. Give me a sec, will you? This plot's only two minutes old."

Very let out a laugh. "I love this guy."

"You're out of luck, wild thing," Des informed him. "He's taken."

"I think I'll run up to the Mohegan Sun after dinner," Yolie said. "Try to nail down what time Beth and Vinnie checked in last night. I'll need pictures of them I can show around."

"You're welcome to whatever you need," Very said. "Want some company?"

"What's that supposed to mean?"

"I could ride along with you."

"Why would you want to do that?"

Des's right foot collided with Yolie's shin under the table.

Yolie looked at her, startled, before she cleared her throat and said, "If you want to ride along, it's fine by me. Happy for the company."

"Cool." Very drained the last of his beer, swiping his mouth with the back of one hand. "Anybody in class have anything else they'd like to share?"

Mitch raised his hand. "Yeah, I do. Dinner's ready. Let's eat."

Later, after Yolie and Lieutenant Very had driven off to the casino in Yolie's cruiser, Des and Mitch walked the island's beach together in the moonlight, enjoying the quiet and each other. They shed their clothes and dove naked into the cool water. Floated on their backs and gazed up at the stars, bobbing up and down on the gentle swells until Des's teeth began to chatter. Back at the cottage they jumped in a hot shower and Mitch soaped her, nose to toes, with a bar of L'Occitane milk soap infused with sinfully rich shea butter. He was very dutiful and thorough, his hands gently massaging and kneading her flesh, lingering lovingly over her booty. And lingering. And . . .

"I think I'm good and clean back there now, Armando."

"Sorry, I got a little captivated. It's like being allowed to stand in the Louvre running your bare hands over the Venus de Milo."

"Yeah, that's me—Venus. Except I've got arms."

"And legs." He knelt behind her, soaping them. "God, you've got legs."

She stood there smiling inside. No man had ever made her smile inside like Mitch did. For sure not Brandon. With Brandon she'd been one big knot.

Upstairs in the sleeping loft, the oil lantern glowing soft and golden, she needed something different from Mitch tonight. Maybe it was that extreme dose of Richie Tedone and his tranny skank Eboni. But when Mitch reached for her, Des took his face in her hands and said, "Do me a special favor, will you?"

"I don't have to wear the handcuffs, do I?"

"Nothing like that. Will you just hold me, squeeze me and never leave me?"

"Done." Mitch gathered her in his arms and hugged her tight. "This is the deal from now on, you know. Our parents aren't getting any younger."

She blinked at him in surprise. It never ceased to amaze her how he *knew* her. "The Deacon just seemed so . . . vulnerable."

"Get used to it. Before long they'll be the ones sitting in a diaper talking gibberish and we'll be the ones spoon-feeding them vanilla pudding."

"You make it sound so appealing, Armando."

"Okay, my turn now. To ask you for a special favor, I mean."

"You want me to do that thing to you with the feather?"

"No. Well, yeah. But no, that's not where I was going. We, that is to say *you*, decided that since I've lost so much weight, my old pet name no longer applied. But the truth is I really, really miss it."

"You *want* me to go back to calling you that?"

"More than anything in the whole, wide world."

She caressed his cheek, kissing him softly. "You got it, doughboy."

"About the Deacon . . ."

"What about him?"

"There's more going on here than you've told me, isn't there?"

She nodded. "The Brass City boys want his job. They're trying to use that scuffle I had with Augie to push him out. If he'll retire then Internal Affairs will drop any investigation into my actions."

"But they have no case against you."

"Doesn't matter. They can put a stink on me that'll stay with me throughout my career. They know he won't let that happen."

"So what are you doing about it?"

"Pushing back. But please don't ask me how, okay? Because I'm not real proud of myself. Which reminds me, I've got a loose end that's driving me crazy. Can you think of any connection between the Dorset Flasher, Augie Donatelli and York Correctional?"

"The women's prison?" Mitch frowned. "Not really—aside from the fact Kimberly teaches yoga there two afternoons a week."

"She does?"

"Yeah, she's a volunteer. Does that mean something?"

"I have no idea. Probably not." Des yawned contentedly, feeling herself getting drowsy. Her eyelids were heavy, circuits fried. She surrendered, snug and safe in Mitch's arms.

Until her cell phone rang on the nightstand.

She answered it and listened. "But I'm on desk detail now,

remember?" And listened some more before she said, "Okay, Oly. I'll be there in five."

"What's up?" Mitch asked as she climbed hurriedly out of bed.

"I'm not entirely sure. But it's nothing good."

She could hear the screams from out on Maple Lane.

It was just past 1:00 a.m. when Des pulled in at the same little dead-end road off of Dorset Street where she'd tripped over Augie's dead body. Oly's cruiser was parked there next to Dorset's volunteer ambulance van. Rut Peck's place was dark, same as last night. Over at Ray Smith's, the porch light was on. Ray stood outside in his bathrobe, pulling on a cigarette and watching the action.

It was going on at Nan Sidell's. Lights were blazing inside the little farmhouse that the blond middle school teacher shared with her two sons.

The screams grew even louder as Des rushed up the front steps to Nan's open screen door. They were the screams of a terrified boy. And she could make out words now: *"We're next, Petey! Look out, we're next!"*

In the parlor, Oly was seated on the sofa with Dawn's wide-eyed ten year-old, Peter, who was wearing a pair of Boston Celtics pajamas. The family's big yellow Lab, Josie, was stretched out at Peter's feet, whining uneasily. The screams were coming from Nan's bedroom, where Des found Nan's gangly older boy, twelve-year-old Phillip, in a state of uncontrolled hysteria.

"Look out, Petey! Look out!" he screamed, his eyes bulging with panic as he scrabbled around on the floor underneath his mother's antique four-poster bed, trying to hide from a monster that he alone could see. Sweat was pouring from him, soaking his pajamas. *"We're next! Run, Petey! Run!"*

A distraught Nan knelt there by the bed in her nightshirt, trying to calm him. "Philly . . . ?Mommy's right here, honey. You're okay. Everything's okay."

But the boy wasn't responding. Didn't hear her. Didn't know her. Just kept screaming: *"Run, Petey! Run!"*

Marge and Mary Jewett, the two no-nonsense sisters in their fifties who ran Dorset's volunteer ambulance service, were standing just inside of the bedroom doorway. It was a small, sparely furnished room. Aside from the unmade bed, which had a patchwork quilt on it, there was a nightstand, a chest of drawers. No art on the walls. No rugs.

"Don't make any sudden movements," Marge cautioned Nan in a quiet voice as the boy continued to scream his head off. "Just be real gentle. Don't grab for him or try to shake him. He'll come out of it on his own."

"Come out of *what*?" Nan sobbed, tears streaming down her face. She was trembling. "What is happening to my son?"

"We're next, Petey! Run, Petey!" Phillip cried out, bug-eyed with terror as he crawled frantically around under the bed. Until, abruptly, he stopped and became quiet. And calm. So calm that he curled into a fetal ball right there on the floor and fell asleep.

Marge knelt before him and felt for his pulse. "Returning to normal," she whispered, lifting one of his eyelids to check his pupil. "Let's get him back into bed." She started to pick Phillip up off of the floor but halted with a grunt of pain. "Dang, my old back isn't what it used to be."

"Here, let me . . ." Des gathered the tall boy up in her arms and carried him into the other bedroom, which had twin beds and Celtics posters all over the walls.

"His bed's the one over by the window," Nan said softly.

Des set him down there. Nan wrestled him out of his sweat-soaked pajamas and into fresh ones. The boy mumbled a bit in his sleep but was docile and compliant. She tucked him in and turned out his bedside light. They backed slowly out of the room into the narrow hallway, shutting the door.

"He'll be okay now, honey," Mary assured Nan.

The tears were still streaming from Nan's blue eyes. She was such a tiny little thing in her bare feet that she looked more like a girl than a full-grown single mother. "Are . . . are you sure?"

"Positive. We've seen this before."

"I-I didn't know what to do. I had no idea. I've never . . ." She ran a hand through her long blond hair, exhaling slowly. "Des, I'm *so* sorry to drag you out of bed like this."

"Not a problem, Nan. What I'm here for. Want to fill me in?"

"Little Petey came in and woke me up about, I don't know, a half hour ago. Told me that Philly was having a terrible nightmare and he couldn't wake him up. That's when I heard Philly screaming. And then *he* came running into my room, too. He followed Petey in there, I swear. His eyes were wide open. He-he was awake. I swear he was awake. And he was screaming and screaming and I-I couldn't get him to stop. *Or* get him out from under my bed. He was panting and gasping and-and . . . well, you saw him. He was *possessed*. So I called the girls." Nan turned to Mary now and said, "You've actually seen this sort of thing before?"

Mary nodded. "They're called night terrors. Not at all uncommon among kids Phillip's age. The episodes can last ten, fifteen minutes. Sometimes longer. It's basically an extreme nightmare."

Nan shook her head. "Philly was awake. You saw him. He was awake."

"They *seem* to be awake," Marge said. "But they're actually asleep. Generally, they return to normal sleep when the episode's over—and they don't remember a thing. That's why it's best not to shake them out of it or frighten them."

"Night terrors," Nan repeated, sounding unconvinced. "I was afraid he'd gotten into drugs of some kind."

"That's a definite no," Mary assured her. "His heart rate slowed right back down. His pupils were normal. He didn't ingest anything."

"But you were smart to play it safe," Marge said. "We had a pissed-off eleven-year-old girl on Whippoorwill just last Wednesday night who swallowed a whole bottle of her mother's Vicodin."

"That's why I wanted *you* here, Des," Nan explained. "You know what these kids are into. Not that Philly has ever given me the slightest reason to think he's . . . I just . . . he was like a totally different person. I'd better let Petey know he's okay. Will you excuse me for a moment?" She darted into the parlor to comfort her other boy.

Des and the Jewett sisters went out onto the front porch. Oly joined them.

"How did it go out there tonight?" Des asked him.

"Nice and quiet," he replied. "Until now."

"No Flasher sightings?"

"Not a one. I think our Flasher's on a slab in the morgue, don't you?"

"Oly, I don't know what to think."

Nan followed them outside a moment later. The boy remained on the sofa with Josie at his feet. "Petey seems just fine."

"Sure he is." Oly smiled at her. "He's a rock, that one."

"Please explain these night terrors to me," she said to the Jewett sisters. "Because Phillip has never, ever had anything even remotely like one before. What causes them?"

Marge and Mary exchanged an uneasy glance. They were, as a rule, careful not to stray too far above their pay grade.

"They're often caused by a psychological trauma of some kind," Marge answered gingerly. "It's entirely possible he won't ever have another one, Nan. But you should phone his pediatrician in the morning. He'll want to see Phillip."

"Did you folks happen to have a family situation this weekend?" Mary asked her.

Nan frowned. "Such as . . . ?"

"Did their father visit them? Not that I mean to pry, but an emotional upheaval like that might explain it."

Nan's face hardened. "Donald hasn't made time for our boys for over a year. He and Heather have a baby girl now who occupies all of his attention."

"I'm standing here wondering about something else," Des said, shoving her heavy horn-rimmed glasses up her nose. "Phillip and Peter were right there in that room of theirs last night when Augie Donatelli was murdered. Something pretty awful was happening out there in the dark. Josie was barking her head off. That's scary stuff. Major bogeyman material. Seems to me it would be perfectly natural for a boy's imagination to get the best of him."

Marge nodded. "I absolutely agree."

"Then again, it's possible there's more to it than that."

Nan studied Des closely. "You think the boys saw something, is that it?"

"Did they, Nan?"

"I honestly don't know. They haven't told me a thing."

"Do you mind if I talk to Peter?"

"No, of course not. As long you don't upset him."

"Not to worry. I won't."

"We're going to take off now," Mary told Nan. "If anything changes, just call us. Don't even hesitate. We're here for you."

Nan walked them to their van, thanking them profusely. Oly climbed into his cruiser and took off.

Des went back inside and joined Peter, who was sitting there petting Josie. The boy had his mother's big blue eyes and soft blond hair, but not her delicacy. His jaw was strong and stubborn, his hands unusually large for a boy of ten.

"Hey, Peter," she said, showing him her smile.

"Hey," he responded sullenly.

"Listen, I need for you to man up. Can you do that for me?"

He peered at her suspiciously. "Man up . . . how?"

"By telling me what's really going on."

The boy shrugged. "Mom said Philly had a bad dream."

"A bad dream about what, Peter?"

He didn't answer her.

"Phillip is real scared about something," she said. "And so are you."

"Am not."

"Yeah, you are."

"How would *you* know?"

"Because I'm a professional, that's how. That's why I get to wear this big hat and carry this big semiautomatic weapon. Because I know things."

He glanced at her uneasily. "*What* things?"

"I know that you boys saw what happened to Mr. Donatelli last night. That's why Phillip had his bad dream. That's why he kept screaming, '*We're next, Petey!*' Because he thinks the killer will come back for the two of you. That's why Phillip's so scared."

"*I'm* not scared," the boy insisted.

"Peter, I can't protect you unless I know what you boys saw."

"We didn't see anything! Philly just had a bad dream is all."

"Tell me the truth, Peter. Who killed Mr. Donatelli?"

"I don't know!" he cried out. "And don't try to make me say I do because I don't. We didn't see *anything*, okay? Not a thing!"

Peter jumped to his feet now and ran out the front door of the house to his mom—leaving Des alone in there with Josie wondering just exactly what in the hell was going on.

If Josie knew anything she sure wasn't talking.

Chapter 15

Waa-eeeeeeeeeeeeeee . . .

Mitch was up at dawn, beloved sky blue Stratocaster in hand, sitting in with Hendrix on "Red House" while his coffee brewed. There was no sleeping late on Big Sister Island. Not with the early morning sun streaming through the skylight over his bed. Not with Augie Donatelli's murder gnawing at him like it was. Because he was missing something. They were all missing something. The key to the whole case was right there in front of them and they weren't seeing it. Mitch was positive of this. But, damn it, he just couldn't figure out what it was.

Eeeee-yahhhhhh . . .

So he played. Standing there in his living room in a sleeveless T-shirt and gym shorts, eyes closed, bare toes wrapped around his wa-wa pedal and Ibanez tube screamer, monster amps cranked all of the way to the proverbial eleven, shaking the cottage to its stone foundation. Reaching for it. Feeling it. Nailing it. Yeah, there it was. Oh, yeah . . .

Scareeeeeeeeeee . . .

He'd awakened alone—unless you count Clemmie pad, pad, padding at his full bladder to let him know that her kibble bowl was emp-emp-empty. Des had gone back to her own place from Nan Sidell's. It had been nearly three a.m. by then. He'd insisted she phone him when she found out what was up—no matter the time—and so he'd heard all about Phillip Sidell's night terrors. Mitch knew the Sidell boys. The pair of them used to be in and out of Rut Peck's house day and night before Rut moved into Essex Meadows. Mitch used to stop by Rut's regularly. The old fellow had been one of the housebound villagers he'd bought groceries for. Phillip and Peter missed having their dad around but they were good kids. Sunny kids full of energy and jostling enthusiasm. Night terrors? No way.

Wa-eeeeeeeeeeee . . .

The coffee was ready. Mitch set his guitar aside, poured himself a cup and discovered he was nearly out of low-fat milk. He had enough for his coffee but not for his healthy Grape-Nuts breakfast. He'd have to go out and get some. He sipped the strong coffee gratefully, gazing out his bay window. It was another warm, humid morning. Not a whiff of a breeze. The sky was the color of dishwater, the Sound as calm as a bathtub. Haze hung low over the water. He could barely make out the Old Saybrook lighthouse just across the river.

Outside the front door, Quirt began yowling impatiently for his breakfast. Mitch let him in—and discovered that Yolie's cruiser was still parked there in the driveway next to Lieutenant Very's Norton Commando.

Well, well . . .

Mitch had loaned Yolie a coded card for the security barricade so she could bring Very back to the island after they'd finished doing their thing at the Mohegan Sun. He'd heard the crunch of her tires on the gravel outside sometime in the middle of the night. The engine idling for a long while before she shut it off. Soft voices as the two of them strolled down the path to the beach, talking easily, laughing. Mitch had fallen back to sleep after that.

Well, well . . .

He raised his coffee mug in silent tribute to them, then padded down to the beach with his coffee and his nagging thoughts about Beth Breslauer. Beth and the Seven Sisters. Beth and Bertha Peck, her grandfather's mistress. Beth and Vinnie Brogna, the great, secret love of her life. Beth and Lieutenant Very, who it turned out was a blood relation. Beth and Kenny. Kenny and Kimberly. Kimberly and J. Z. Kimberly and Hal . . .

As Mitch strolled in the direction of the lighthouse, lost in his thoughts, he came upon Yolie and Lieutenant Very seated together on a driftwood log watching the sun come up.

"Morning, kids!" he called out to them.

"Oh, hey, dude. . . ." Very seemed surprised to see him. Also a bit guilty.

So did Yolie. She lowered her gaze, shifting around on the log.

"Whoa, is it six-thirty already?" Very said with a glance at his watch. "I had no idea. Although I did hear some righteous heavy metal a few minutes back. Somebody really bringing it."

"That was me. And it was blues, actually."

"No way. I definitely heard Leslie West's opening riffs to 'Mississippi Queen' in there."

"You know you your vintage axe men, Lieutenant. I'd offer you breakfast but Bitsy is no doubt building you a lumberjack special as we speak."

"Yeah, I'd better head on over there. I want to hit the road soon." He climbed to his feet. "Yolie, I'll call you from the City as soon as I've had a go at Vinnie."

"You do that," she said quietly, her eyes large and soft.

"And, dude, I'll holler good-bye before I shove off. If you're still home, I mean." Very gazed around at the idyllic Yankee Eden that was Big Sister Island, one knee jiggling, head nodding, nodding. "And here I thought nothing ever happened in a small town like this."

"You thought wrong, Lieutenant. We play with live ammo here. If you want some real action come back to Dorset."

"I hate to admit it," he said, "but this place is cool."

"Very."

The lieutenant frowned at him. "Yeah, dude?"

Mitch sighed. "It's very cool."

"You got that right."

Detective Lieutenant Romaine Very started his way up the beach toward Bitsy's place. Yolie watched him go. Mitch sipped his coffee, saying nothing.

She got up off of the log, swiping the sand from her trousers. "It's not how it looks, okay? I don't give it up for men I barely know. I'm not like that."

"Did I say you were?"

"Didn't have to. That smirk is saying it for you."

"I'm not smirking. I'm *kvelling*."

"*Kvelling*? What's that mean?"

"It means I'm happy for you. Can't I be happy for you?"

"Whatever. We just talked is all. Talked all night. It's been a long time since I've done that. We spent a good two hours on politics. He's a borderline socialist, you want my honest opinion. Then a solid hour on the works of Mr. Albert Camus, who he's read in the original French. Not bragging on himself. Well, maybe just a little. Then, shortly before sunrise, he started reciting *Howl* by Mr. Allen Ginsberg, which I swear he knows entirely by heart."

"It's worth knowing by heart."

"Hey, I'm there." She glanced down the beach at Very's retreating figure. "He's a sweet guy. Smart, interesting. Drop-dead cute."

"That nodding thing doesn't bother you?"

"What nodding thing?"

"Nothing. Pay no attention to me."

"I wonder what's wrong with him."

"Why does anything have to be wrong with him?"

"He told me he hasn't been in a steady relationship in years."

"Neither have you."

"We were talking about *him*, not me. He's probably the type who just smiles and dials whenever he feels like it. Except he doesn't *seem* like the player type. Listen to me, will you? You're all players."

"I'm not."

"You're a freak."

"Thank you large for noticing." They started back up the beach toward his house. "What'd you find out last night at the casino?"

"Beth and Vinnie were definitely there Saturday night. Checked in at the front desk at nine-thirty. The hotel has them right there on their time-coded surveillance cameras. That means they had to be on the road somewhere between here and Uncasville at the time of Augie's death."

"So they're in the clear."

"Unless Vinnie put out a hit on him, like Very thinks. Where's our girl?"

"Halfway to Boston by now, knowing her."

"I should get rolling, too. I *have* to break this case open."

"Can I pour you a cup of coffee? I just made it."

"You talked me into it. And maybe I ought to change these stanky clothes before I have a go at Beth. I *think* I still have some clean ones left in the trunk of my ride."

"You're welcome to use my shower."

"I believe I will. Find out for myself what all of the fuss is about."

"Which fuss is that?"

She smiled at him. "Oh, I've heard about what goes on in there." Then she came to a halt, turning serious. "I don't want you thinking what you're thinking, Mitch. We didn't spend the night together."

"Come here, you big lug." He put his arm around her shoulder. It was like grabbing hold of a boulder. "You don't owe me an explanation. I'm not your father. I'm your friend."

"In that case I do have something to tell you. . . ."

"What is it, Yolie?"

"I want to get with that boy so bad I can barely breathe. If he doesn't come back here and bust a move, I swear I will explode."

"There, you see? That wasn't so hard."

Chapter 16

"The Tokyo markets opened three percent higher today," Des announced brightly as she leaned against her cruiser in Captain Richie Tedone's driveway, holding his freshly delivered Monday morning edition of the *Hartford Courant* out to him.

The human lug nut stood there in his terry-cloth bathrobe, blinking at her sleepily. Unshaven and uncombed, Richie looked a whole lot more like a wild boar than Des was cool with. "What can I do for you, Master Sergeant Mitry?"

"Actually, it's what I can do for you, sir."

"And that is . . . ?"

"I think I just may be able to save your life."

"What in the hell are you talking about?"

"I'm talking about your career, your marriage, family. . . . Pretty much everything you hold near and dear, Captain."

Richie shot a quick glance at the house before he turned back to her, his chest all puffed out. "Look, I don't know if you've been on an all-night bender or what, but showing up here at six o'clock in the morning blowing smoke at me is not what I'd classify as a real smart career move. I'm heading inside to have my breakfast now. You want to have a conversation with me, you call and make an appointment. Mondays are usually skunky but I'll try to squeeze you in. Now if you'll excuse me . . ."

"I wouldn't go inside for that breakfast yet, Captain. Not if I were you."

He heaved a sigh of disgust. "All right, let's have it. And make it fast."

She held the manila envelope out to him. He took it from her and opened it. Inside were copies of the digital photos she'd printed out of Richie standing in the doorway of apartment C of the Edgewood Vista apartments, exchanging slurpy kisses with a half-naked Michael Reginald Toomey, aka Eboni.

Richie grew redder and redder as he riffled through them. "Why, you sneaky bitch. What in the hell do you think you're . . . ?"

"I ran Toomey's arrest record. Turns out he has a long history of arrests for prostitution and drug possession. He was also up to his eyeballs in the Suburban Madam case, remember? The madam alleged that a member of the task force accepted sexual favors from one of her prostitutes. After conducting a thorough interrogation of said prostitute you determined that there was no merit to the charge. Case closed. Aside from the fact that you're now paying the rent on said prostitute's apartment *and* bought said prostitute that cute little red Beemer."

He glared at her long and hard. "Are you trying to make a point?"

"Well, yeah. You're keeping house with a key witness in a case you personally investigated. A pro, as it happens. A *tranny* pro, in fact. Not that I'm passing judgment on your lifestyle. But it's really, really not the sort of behavior that Internal Affairs looks too kindly on."

"Did you come here to *threaten* me?" he blustered in response. "You did, didn't you? You are actually trying to threaten me. Let me tell you something, Master Sergeant Mitry. You just made the biggest mistake of your miserable life. Because you are done, hear me? You will never work in law enforcement again!"

"Um, okay, this is the part where I talk and you listen," Des said in a calm, steady voice. "I don't give a damn who you're related to. All I have to do is hand these around at the headmaster's house and you are toast." She gazed at him, smiling. "I can see those little wheels starting to turn in your head. Don't waste your brain power. The memory card is stashed somewhere safe. It won't do you any good to nuke my computer. Or search my house. Or burn it to the ground. The card's not there." She'd hidden it at Mitch's place last night. Taped it under a kitchen drawer. "And if by some weird chance anything tragic should happen to me—like if I were to die a sudden death in a random drive-by shooting—this all gets sent directly to Superintendent Crowther. The arrangements have already been made." She'd e-mailed the detailed instructions to her lawyer before she'd headed here. "You're the one who's done, Captain. I own your ass from now on, hear me? You're mine. All mine."

"What d-do you *want* from me?" he sputtered, his barrel chest heaving with rage.

"For starters, this so-called case of yours regarding my conduct toward Augie Donatelli disappears right now. I want back on normal duty by the end of today. More importantly, when Deputy Superintendent Mitry returns from medical leave in a few weeks—and he *will* return—he will serve out the remainder of his long, distinguished career in whatever capacity he chooses. He's fought for that right. And he deserves it. What he doesn't deserve is to have a pack of jackals nipping at his heels while he's being wheeled into the operating room. If you try to mess with my father *ever* again, I swear I'll go public with these photos. And I'll make sure your lovely wife gets a complete set, too."

Richie breathed in and out heavily, struggling to control himself. Clearly, he wanted to dive at Des and strangle her with his bare hands. "You'll *never* get away with this."

"Yes, I will. There's a pretty little girl with a pink tricycle who's got my back. You don't want to lose her, do you?"

"How dare you mention my daughter? You *don't* go after a man's family. That's way out of line."

She let out a laugh. "Oh, is that right?"

He narrowed his eyes at her. "You're on the job. That's different."

"So are you, Captain. Real different. And I wouldn't invoke the sanctity of your happy family right now if I were you because you're on super-shaky ground. Tell me, do you wear a condom when you're with little Eboni? I certainly hope you do. I'd hate to think you're jeopardizing your wife's health."

He shook a stubby finger at her. "It's Yolie, isn't it? Yolie Snipes is behind this. She's *always* had it in for me."

"Yolie doesn't know a thing about this. Nor does your cousin Rico, if that's where you're going next. You're looking for hate in all the wrong places, Captain. Try checking out the mirror. Now do we have a deal or don't we? Because if we don't, I'm going to knock on that front door and show your missus these pictures right freaking now."

He glowered at Des, the very model of macho defiance. Until, slowly, Captain Richie Tedone of Internal Affairs began to deflate right before her eyes. His shoulders slumped. His pumped-up muscles seemed to shrivel. "I-I can't get Eboni out of my system," he confessed miserably. "You think I don't know how wrong it is? I'd give anything to be free of that crazy little tramp. I-I've tried to walk away a million times. Believe me, I've tried. But I keep coming back. It's like a sickness or something."

She offered him her cell phone. "Call somebody who cares. I don't. If you choose to spend your free time with a drugged-out tranny skank instead of with your beautiful wife and children that's your business. Just know that today's the day it bit you in the ass."

"You're one cold-hearted bitch, know that?"

"If it makes you feel any better to think so go right ahead," she responded. "Now do we have a deal or do I go knocking on your door?"

"All right, all right," he growled at her. "You win—this round.

But I promise you, Master Sergeant Mitry, if you ever come near my house again I *won't* be responsible for my behavior."

"No offense, Captain, but you crossed that particular bridge a long, long time ago."

Chapter 17

What am I missing?

It kept gnawing at Mitch as he toodled down Dorset Street in his pickup en route to the A&P. The *something*, whatever it was, that he wasn't seeing. The key to Augie's murder. The link between Augie's death and the Dorset Flasher. Because there *was* a link, he told himself, munching on the last of the four apple-cider doughnuts he'd picked up at McGee's diner on his way to the market. At a time like this he needed to be fortified by one of his native fat-boy food groups. Well, two actually. Here lay the sheer genius of doughnuts—they counted as both sugar *and* grease. The Dorset Flasher, he was convinced, was not just some random kid from the neighborhood. This whole mess was linked together somehow. Had to be. Because this was Dorset—ground zero for hidden links that went back God knows how many generations. Like that whopper of a hookup between Beth and Bertha, her grandfather's one-time tootsie. Therefore, the identity of the Dorset Flasher was critical. Had to be. The Flasher had not indulged in any targeted weenie waving last night, according to Yolie. Not a single sighting of him. Which signified what—that he was dead? That Augie *had* been the culprit? *Or* that he was alive and in hiding now?

What am I missing?

Maybe nothing. Maybe he just had a case of Chattering Monkey Brain, as Kimberly called it in yoga class. His head spinning around and around. No outlet for his jumbled thoughts. Nowhere to run with them. He was the only one of them who had no assignment this morning. Des was on her way to Boston to check the tollbooth security cameras for Kenny's comings and goings. Very was on his way back to New York City to grill Vinnie Brogna. Yolie was preparing to take another crack at Beth, who Very was convinced had been holding out on him. Mitch? He was heading to the supermarket for a half gallon of low-fat milk. And then it was back to his computer to flesh out this week's column on icebox questions. After he'd filed that he had a mountain of spade work to do on his new film encyclopedia. This was his chosen profession. He wrote about movies. He didn't solve crimes. Augie's death was strictly a job for the pros.

What am I missing?

Or maybe he was just shook up from meeting the real Beth after all of these years. The Beth who was a member of the crime family known as the Seven Sisters. The Beth whose first husband, Sy Lapidus, had been in jail for bookmaking back when Mitch befriended Kenny in Stuyvesant Town. The Beth who had been carrying on a ten-year affair with a married mobster. No doubt about it—the first great love of Mitch Berger's life had never been the woman he'd thought she was. And maybe a man doesn't just shrug off something like that. Maybe it was hitting home more than he wanted to admit. Same as the Deacon's impending coronary bypass surgery was. It was body blows like these that made Mitch miss the blissfully clueless innocence of his youth. Before he'd loved and lost Maisie. Before he'd become acutely aware of the pain and pitfalls that lay before him in the years to come—no matter how careful or smart or lucky he might be. Real life in all of its ugly glory. No grand finale. No stirring John Williams musical score. Just a small, quiet fadeout.

Maybe that was it, Mitch reflected, as he eased his old truck through the Historic District. Kids were out enjoying their last week of summer freedom. A couple of giddy thirteen-year-old girls were riding their bicycles. A boy on a skateboard was showing off for them. The girls were pretending they weren't watching him. As he cruised past the firehouse, Mitch saw the Sidell boys, Phillip and Peter, walking down the street together, the pair of them playing a spirited little game on the sidewalk as they ambled along, chattering away. He honked and waved to them. They looked up and waved back, the pair of them seemingly as happy as could be. Less than eight hours ago Phillip had been screaming in blind terror. And yet now he seemed fine. Bright eyed and carefree as he strolled in the morning sunshine with his younger brother, totally absorbed in their game, smiling and laughing and . . .

Mitch hit the brakes right there in the middle of Dorset Street, the hairs on the back of his neck standing up. Of course! Why hadn't he seen it before? Why hadn't *any* of them? He sat there watching the boys in his rearview mirror, his eyes bulging, head spinning. Then he pulled over and grabbed his cell phone. Des answered on the second ring.

"Listen, how close are you to Boston right now?"

"I had to make a pit stop in Glastonbury. I'm not even in Hartford yet. Why are you asking?"

"How long will it take you to get back here?"

"A half hour. Twenty minutes if I put my cherry on."

"Put it on, girlfriend."

"Why, Mitch?"

"Because I need your help. And you'll want to call Yolie. She needs to be there, okay?"

"Needs to be *where*? Mitch, what in the hell is going on?"

"I'm about to tell you. But first answer me this: Can you get your hands on a good, sturdy pair of bolt cutters?"

He'd never been inside of their place before.

It was exceedingly formal. A stately grandfather clock ticktocked discreetly just inside of the front door. Oil portraits of dead ancestors hung from the living room walls. The gleaming antique furniture smelled faintly of lemon oil polish.

"What a wonderful surprise, Mitch," Maddee exclaimed as she led him inside. She wore a floral print summer dress today. And her pearls. And a fresh coating of her alarming magenta lipstick. "Dex will be so pleased to see you."

"I was out running errands. Hope it's not too early to pay a social call."

"Not at all. Dex still keeps Wall Street hours. Once an early riser always an early riser. He's already done his calisthenics and eaten his breakfast. And Kimberly's left for her eight o'clock Vinyasa class." Maddee eyed him critically. "Nonetheless, I'm terribly cross with you."

"You are? Why is that?"

"You're empty-handed. Are you honestly telling me you couldn't find *one* item of old clothing to pass along to the Nearly New shop?"

"I'm still searching, ma'am."

"Please keep at it, Mitch. There are people out there who are hurting. They depend on us."

Dex Farrell was parked at a teak table on the screened-in porch with a cup of coffee and the *Wall Street Journal*. He wore a crisp white shirt, blue-and-gold bow tie, pressed khaki slacks and white bucks. Maddee had been seated across from him clipping supermarket coupons from the local shoreline weekly newspaper, Mitch gathered. Her coffee cup sat next to a tidy stack of coupons and a small, pointy pair of scissors.

"Why, good morning, Mr. Berger," Dex said, gazing at him over his rimless eyeglasses.

"Good morning, sir. You suggested I drop by some time for a chat."

"And here you are. I'm glad. Pull up a chair."

"Can I get you anything?" Maddee offered as Mitch sat at the table. "Coffee, lemonade?"

"No, thanks. I'm fine."

"Then I'll leave you two boys to talk. I have my Meals on Wheels duty this morning."

"I wish you wouldn't go just yet, Mrs. Farrell. Can you stay a few minutes? There's something I wanted to ask you about."

"Certainly." Maddee sat back down across from her husband and resumed her coupon clipping. She performed the little task same way she gardened—with focused tenacity. Whipping through an ad supplement before she paused, zeroed in, and pounced. Her sharp little scissors going *snip-snip-snip* in the morning quiet. "Look at this, Dex, the IGA at Four Corners has ten cans of Bumble Bee tuna for ten dollars." *Snip-snip-snip.* "You say there's something you wish to ask me about, Mitch?"

"Yes, ma'am."

"Well, don't be shy. It's a sign of weakness. I've always encouraged Kimberly to speak right up and tell me what's on her—"

"How long have you known that your husband is the Dorset Flasher?"

Dex Farrell didn't so much as blink. Just stared straight ahead, his face impassive.

But Maddee paled instantly, her eyes darting wildly about the porch. "Why, whatever do you mean . . . ?"

"I mean that our Flasher isn't a sexually frustrated kid. Or an overheated man child like Hal Chapman or J. Z. Cliffe. It's Dex who has been exposing himself to various prominent ladies in the Historic District, and leaving little presents on their doorsteps." Mitch looked at him. The man still hadn't moved a muscle. "Actually, this whole crazy business fell right into place once I realized it was you. For one thing, the Flasher never seems to—how shall I put it—rise to the occasion. Makes total sense. You're, what, sixty-seven years old? That's not to say you *can't* stand and deliver from time to time. I certainly hope you can. Otherwise I don't have a whole lot to look forward to in the years ahead. But sex has never been what this was about. Has it, sir?"

Dex reached for his coffee and took a small sip, his hand steady as a rock. He didn't respond. Or look at Mitch. Just gazed out the porch screen at the rosebushes that flanked the Captain Chadwick House's front path. The Blush Noisettes that Maddee tended to so passionately.

"I've been asking myself why the Flasher always strikes on weekends—which just happens to be when Kenny's in town visiting Kimberly. I kept thinking there had to be some connection. Again, the obvious answer fell right into place: You do your thing on the weekend because Kimberly isn't *here* on the weekend. She's out of the apartment—over at Beth's place with Kenny. Plus, who knows, maybe you're a teensy bit conflicted about that. Daddy's little girl across the hall, lying in bed naked in some geeky young stranger's arms. But, hey, that's a little Freudian for me so I don't think I'll go there. Armchair psychology is not my thing. I've never been a big fan of *Spellbound*, have you?"

Dex continued to stare out at the rosebushes. He was very still. Scarcely seemed to be breathing.

"Which isn't to say that it belongs in the pantheon of Hitchcock's truly awful films," Mitch went on. "Such as, say, *The Paradine Case*. Which, interestingly enough, also happens to star Gregory Peck. He and Hitch were clearly not a match made in Selznick heaven. But *Spellbound* has never appealed to me. So heavy-handed. And, wowser, talk about icebox questions."

"Talk about . . . *what*?" Maddee asked hoarsely.

"You still haven't answered my question, ma'am. How long have you known? You may as well tell me. I can help you. I certainly don't wish to hurt you. I'm a friend of the family. And we both know that Mr. Farrell already has a well-documented history of behaving, shall we say, eccentrically in public."

Maddee lunged for her coffee cup and took a sip, her own hand shaking so badly that Mitch could hear the cup *clonk* against her front teeth. "I think you'd better leave, Mitch. I think you'd better leave right this minute. I refuse to sit here and allow you to speak such—such vile, awful, despicable . . ."

"Please stop talking now, dear," Dex spoke up, his voice quiet but firm. "Kindly shut your mouth and keep it shut. Mr. Berger has shown me the courtesy of paying us a personal call on this matter. In return, I owe him the courtesy of the truth. It's the only honorable thing to do. Although I'm afraid, young man, that you won't understand the purpose behind this little undertaking of mine."

"I'd like to, sir. I really would."

"Very well. I'll do my best to explain it to you," he said to Mitch as Maddee sat there across the table from him in obedient silence, a stricken expression on her face. "Over the years, Mr. Berger, there have been occasions in my life that have called for me to act in an extraordinary fashion."

"By extraordinary you mean . . . ?"

"Kindly don't interrupt me. I assure you that I will answer all of your questions at the appropriate time." Dex folded his hands before him on the table and resumed. "Occasions that have forced me to invent an alter ego so as to do what needed doing. Whether it be escaping the bonds of a rigid, recalcitrant authority or the righting of egregious wrongs. Wrongs that could not be dealt with by traditional means. Maddee and I have endured a great deal of personal humiliation since we've returned to Dorset. Perfectly understandable. I put my faith in the wrong men and cost a lot of innocent people a lot of their hard-earned money. I ask for no sympathy. I fully deserve the scorn and derision that is directed at me wherever I go. But *not* Maddee. It isn't fair that this good woman has been made to suffer along with me. She had no part in the institutional failures of Farrell and Co. She was an innocent bystander who wished nothing more than to retire in peace to this village that she loved. That's not so much to ask for, is it? And yet I *saw* how the old biddies whispered about her behind her back. Shunned her, humiliated her. Made her grovel to regain their precious approval. A fine, caring lady like my Maddee. Someone of breeding and taste. Her folks were very, very fine people. She was quite a stunner in her day, too, my Maddee. You should have seen her in a bathing suit, Mr. Berger. She would have taken your breath away. And yet just look at how these awful women have treated her. They've made her sort through other people's soiled clothing like a ragpicker. Deliver meals around town just like one of those high-school dropouts who drive for Domino's Pizza. All because she wanted to book the Yacht Club for Kimberly's wedding. I'll have you know I paid for that club's new dock out of my own pocket seven years ago. Yet now my Maddee has to beg her way back into their good graces. They're intolerably vicious and cruel, these women. Believe me, each and every one of them richly deserved a dose of her own medicine. And that's exactly what I gave them."

"What about that poop sample you left on resident trooper Mitry's welcome mat? Did she 'deserve' that?"

Dex's jaw muscles tightened but he didn't respond. Didn't care for inconvenient questions. Just sat there gazing at Mitch.

"The resident trooper referred to Dex as 'seriously disturbed' on Channel Eight News," Maddee explained, her voice quavering slightly. "It was very hurtful. Dex has been under a doctor's care for these past two years. He knows—*we* know—that he has a problem with his . . . moods. He's coping with his condition bravely. And, believe me, he's never harmed a soul."

Dex nodded in agreement. "I've done no actual harm to any of the ladies, Mr. Berger. Merely taken it upon myself to mete out an appropriate measure of justice. You can see that, can't you?"

"Absolutely, sir. You've been making a statement."

"That's correct. A statement."

"And no harm has come to anyone. Unless, of course, you count Augie Donatelli getting his brains bashed in. A man is dead, Mr. Farrell. That kind of throws your whole tit-for-tat thing out the window, doesn't it?"

Dex clucked at him reproachfully. "You don't understand a thing."

"No, sir, I understand perfectly. It's like Mrs. Farrell just said—you've never hurt a soul. And she's the one person in the world who's in a position to know that for sure."

"Because I love my husband," Maddee said, gazing warmly across the table at him.

"I don't doubt that for one second, Mrs. Farrell. Tell me, when did you first realize that you weren't the only one who was following Dex around on his nightly excursions?"

Maddee shook her head at him. "I'm afraid you've lost me."

"Did you know that it was Augie from the get-go?"

She didn't answer him. Went back to clipping her coupons instead. *Snip-snip-snip.* Her entire being focused on the task at hand. *Snip-snip-snip.*

Mitch pushed harder. "I'm curious—how did Augie get onto him?"

Again, no reply. Just that same *snip-snip-snip. . . .*

"Did Augie have the building staked out?" *Snip-snip-snip.* "Did he spot Dex sneaking home one night in his ski mask?" *Snip-snip-snip.* "Is that why you decided you had to kill him?"

Maddee halted, gazing up at Mitch. She seemed quite calm. Almost serenely so. She was smiling at him. A kindly, motherly smile. As Maddee sat there like that, smiling, a strange noise began to emanate from her. A low moan that seemed to originate way down deep in her diaphragm. As it traveled its way up her throat, the moan became a feline roar—a roar that erupted out of her mouth at the same moment she sprang to her feet, kicking over her chair. "You've been *spying* on us, too, haven't you?" she snarled at him, clutching those sharp little scissors in her fist. Her eyes bulged with rage. "Yes, you have. You're a nosy little spy, just like that awful, filthy man was. *Lurking* there in the darkness. Do you *know* what happens to nosy little spies?" Now she raised those scissors high over her head. "They get their eyes poked out!"

"I wouldn't try that if I were you, Mrs. Farrell," Mitch said quietly. "Not if you value your health and well-being."

Her husband said nothing. Just sat there.

"Put those scissors down on the table right now, ma'am. You're in a great deal of danger."

Maddee gaped at him in disbelief. "From who? *You*?"

"Not exactly, no."

"That would be from us, Mrs. Farrell."

Maddee whirled—and discovered that Des and Yolie were standing shoulder to shoulder just outside of the screened-in porch with their SIGs aimed right at her.

"Drop those scissors," Yolie ordered her. "Drop them right now."

Maddee wouldn't. Just continued to stand there brandishing them high overhead.

"Please put them down, Mrs. Farrell," Des said.

Maddee refused. She even took a step *toward* the two of them, opening the screen door wide. This was when the awful words "officer-assisted suicide" jumped into Mitch's head.

"Don't do this, Mrs. Farrell," Des pleaded. "We don't want to hurt you. Just put those scissors down."

Maddee hesitated, glancing fondly over at her husband, then she turned back to Des and Yolie, her jaw clenching.

"Put 'em down!" Yolie said once more.

Now Mitch heard it again—that same low moan coming out of Maddee. The one that would soon turn into a roar. She was going to charge them.

"Don't do it," Des warned as Maddee took another step toward them. "*Please*, Mrs. Farrell."

This was when Mitch dove for her. He tackled Maddee to the wooden deck, her body under his. She went down hard—but not without a fight. She wrestled with him, snarling and gasping. His hand found her right fist, the one that was wrapped around those scissors. He pinned her fist to the floor. But she still wouldn't let go of the damned things. She was amazingly strong.

By now Des and Yolie had charged inside. Des stomped on Maddee's wrist with her shoe. Maddee's hand immediately went dead, her fist opening like a clamshell. Yolie snatched the scissors away from her.

"You see, Des, this is why I've never gone in for coupon clipping," Mitch explained. "It's much too dangerous a hobby. What took you so long anyhow?"

"We had to search through two whole bins before we hit the jackpot," responded Yolie, who was still wearing a pair of white latex crime-scene gloves.

"But I was right, wasn't I?"

Yolie nodded at him. "You were right—about all of it. Dunno how."

"I don't either." Des looked at him in amazement. "I swear, boyfriend, sometimes you scare me."

Yolie went back outside for a pair of bulging, black plastic trash bags and dumped them on the floor.

Maddee's eyes widened when she caught sight of them. And the last bit of resistance went out of her. Her body slackened. She was subdued now. And unhurt—aside from a bruised wrist. Mitch helped her back up onto her feet and into her chair.

Her husband continued to take all of this in with no expression. In fact, Dex Farrell barely seemed to notice the two large, gun-toting black women who were standing there on his porch.

"Happily, you ladies got here just in time," Mitch informed them. "Mrs. Farrell was just about to tell me how and when she realized Augie was following Mr. Farrell around."

"I knew about Dex's activities from the beginning. That very first night he slipped out of our condo," Maddee explained quietly. She sounded weary now. Utterly exhausted. "We retire early. By nine, nine-thirty at the latest. Always have. Wall Street men keep early hours. Dex thought I was asleep, but I don't sleep very well. I haven't in years. I heard him go into the bathroom and get dressed. I had no idea what he was up to but he was being so—so *secretive* that I became concerned. I threw on some dark clothes, put a scarf over my head and followed him. Not that I would have recognized him unless I'd seen him leave our unit with my own two eyes. He wasn't dressed at all like his usual self. He had on a black nylon windbreaker, jeans, a pair of sneakers . . ."

"And don't forget the ski mask," Mitch said.

"He could have been anyone. Except he *wasn't* anyone. He was the man I've loved for thirty-seven years." Maddee reached across the table and put her hand over Dex's, smiling at him.

"A real stunner, Mitch," he said softly, his eyes blank and lusterless. "She would have taken your breath away."

Yolie glanced down at the trash bags on the floor. "I'm not going to open up these bad boys again. Don't want to compromise any evidence. But the Flasher's whole outfit is bundled up in this one here," she said, poking it with her foot. "Including a mud-caked pair of Chuckie T. All Stars *and* the ski mask, which will provide us with excellent samples of Mr. Farrell's DNA—his saliva, nasal secretions, hairs from his head. A ski mask is what the forensics people call a target-rich environment. Your own outfit is in that other bag, Mrs. Farrell. Dark blue slacks, long-sleeved blouse, purple scarf. Your garden gloves, hiking shoes. Everything you were wearing on Saturday night when you were out there keeping watch over your husband. I have zero doubt that we'll find traces of Augie Donatelli's blood all over them. You're bound to produce blood spray when you beat a man's head in with a baseball bat." She turned to Mitch. "Lay it on me, hon. How did you know where we'd find this stuff?"

"Basic human nature, Yolie. It's all perfectly good clothing—including the ski mask. Mrs. Farrell couldn't destroy it. Not when there are needy souls out there who could wear it. It's just not in her nature to waste anything." To Maddee he said, "You delivered a load of used clothing to the Nearly New shop at St. Anne's yesterday morning. Kimberly told us she helped you load up your car before church. You're a smart, careful person. You didn't dare bring that ski mask and clothing to the Nearly New. We're talking about incriminating evidence. But you *could* toss it in one of those Goodwill bins behind Christiansen's Hardware, figuring it would get carted halfway across the country and no one would ever be the wiser. Clever move, ma'am."

"Hell, you've been nothing but clever," Des said to her. "When I answered Bertha's 911 here on Friday you went out of your way to play the frightened victim. Telling me how scared you were you'd be the Flasher's next victim. But you made one small mistake, Mrs. Farrell. The Goodwill truck only empties out those bins once a week—on Tuesdays. So the evidence hadn't left town yet. It's just been sitting in that bin ever since you dropped it there yesterday on your way to church. It would still be sitting there if Mitch hadn't put two and two together. He's the one who advised us to pop the locks and start searching. Sure enough, there it was. But I still don't get it, Mitch. How did you know?"

"Because of something Mrs. Farrell said to me yesterday when I was here with Lieutenant Very. She was out in the backyard working on the Captain Chadwick roses. I happened to say how nice they looked. And she said it wasn't easy, what with the insects and diseases and ball-playing louts. I kept thinking *what* ball-playing louts? There's nobody living here but well-heeled older adults, right?"

Des studied him curiously. "Right . . ."

"Until, wham, it hit me just now as I was driving down Dorset Street. That's when I saw them."

"Saw *who*?"

"Phillip and Peter Sidell moseying down the sidewalk kicking a soccer ball back and forth to each other. Phillip and Peter who live two doors over in a small place that doesn't have much of a backyard. Certainly nothing like the four acres or so of lawn that this place has. Phillip who suffered a full-blown freak-out last night."

Des nodded her head slowly. "Because he knows who killed Augie. They both do. They looked out of their bedroom window and saw her running from the scene. Must have. But I couldn't get them to admit anything."

"Because they're totally petrified of this lady. Why is that, Mrs. Farrell?"

"Those boys trampled one of my Blush Noisettes just like a pair of wild animals," Maddee explained matter-of-factly. "They uprooted it. Broke its branches. Nearly killed the poor thing. So I told the little hooligans that if I *ever* caught them kicking their damned soccer ball into my roses again I'd sneak into their bedroom in the night and take my pruners to their little dickies."

Mitch drew his breath in. "Okay, that sure would have given me night terrors when I was twelve. In fact, it still may. But I'm not clear about one thing: How did you come to be in possession of Augie's Louisville Slugger?"

"I can answer that," Des said. "Augie told me he'd found her in his apartment Friday morning searching through his trash for recyclables. Or so she claimed. What he didn't tell me—what he didn't know—was that the real purpose of her visit was to grab that bat from under his bed. How did you know it was there, Mrs. Farrell?"

"Augie told me it was," Maddee replied. "He said that even though he felt completely safe in this neighborhood he'd slept with his Mickey Mantle bat under his bed for thirty years and was not about to change his ways. He was a stubborn man. Also a filthy one. There was dust everywhere. Stacks of dirty dishes, soiled underwear . . ."

"You stashed it here," Des continued. "And when Dex slipped out on Saturday night you brought it with you to use as a weapon on Augie. Augie was on to him and you had to do something about that. I was tailing Augie myself that night. He left his apartment, crossed the backyard and perched there in the darkness, waiting. I didn't know why. Now I do—he was waiting for Dex to come tiptoeing out of the building. When Dex took off into the night Augie went after him. I tailed Augie. And *you* were tailing all three of us. As soon as you had a clear swing at him you used that bat to take him out."

"He fell to his knees, groaning, when I struck him," Maddee recalled. "I surprised him more than I hurt him, I do believe. It was so dark I wasn't sure *where* I'd hit him. So I hit him again—this time with greater force and accuracy. After that, he didn't make a sound. I dropped the bat and ran back to the house. Bagged up my clothes, washed myself off and waited for Dex to return, hoping and praying that he'd make it home safe. And he did." She gazed at him, her eyes shining with love. "My husband needed me, Master Sergeant Mitry. That awful man meant to do great harm to my Dex. It was up to me to protect him. I'd do it again if I had to."

"Sir, did you know what your wife did?" Yolie asked him.

Dex didn't answer her. Just sat there, gazing out at the Blush Noisettes.

Yolie tried again. "Mr. Farrell . . . ?"

He blinked several times before he said, "We always talk things over. It's the key to a successful marriage. That's something you young people ought to remember for the future. Never keep secrets. Never go to bed angry. Talk everything out."

"So you *did* know?"

"He just told you, Sergeant. We don't keep secrets. We've been through so many ups and downs over these past thirty-seven years, haven't we, Dex? This little episode—this is just one more thing."

"It's the *only* thing," Yolie countered. "You murdered another human being, lady. Don't you understand that?"

"What I understand," Maddee replied, "is that I made a sacred vow to this man the day I married him. For richer, for poorer. In sickness and in health. This right here is the sickness part. My Dex isn't well. But I wasn't about to abandon him when he needed me most. What kind of a wife would that make me?"

"The kind who has to take a little ride to New London with me," Yolie said to her. "You and your husband both. Maddee Farrell, you are under arrest for the murder of Augie Donatelli. Dexter Farrell, you are under arrest for being an accomplice to the murder after the fact—as well as for multiple counts of public indecency, criminal trespass and malicious mischief. You both have the right to remain silent. Anything you say can and will be used against you in a court of law. You have the right to speak to an attorney and to have—"

"I'd like to phone ours before we leave," Maddee told her. "And to finish dressing as well."

"Of course."

"Dex, do you want your seersucker or your madras?" Maddee asked him, as if they were off to the country club for a game of bridge.

He considered his reply carefully. "The seersucker, I think."

Maddee went into the kitchen to make her phone call, which was quite brief. Then she went down the hall to their bedroom. Yolie stayed right with her, not trusting her one bit. When they returned Maddee had a yellow cotton sweater on over her summer dress. She was carrying her purse and her husband's seersucker sports jacket.

As she helped him on with it Maddee said, "Sergeant, you don't need to handcuff us, do you?"

"No, ma'am. That won't be necessary. We're just taking a little ride."

"You're very considerate. Thank you."

They all left together by way of the front door. Yolie toting the black plastic trash bags of evidence. Maddee pausing to make sure the door was locked behind them.

Beth and Bertha stood there waiting for them in the hallway of the building. They'd seen Des and Yolie pull up outside in their cruisers, apparently. Bertha had a defiant look on her wrinkled little face. Beth, on the other hand, seemed uneasy. Her eyes avoided Mitch's. She couldn't, wouldn't look at him.

"I was *hoping* to run into you, Bertha," Maddee exclaimed brightly. "Could you phone Cissy and tell her I won't be able to help with Meals on Wheels today? It would be terribly inconsiderate not to call."

"Certainly, Maddee."

"And if I'm not back by late this afternoon will you please make sure my roses get a good watering? It's been terribly dry. Also, the recyclables go out tonight and Augie isn't around to . . ."

"Don't worry about a thing, Maddee," Bertha said. "I'll find someone to do it. Hell, I'll do it myself if I have to. Won't be the first time I've pitched garbage."

"Thank you, dear. Come along, Dex." And with that Maddee Farrell marched out the front door of the Captain Chadwick House, her head held high, her husband's hand in hers. Yolie trailed along behind them.

Mitch stayed there in the hallway with Des.

"Lieutenant Very was convinced that you two were holding out on us," he said to Beth and Bertha. "You knew who the Dorset Flasher was all along, didn't you? You knew that Maddee killed Augie to protect him. You knew everything."

"Of course," Bertha responded airily. "Nothing goes on in this town that I don't know about."

"Why didn't you speak up, Mrs. Peck?" Des demanded.

"Because we look out for one another in Dorset, that's why. All we have is each other. We're not perfect. Lord knows, the men who we choose to marry certainly aren't. We do the best we can with them. We prop them up, stroke them, coddle them. And yet it happens anyway—in the blink of an eye they go from Mr. Dependable to Mr. Depends. That's what happened to my Guy. And now it's Maddee's Dex. She was simply looking out for him. I can't condemn her for that."

"She *killed* a man," Des pointed out.

Bertha made a face. "Oh, please. Augie was a drunken, leering boor. A predator who took pictures of my friend when she was undressed."

"You knew about that?" Mitch asked Beth.

"Of course," she replied, shivering slightly. "Women always know when we're being watched."

Mitch considered this for a moment, wondering if that meant Beth knew he used to watch her outside his bedroom window every morning as she left for work, her hips swaying, her blond hair shimmering in the sunlight. He didn't want to know the answer. It fell under the category of Don't Ask, *Please God* Don't Tell.

"Augie hounded Beth everywhere she went," Bertha went on. "He was determined to destroy her and her lover. Just as he was determined to unmask Dex Farrell and take away what little dignity the man had left. Dex has already suffered enough from the financial scandals. Maddee certainly has. She's been ostracized by everyone who quote-unquote matters, poor woman. I've never considered her a close friend. I like to be around people who are light-spirited and fun. Maddee isn't. She's a pain, quite frankly. But she's a decent lady. And she didn't deserve this."

"Mitch, I'm so sorry I wasn't more candid with you yesterday," Beth said, her big, brown eyes gleaming. "I owed you the truth. But I gave Bertha my word that I'd keep quiet about it."

"I understand, Beth."

She tilted her head at him. The old Natalie Wood tilt. "You *say* you understand, but you don't. You're disappointed in me. I can see it in your eyes. And it really hurts, Mitch. Please phone me this week, will you? We can meet at The Works for coffee, okay?"

"Sure. If you'd like."

"I would, very much. I want us to stay friends—for Kenny's sake. And for Kimberly, whose life is about to become a total nightmare."

"I'm heading to the fitness center right now to give her the news," Des said. "And I'll let Lieutenant Very know that he no longer needs to question your friend Vinnie. It's all over."

"Thank you, Des. That's very good of you."

"Just doing my job."

Out in front of the Captain Chadwick House, Yolie had gotten the Farrells settled in the backseat of her cruiser. She waved good-bye to Des and Mitch, then hopped in and took off down Dorset Street.

"I could see it, too, you know," Des said, standing there on the front steps.

"See what?"

"The disappointment in your eyes."

"It was that obvious, was it?" He glanced over at her. "You're smiling. Why are you smiling?"

"Can't help it. I'm *kvelling*."

"*Kvelling*? That's a new one on me. Where'd you pick up such a funny sounding . . . Okay, ow, that hurt."

"You aced it, doughboy. Figured this whole thing out all by yourself. I guess you don't need me anymore."

"Guess again."

"No, no, it's finally happened. You're all grown up now. Cracking cases on your own. Tackling armed suspects to the floor . . ."

"Yeah, right. An old lady with a pair of coupon scissors. I was afraid she *wanted* you to shoot her."

"There, you see? Nothing gets by you. Your eyes are wide open now. You realize that your one and only dream girl is human. Hell, you don't even blush anymore when we talk about her."

"I *never* blushed."

"Oh, right. You were having hot flashes. Maybe you should have your doctor check that out."

"Des, if I didn't know you better I'd swear you were jealous."

"Not a chance."

"Besides, you couldn't be more wrong about my one and only dream girl. Would you like me to tell you a little bit about her?"

"I'm listening."

"Okay, here goes. She's a long, lean, bootylicious Connecticut state trooper. She has amazing legs. I'd trust her with my life, and have on numerous occasions. She's a tremendously gifted artist. She has amazing legs. Or did I already—?"

"I don't mind if you repeat yourself."

"Plus I happen to know she's *plenty* human and . . ."

Des raised an eyebrow at him. "And . . . ?"

"I wouldn't have it any other way, thinny."

Epilogue

(two days later)

Maddee Farrell was arraigned in New London Superior Court the morning after her arrest, and charged with murder in the first degree. The courtroom was packed with national media people. Reporters from the major newspapers, TV networks and cable news channels slavered all over it. It wasn't every day that the patrician wife of a world-famous Wall Street swindler—Dex "Quacks Like a Duck" Farrell—was charged with murdering a retired New York City police detective. Or that Dex Farrell himself was hauled in and charged with being the serial weenie waver who'd been terrorizing the good ladies of Dorset, Connecticut for weeks. The whole scene was one giant made-for-cable newsapalooza. Maddee's lawyer requested that she be released on bail. The judge denied the request. Judges tend to take a dim view of premeditated acts of murder, even those committed by rich old ladies who wear pearls and magenta lipstick. Dex, meanwhile, was being held at Connecticut Valley Hospital in Middletown pending the findings of a psychological evaluation by a court-appointed psychiatrist.

Des highly doubted that the shrink would find Dex Farrell competent to stand trial. But she had to admit that the Dorset Flasher had been right about one thing: the weather. A blast of fresh, cool Canadian air blew in late Tuesday night, just like he'd predicted. It was the first hint that fall wasn't far off. And it meant that the Deacon was wearing a hooded state police sweatshirt as he stood there at 5:00 a.m. on his front porch waiting for Des to take him to Yale-New Haven Hospital. He was due in pre-op at 5:45. The

Deacon wore pressed chinos and walking shoes with his sweatshirt, and had an overnight bag at his feet. He looked like a kid going off to camp. Lights were on inside of the house. Her aunt Charlene had arrived from Scranton last night and intended to spend the day scrubbing the place from floor to ceiling with Clorox. How she dealt.

Des was alone in the car. Mitch had wanted to come along but she'd told him she'd rather fly solo.

"Is this a Mitry thing or a *you* thing?"

"Is what?"

"Suffering all alone."

"Mitch, I'll be fine. Just step off, okay?"

And so he had.

"My affairs are entirely in order, Desiree," the Deacon informed her after he'd settled in beside her, his seat belt buckled. He was reserved and calm. Himself. "You'll find my will and other pertinent personal papers in the top left drawer of my desk in the den. The house goes to you. I own it free and clear. You can sell it or rent it out. Entirely your call."

"All right," she said as she steered them onto I-91. There were very few cars on the highway that early.

"I've left some money to your mother. Also to my church. The bulk of it goes to you. My investment portfolio and life insurance policy. My wedding ring, wristwatch . . ."

"Daddy, can we please not have this conversation?"

"I merely wanted you to know that I've taken care of everything."

"I never doubted that for a second. Now will you please shut up about it?"

"Fine." But he wasn't done talking. "Girl, what did you go and do?"

"What do you mean by that?"

"I mean that our dear friend Captain Richie Tedone called me last night just to tell me what an exemplary state trooper you are. The man could not say enough nice things about you. Why, he practically called you a credit to your race. Wanted me to know that Internal Affairs has no further interest in the Augie Donatelli matter. He also wanted to wish me a speedy recovery." He gazed at her sternly. "You have something on him, don't you?"

"Daddy, let's not have this conversation either, okay?"

"I don't approve, Desiree. You never come out ahead when you tussle with a Tedone."

"I wasn't trying to come out ahead. Just level the playing field a little."

He stuck out his chin. "You shouldn't have done it."

"Well, it's done. Richie will never bother us again. None of the Waterbury boys will. You can put that in the bank."

"What on earth did you get on him?"

"It's better if you don't know. The mental image will set back your recovery by weeks."

They got to the hospital in plenty of time. The Deacon signed in. They sat there together in the small pre-op waiting room for an hour.

When his name was finally called he stood and handed Des his wallet and shield. "Hold on to these for me, will you?"

She hugged him and gave him a kiss on the cheek. "I'll be here, Daddy."

"See you in a little while," he said, his voice turning husky. Then he strode through the door to get ready for surgery.

Des moved to the patient-recovery waiting room, a much larger area that was filled with people who were camped out there for however long it took. Which, in the Deacon's case, would be at least six hours, maybe eight. But Des wasn't going anywhere. As she sat down she realized she was still clutching his shield and wallet in her hand. She stuffed the shield in her shoulder bag. Opened his wallet and glanced through it. He carried the usual credit and ID cards. Also two fading color snapshots. One was of Des and her mother standing together at Des's West Point graduation. Des in uniform, all straight and proud. Her mother dressed up, looking beautiful. The other snapshot was an appallingly geeky high school yearbook photo of Des. She'd worn her hair like the business end of a felt tip marking pen in those days, the better to show off the sprinkling of pimples on her forehead and her oh-so stylish Urkel glasses. There were no current photographs in the Deacon's wallet.

She put it away and took out her sketchbook, graphite stick and the crime scene photos that Yolie had given her. She began to draw, deconstructing the horror that she'd been a part of on Saturday night. Converting Augie's bashed-in skull and splattered brain matter into lines and shapes and shadows. Her way of trying to deal with the ghastly reality of what Maddee Farrell had done to protect the man she loved. Was proud to do. Would do all over again if she had to. Des wanted to understand. Needed to understand. But Maddee and Dex Farrell would haunt her for a long, long time and she knew it.

She drew like mad for hours, one page after another, so absorbed in what she was doing that she almost didn't notice someone standing there before her.

"That's one of the crazy things about hospitals," Mitch exclaimed, grinning at her maddeningly. "You just never know who you might run into."

"Mitch, I *told* you I'd be fine on my own," she growled.

"I know you did."

"So what are you doing here?"

"I'm not here. Well, obviously I am. But I'm not. I happen to be on my way to Pepe's Pizza for my monthly pig out."

"Your monthly what?"

"It's a private thing that I do. Something personal. I feel it's very important to stay connected to my inner fat boy. So once a month I make a pilgrimage to the Elm City and stuff my face on Pepe's white clam pizza."

"I didn't know this."

"We all have our little secrets. I just got an idea—why don't you come along? It's world-class pie. And you could use a break."

"I'd better wait here. They said they'd page me when they had something to report."

Mitch glanced at his watch. "That won't be for at least another two, three hours."

"Mitch, I'm not leaving."

"Cool." He flopped down in the chair next to hers. "If you want to stay here, we'll stay here."

"What about your monthly hajj to fat boy Mecca?"

"Hell, I can do that any time. Oh, hey, would you like to come to a wedding on Friday? It'll be ultracasual. Shoes are optional. I highly doubt that the bride will be wearing any."

"Kimberly and Kenny?"

He nodded. "They want to get married right away. Kimberly really needs something positive in her life right now. Kenny is totally up for it. The oh-so-exclusive Dorset Yacht Club, however, is not."

"So where are they . . . ?"

"My little slice of beach on Big Sister. They'll exchange vows at sunset at the water's edge. Kimberly's yoga mentor, Anna, will do the honors. She also happens to be a practicing periodontist *and* justice of the peace. Not your typical career path but, hey, it's Dorset. A few close friends will be there. No more than twenty people. There will be, I'm told, various musical selections by the Grateful Dead. Some champagne and finger food, courtesy of Beth. Kimberly's best friend is coming down from Vermont to be her maid of honor. We already know who the best man is."

"Mitch, I wouldn't miss it. And I'm bringing Bella. She loves weddings."

"Good. It'll be a happy occasion."

"Speaking of happy occasions, Tawny Tedone gave birth at three o'clock this morning—a seven pound, three-ounce girl named Adriana. Rico woke Yolie out of a sound sleep to give her the news. Couldn't wait to tell her."

"He's one mondo-proud papa, I take it."

"One mondo-insecure papa is more like it. Yolie cracked this case without him. Grabbed a ton of face time on national TV. Big-time props up at the headmaster's house. She'll probably make lieutenant now, which she totally deserves. Little man's freaking out."

"And how about Yolie? Is she planning a little trip to New York City any time soon?"

"Not that I know of."

"Really? I'm surprised."

"Don't be. Lieutenant Very's on his way back to Dorset as we speak. Has to clean out Augie's apartment. He's the man's executor and sole heir. Not that Augie left him much of value."

"That GTO isn't exactly chopped liver. And you should see Augie's collection of vintage *Playboy* magazines."

"I'll pass on those, thanks. Very is planning to stay in the apartment for a few days."

"Is Yolie pumped about it?"

"Actually, she told me she keeps feeling as if she's about to throw up."

"That's not necessarily a bad sign."

"Yeah, it is. He's making her dinner there Saturday night."

"Get out, the guy *cooks*, too?"

"That's just what I said." Des took a deep breath and let it out slowly. "Mitch, it was sweet of you to do this but you really don't have to stay."

"Will you stop being such a butthead already?"

"I'm sorry, what did you just say?"

"I *want* to be here with you. Don't you get it? This is what people who love each other do. I'm not going anywhere, period. So just deal with it, tough guy." He fished a dog-eared paperback from his back pocket. "If it'll make things any easier you can just pretend I'm not here, okay?"

"What's that you're reading?"

"A collection of essays by the late, great H. L. Mencken."

"Since when are you into him?"

"I'm not. Let's just say my curiosity was piqued recently."

He turned his attention to his book. Des returned to her drawing, focusing on Augie's facial expression—the total shock that was frozen there for all time. She drew. Mitch read his book. She kept on drawing. Mitch kept on reading. Each of them in their separate spaces. Until, slowly, Des reached over and found Mitch's hand with hers. He gave it a squeeze and held on to it. And, together, they waited.